DOVER · THRIFT · EDITIONS

The Legend of Sleepy Hollow

and Other Stories

WASHINGTON IRVING

DOVER PUBLICATIONS, INC.
Mineola, New York

DOVER THRIFT EDITIONS

GENERAL EDITOR: MARY CAROLYN WALDREP
EDITOR OF THIS VOLUME: JANET BAINE KOPITO

Copyright

Copyright © 2008 by Dover Publications, Inc.
All rights reserved.

Bibliographical Note

This Dover edition, first published in 2008, is an original compilation of unabridged stories from standard editions. An introductory Note has been specially prepared for the present edition.

Library of Congress Cataloging-in-Publication Data

Irving, Washington, 1783–1859.
    The legend of Sleepy Hollow and other stories / Washington Irving.
        p. cm. — (Dover thrift editions)
    This edition is an original compilation of unabridged stories from standard editions.
    ISBN-13: 978-0-486-46658-3
    ISBN-10: 0-486-46658-2
        I. Title.

PS2067.A1 2008
813'.2—dc22

2007050526

Manufactured in the United States by Courier Corporation
46658204   2013
www.doverpublications.com

Note

AN ENDURING FIGURE of American letters— and a keen observer of life abroad—Washington Irving was born in New York City in 1783, the same year that marked the end of the American Revolution and the founding of the United States. Irving, the youngest of eleven children, was, in fact, named after George Washington (the subject of his final work, *The Life of George Washington* [1859]).

After studying law and passing the bar examination, Irving instead chose to follow his flair for writing. By his late teens, he was a published author, contributing stories to local publications such as the *Morning Chronicle* (edited by his brother Peter). In spite of personal setbacks —the death of his fiancée, Matilda Hoffman, in 1809, and his involvement with the faltering family import business—Irving enthusiastically entered the contemporary literary scene, gaining the support of Sir Walter Scott, Lord Byron, Mary Shelley, and Henry Wadsworth Longfellow. His travels in Europe led to the publication of humorous sketches in *Salmagundi; or, The Whim-Whams and Opinions of Launcelot Langstaff, Esq. & Others.* (Later writings inspired by Irving's Europe experiences appeared in 1824 in *Tales of a Traveller.*) In 1826 he took up a post with the American Embassy in Madrid, and his curiosity about Spain led him to write *The Conquest of Granada* (1829) and *The Alhambra* (1832). After returning home, Irving traveled around the American West, recording his impressions in *A Tour of the Prairies* (1835). He took another governmental post in Spain in the 1840s. Irving, who never married, thereafter took up residence—along with an array of family members—at Sunnyside, his house near Tarrytown, New York. He completed the final volume of his biography of Washington in March 1859; he died the following November.

The present edition leads off with Irving's best-known tales, "The Legend of Sleepy Hollow" and "Rip Van Winkle," which appeared originally in the collection *The Sketch-Book of Geoffrey Crayon, Gent.* (1819). Who can forget the startling image of Ichabod Crane striding through the "drowsy shades of Sleepy Hollow" with "hands that dangled a mile out of his sleeves" and "feet that might have served for shovels"? Equally familiar to the reader is Rip Van Winkle, a "simple good natured man" who would rather "starve on a penny than work for a pound"—and whose long slumber in the mountains of New York State propels him from the realm of King George and the "yoke of Old England" to the newly minted United States of George Washington. These works, and the eleven others that accompany them, offer a broad range of genres: satire, parable, suspense, and tales of the supernatural. They are evidence that the versatility of the author was enriched by his fascination with history—both American and European—and his ability to depict character, mood, and plot with a sure, engaging, and highly entertaining hand.

Contents

The Legend of Sleepy Hollow [1820] 1

Rip Van Winkle [1820] 26

The Spectre Bridegroom [1820] 42

The Mutability of Literature [1820] 54

Westminster Abbey [1820] 62

The Wife [1820] 75

Mountjoy [1820] 81

Adventure of the German Student [1824] 113

Adventure of the Mysterious Stranger [1824] 118

The Adventure of My Uncle [1824] 125

The Adventure of My Aunt [1824] 135

The Story of the Young Italian [1824] 139

The Devil and Tom Walker [1824] 161

THE LEGEND OF SLEEPY HOLLOW

(Found among the Papers of the late Diedrich Knickerbocker)

> A pleasing land of drowsy head it was,
> Of dreams that wave before the half-shut eye;
> And of gay castles in the clouds that pass,
> Forever flushing round a summer sky.
>
> *Castle of Indolence*

IN THE BOSOM of one of those spacious coves which indent the eastern shore of the Hudson, at that broad expansion of the river denominated by the ancient Dutch navigators the Tappaan Zee, and where they always prudently shortened sail and implored the protection of St. Nicholas when they crossed, there lies a small market town or rural port, which by some is called Greensburgh, but which is more generally and properly known by the name of Tarry Town. This name was given, we are told, in former days, by the good housewives of the adjacent country, from the inveterate propensity of their husbands to linger about the village tavern on market days. Be that as it may, I do not vouch for the fact, but merely advert to it, for the sake of being precise and authentic. Not far from this village, perhaps about two miles, there is a little valley, or rather lap of land among high hills, which is one of the quietest places in the whole world. A small brook glides through it, with just murmur enough to lull one to repose; and the occasional whistle of a quail, or tapping of a woodpecker, is almost the only sound that ever breaks in upon the uniform tranquillity.

I recollect that, when a stripling, my first exploit in squirrel-shooting was in a grove of tall walnut-trees that shades one side of the valley. I had wandered into it at noon time, when all nature is peculiarly quiet, and was startled by the roar of my own gun, as it broke the sabbath stillness around, and was prolonged and reverberated by the angry echoes. If ever I should wish for a retreat, whither I might steal from the world and its distractions, and dream quietly away the remnant of a troubled life, I know of none more promising than this little valley.

From the listless repose of the place, and the peculiar character of its inhabitants, who are descendants from the original Dutch settlers, this sequestered glen has long been known by the name of SLEEPY HOL-LOW, and its rustic lads are called the Sleepy Hollow Boys through-out all the neighboring country. A drowsy, dreamy influence seems to hang over the land, and to pervade the very atmosphere. Some say that the place was bewitched by a high German doctor, during the early days of the settlement; others, that an old Indian chief, the prophet or wizard of his tribe, held his powwows there before the country was discovered by Master Hendrick Hudson. Certain it is, the place still continues under the sway of some witching power, that holds a spell over the minds of the good people, causing them to walk in a continual reverie. They are given to all kinds of marvellous beliefs, are subject to trances and visions, and frequently see strange sights, and hear music and voices in the air. The whole neighborhood abounds with local tales, haunted spots, and twilight superstitions; stars shoot and meteors glare oftener across the valley than in any other part of the country, and the night mare, with her whole nine fold, seems to make it the favorite scene of her gambols.

The dominant spirit, however, that haunts this enchanted region, and seems to be commander-in-chief of all the powers of the air, is the apparition of a figure on horseback without a head. It is said by some to be the ghost of a Hessian trooper, whose head had been carried away by a cannon ball, in some nameless battle during the revolution-ary war, and who is ever and anon seen by the country folk, hurrying along in the gloom of night, as if on the wings of the wind. His haunts are not confined to the valley, but extend at times to the adjacent roads, and especially to the vicinity of a church at no great distance. Indeed, certain of the most authentic historians of those parts, who have been careful in collecting and collating the floating facts con-cerning this spectre, allege, that the body of the trooper having been buried in the churchyard, the ghost rides forth to the scene of battle in nightly quest of his head, and that the rushing speed with which he sometimes passes along the hollow, like a midnight blast, is owing to his being belated, and in a hurry to get back to the churchyard before day break.

Such is the general purport of this legendary superstition, which has furnished materials for many a wild story in that region of shadows; and the spectre is known, at all the country firesides, by the name of The Headless Horseman of Sleepy Hollow.

It is remarkable, that the visionary propensity I have mentioned is not confined to the native inhabitants of the valley, but is uncon-sciously imbibed by every one who resides there for a time. However wide awake they may have been before they entered that sleepy region, they are sure, in a little time, to inhale the witching influence of the air, and begin to grow imaginative—to dream dreams, and see apparitions.

I mention this peaceful spot with all possible laud; for it is in such little retired Dutch valleys, found here and there embosomed in the great state of New York, that population, manners, and customs remain fixed, while the great torrent of migration and improvement, which is making such incessant changes in other parts of this restless country, sweeps by them unobserved. They are like those little nooks of still water, which border a rapid stream, where we may see the straw and bubble riding quietly at anchor, or slowly revolving in their mimic harbor, undisturbed by the rush of the passing current. Though many years have elapsed since I trod the drowsy shades of Sleepy Hollow, yet I question whether I should not still find the same trees and the same families vegetating in its sheltered bosom.

In this by place of nature there abode, in a remote period of American history, that is to say, some thirty years since, a worthy wight of the name of Ichabod Crane, who sojourned, or, as he expressed it, "tarried," in Sleepy Hollow, for the purpose of instructing the children of the vicinity. He was a native of Connecticut, a state which supplies the Union with pioneers for the mind as well as for the forest, and sends forth yearly its legions of frontier woodmen and country schoolmasters. The cognomen of Crane was not inapplicable to his person. He was tall, but exceedingly lank, with narrow shoulders, long arms and legs, hands that dangled a mile out of his sleeves, feet that might have served for shovels, and his whole frame most loosely hung together. His head was small, and flat at top, with huge ears, large green glassy eyes, and a long snipe nose, so that it looked like a weathercock perched upon his spindle neck, to tell which way the wind blew. To see him striding along the profile of a hill on a windy day, with his clothes bagging and fluttering about him, one might have mistaken him for the genius of famine descending upon the earth, or some scarecrow eloped from a cornfield.

His school house was a low building of one large room, rudely constructed of logs; the windows partly glazed, and partly patched with leaves of old copy books. It was most ingeniously secured at vacant hours, by a withe twisted in the handle of the door, and stakes set against the window shutters; so that though a thief might get in with perfect ease, he would find some embarrassment in getting out; an idea most probably borrowed by the architect, Yost Van Houten, from the mystery of an eelpot. The school house stood in a rather lonely but pleasant situation, just at the foot of a woody hill, with a brook running close by, and a formidable birch tree growing at one end of it. From hence the low murmur of his pupils' voices conning over their lessons, might be heard of a drowsy summer's day, like the hum of a bee hive; interrupted now and then by the authoritative voice of the master, in the tone of menace or command, or peradventure, by the appalling sound of the birch, as he urged some tardy loiterer along the flowery path of knowledge. Truth to say, he was a conscientious man, and ever bore in mind the golden maxim, "spare the rod and spoil the child."—Ichabod Crane's scholars certainly were not spoiled.

I would not have it imagined, however, that he was one of those cruel potentates of the school, who joy in the smart of their subjects; on the contrary, he administered justice with discrimination rather than severity; taking the burden off the backs of the weak, and laying it on those of the strong. Your mere puny stripling, that winced at the least flourish of the rod, was passed by with indulgence; but the claims of justice were satisfied, by inflicting a double portion on some little, tough, wrong headed, broad-skirted Dutch urchin, who sulked and swelled and grew dogged and sullen beneath the birch. All this he called "doing his duty by their parents"; and he never inflicted a chastisement without following it by the assurance, so consolatory to the smarting urchin, that "he would remember it and thank him for it the longest day he had to live."

When school hours were over, he was even the companion and playmate of the larger boys; and on holiday afternoons would convoy some of the smaller ones home, who happened to have pretty sisters, or good housewives for mothers, noted for the comforts of the cupboard. Indeed, it behooved him to keep on good terms with his pupils. The revenue arising from his school was small, and would have been scarcely sufficient to furnish him with daily bread, for he was a huge feeder, and though lank, had the dilating powers of an Anaconda; but to help out his maintenance, he was, according to country custom in those parts, boarded and lodged at the houses of the farmers, whose children he instructed. With these he lived successively a week at a time, thus going the rounds of the neighborhood, with all his worldly effects tied up in a cotton handkerchief.

That all this might not be too onerous on the purses of his rustic patrons, who are apt to consider the costs of schooling a grievous burden, and schoolmasters as mere drones, he had various ways of rendering himself both useful and agreeable. He assisted the farmers occasionally in the lighter labors of their farms, helped to make hay, mended the fences, took the horses to water, drove the cows from pasture, and cut wood for the winter fire. He laid aside, too, all the dominant dignity and absolute sway, with which he lorded it in his little empire, the school, and became wonderfully gentle and ingratiating. He found favor in the eyes of the mothers, by petting the children, particularly the youngest, and like the lion bold, which whilome so magnanimously the lamb did hold, he would sit with a child on one knee, and rock a cradle with his foot for whole hours together.

In addition to his other vocations, he was the singing master of the neighborhood, and picked up many bright shillings by instructing the young folks in psalmody. It was a matter of no little vanity to him on Sundays, to take his station in front of the church gallery, with a band of chosen singers; where, in his own mind, he completely carried away the palm from the parson. Certain it is, his voice resounded far above all the rest of the congregation, and there are peculiar quavers still to be heard in that church, and which may even be heard half a mile off, quite to the opposite side of the mill pond, of a still Sunday morning, which are said to be legitimately descended from the nose of Ichabod Crane. Thus, by diverse little make shifts, in that ingenious way which is commonly denominated "by hook and by crook," the worthy pedagogue got on tolerably enough, and was thought, by all who understood nothing of the labor of headwork, to have a wonderfully easy life of it.

The schoolmaster is generally a man of some importance in the female circle of a rural neighborhood, being considered a kind of idle gentleman like personage, of vastly superior taste and accomplishments to the rough country swains, and, indeed, inferior in learning only to the parson. His appearance, therefore, is apt to occasion some little stir at the tea table of a farm house, and the addition of a supernumerary dish of cakes or sweetmeats, or, peradventure, the parade of a silver tea pot. Our man of letters, therefore, was peculiarly happy in the smiles of all the country damsels. How he would figure among them in the church yard, between services on Sundays; gathering grapes for them from the wild vines that overrun the surrounding trees; reciting for their amusement all the epitaphs on the tombstones, or sauntering, with a whole bevy of them, along the banks of the adjacent mill pond; while the more bashful country bumpkins hung sheepishly back, envying his superior elegance and address.

From his half-itinerant life, also, he was a kind of traveling gazette, carrying the whole budget of local gossip from house to house; so that his appearance was always greeted with satisfaction. He was, moreover, esteemed by the women as a man of great erudition, for he had read several books quite through, and was a perfect master of Cotton Mather's "History of New England Witchcraft," in which, by the way, he most firmly and potently believed.

He was, in fact, an odd mixture of small shrewdness and simple credulity. His appetite for the marvellous, and his powers of digesting it, were equally extraordinary; and both had been increased by his residence in this spell bound region. No tale was too gross or monstrous for his capacious swallow. It was often his delight, after his school was dismissed of an afternoon, to stretch himself on the rich bed of clover, bordering the little brook that whimpered by his school house, and there con over old Mather's direful tales, until the gathering dusk of evening made the printed page a mere mist before his eyes. Then, as he wended his way, by swamp and stream and awful woodland, to the farm house where he happened to be quartered, every sound of nature, at that witching hour, fluttered his excited imagination: the moan of the whip-poor-will from the hill side, the boding cry of the tree toad, that harbinger of storm; the dreary hooting of the screech owl; or the sudden rustling in the thicket, of birds frightened from their roost. The fire flies, too, which sparkled most vividly in the darkest places, now and then startled him, as one of uncommon brightness would stream across his path; and if, by chance, a huge blockhead of a beetle came winging his blundering flight against him, the poor varlet was ready to give up the ghost, with the idea that he was struck with a witch's token. His only resource on such occasions, either to drown thought, or drive away evil spirits, was to sing psalm tunes;—and the good people of Sleepy Hollow, as they sat by their doors of an evening, were often filled with awe, at hearing his nasal melody, "in linked sweetness long drawn out," floating from the distant hill, or along the dusky road.

Another of his sources of fearful pleasure was, to pass long winter evenings with the old Dutch wives, as they sat spinning by the fire, with a row of apples roasting and sputtering along the hearth, and listen to their marvellous tales of ghosts and goblins, and haunted fields and haunted brooks, and haunted bridges and haunted houses, and particularly of the headless horseman, or galloping Hessian of the Hollow, as they sometimes called him. He would delight them equally by his anecdotes of witchcraft, and of the direful omens and portentous sights and sounds in the air, which prevailed in the earlier times of Connecticut; and would frighten them woefully with speculations upon comets and shooting stars, and with the alarming fact that the world did absolutely turn round, and that they were half the time topsy-turvy!

But if there was a pleasure in all this, while snugly cuddling in the chimney corner of a chamber that was all of a ruddy glow from the crackling wood fire, and where, of course, no spectre dared to show its face, it was dearly purchased by the terrors of his subsequent walk homewards. What fearful shapes and shadows beset his path, amidst the dim and ghastly glare of a snowy night!—With what wistful look did he eye every trembling ray of light streaming across the waste fields from some distant window!—How often was he appalled by some shrub covered with snow, which like a sheeted spectre, beset his very path!—How often did he shrink with curdling awe at the sound of his own steps on the frosty crust beneath his feet; and dread to look over his shoulder, lest he should behold some uncouth being tramping close behind him!—and how often was he thrown into complete dismay by some rushing blast, howling among the trees, in the idea that it was the galloping Hessian on one of his nightly scourings.

All these, however, were mere terrors of the night, phantoms of the mind, that walk in darkness; and though he had seen many spectres in his time, and been more than once beset by Satan in diverse shapes, in his lonely perambulations, yet daylight put an end to all these evils; and he would have passed a pleasant life of it, in despite of the Devil and all his works, if his path had not been crossed by a being that causes more perplexity to mortal man, than ghosts, goblins, and the whole race of witches put together, and that was—a woman.

Among the musical disciples who assembled, one evening in each week, to receive his instructions in psalmody, was Katrina Van Tassel, the daughter and only child of a substantial Dutch farmer. She was a blooming lass of fresh eighteen; plump as a partridge; ripe and melting and rosy cheeked as one of her father's peaches, and universally famed, not merely for her beauty, but her vast expectations. She was withal a little of a coquette, as might be perceived even in her dress, which was a mixture of ancient and modern fashions, as most suited to set off her charms. She wore the ornaments of pure yellow gold, which her great great grandmother had brought over from Saardam; the tempting stomacher of the olden time, and withal a provokingly short petticoat, to display the prettiest foot and ankle in the country round.

Ichabod Crane had a soft and foolish heart towards the sex; and it is not to be wondered at, that so tempting a morsel soon found favor in his eyes, more especially after he had visited her in her paternal mansion. Old Baltus Van Tassel was a perfect picture of a thriving, contented, liberal hearted farmer. He seldom, it is true, sent either his eyes or his thoughts beyond the boundaries of his own farm; but within those every thing was snug, happy, and well conditioned. He was satisfied with his wealth, but not proud of it; and piqued himself upon the hearty abundance, rather than the style in which he lived. His strong hold was situated on the banks of the Hudson, in one of those green, sheltered, fertile nooks in which the Dutch farmers are so fond of nestling. A great elm tree spread its broad branches over it, at the foot of which bubbled up a spring of the softest and sweetest water, in a little well, formed of a barrel, and then stole sparkling away through the grass, to a neighboring brook, that babbled along among elders and dwarf willows. Hard by the farm house was a vast barn, that might have served for a church; every window and crevice of which seemed bursting forth with the treasures of the farm; the flail was busily resounding within it from morning to night; swallows and martins skimmed twittering about the eaves; and rows of pigeons, some with one eye turned up, as if watching the weather, some with their heads under their wings, or buried in their bosoms, and others, swelling, and cooing, and bowing about their dames, were enjoying the sunshine on the roof. Sleek unwieldy porkers were grunting in the repose and abundance of their pens, from whence sallied forth, now and then, troops of sucking pigs, as if to snuff the air. A stately squadron of snowy geese were riding in an adjoining pond, convoying whole fleets of ducks; regiments of turkeys were gobbling through the farm yard, and guinea fowls fretting about it like ill-tempered housewives, with their peevish, discontented cry. Before the barn door strutted the gallant cock, that pattern of a husband, a warrior, and a fine gentleman, clapping his burnished wings and crowing in the pride and gladness of his heart—sometimes tearing up the earth with his feet, and then generously calling his ever hungry family of wives and children to enjoy the rich morsel which he had discovered.

The pedagogue's mouth watered, as he looked upon this sumptuous promise of luxurious winter fare. In his devouring mind's eye, he pictured to himself every roasting pig running about with a pudding in his belly, and an apple in his mouth; the pigeons were snugly put to bed in a comfortable pie, and tucked in with a coverlet of crust; the geese were swimming in their own gravy; and the ducks pairing cosily in dishes, like snug married couples, with a decent competency of onion sauce; in the porkers he saw carved out the future sleek side of bacon, and juicy relishing ham; not a turkey, but he beheld daintily trussed up, with its gizzard under its wing, and, peradventure, a necklace of savory sausages; and even bright chanticleer himself lay sprawling on his back, in a side dish, with uplifted claws, as if craving that quarter, which his chivalrous spirit disdained to ask while living.

As the enraptured Ichabod fancied all this, and as he rolled his great green eyes over the fat meadow lands, the rich fields of wheat, of rye, of buckwheat, and Indian corn, and the orchards burdened with ruddy fruit, which surrounded the warm tenement of Van Tassel, his heart yearned after the damsel who was to inherit these domains, and his imagination expanded with the idea, how they might be readily turned into cash, and the money invested in immense tracts of wild land, and shingle palaces in the wilderness. Nay, his busy fancy already realized his hopes, and presented to him the blooming Katrina, with a whole family of children, mounted on the top of a wagon loaded with household trumpery, with pots and kettles dangling beneath; and he beheld himself bestriding a pacing mare, with a colt at her heels, setting out for Kentucky, Tennessee, or the Lord knows where!

When he entered the house, the conquest of his heart was complete. It was one of those spacious farm houses, with high ridged but lowly sloping roofs, built in the style handed down from the first Dutch settlers. The low, projecting eaves formed a piazza along the front, capable of being closed up in bad weather. Under this were hung flails, harness, various utensils of husbandry, and nets for fishing in the neighboring river. Benches were built along the sides for summer use; and a great spinning wheel at one end, and a churn at the other, showed the various uses to which this important porch might be devoted. From this piazza the wondering Ichabod entered the hall, which formed the centre of the mansion, and the place of usual residence. Here, rows of resplendent pewter, ranged on a long dresser, dazzled his eyes. In one corner stood a huge bag of wool ready to be spun; in another a quantity of linsey-woolsey just from the loom; ears of Indian corn, and strings of dried apples and peaches, hung in gay festoons along the walls, mingled with the gaud of red peppers; and a door left ajar gave him a peep into the best parlor, where the claw-footed chairs and dark mahogany tables, shone like mirrors; andirons, with their accompanying shovel and tongs, glistened from their covert of asparagus tops; mock oranges and conch shells decorated the mantelpiece; strings of various-colored birds' eggs were suspended above it; a great ostrich egg was hung from the centre of the room, and a corner cupboard, knowingly left open, displayed immense treasures of old silver and well mended china.

From the moment Ichabod laid his eyes upon these regions of delight, the peace of his mind was at an end, and his only study was how to gain the affections of the peerless daughter of Van Tassel. In this enterprise, however, he had more real difficulties than generally fell to the lot of a knight errant of yore, who seldom had any thing but giants, enchanters, fiery dragons, and such like easily conquered adversaries, to contend with; and had to make his way merely through gates of iron and brass, and walls of adamant, to the castle keep, where the lady of his heart was confined; all which he achieved as easily as a man would carve his way to the centre of a Christmas pie, and then the lady gave him her hand as a matter of course. Ichabod, on the contrary, had to win his way to the heart of a country coquette, beset with a labyrinth of whims and caprices, which were forever presenting new difficulties and impediments, and he had to encounter a host of fearful adversaries of real flesh and blood, the numerous rustic admirers, who beset every portal to her heart, keeping a watchful and angry eye upon each other, but ready to fly out in the common cause against any new competitor.

Among these, the most formidable, was a burly, roaring, roystering blade, of the name of Abraham, or, according to the Dutch abbreviation, Brom Van Brunt, the hero of the country round, which rung with his feats of strength and hardihood. He was broad shouldered and double jointed, with short curly black hair, and a bluff, but not unpleasant countenance, having a mingled air of fun and arrogance. From his Herculean frame and great powers of limb, he had received the nick name of BROM BONES, by which he was universally known. He was famed for great knowledge and skill in horsemanship, being as dexterous on horseback as a Tartar. He was foremost at all races and cock fights, and with the ascendancy which bodily strength acquires in rustic life, was the umpire in all disputes, setting his hat on one side, and giving his decisions with an air and tone admitting of no gainsay or appeal. He was always ready for either a fight or a frolic; but had more mischief than ill will in his composition; and with all his overbearing roughness, there was a strong dash of waggish good humor at bottom. He had three or four boon companions, who regarded him as their model, and at the head of whom he scoured the country, attending every scene of feud or merriment for miles round. In cold weather he was distinguished by a fur cap, surmounted with a flaunting fox's tail, and when the folks at a country gathering descried this well known crest at a distance, whisking about among a squad of hard riders, they always stood by for a squall. Sometimes his crew would be heard dashing along past the farm houses at midnight, with whoop and halloo, like a troop of Don Cossacks; and the old dames, startled out of their sleep, would listen for a moment till the hurry scurry had clattered by, and then exclaim, "aye, there goes Brom Bones and his gang!" The neighbors looked upon him with a mixture of awe, admiration, and good will; and when any mad cap prank, or rustic brawl, occurred in the vicinity, always shook their heads, and warranted Brom Bones was at the bottom of it.

This rantipole hero had for some time singled out the blooming Katrina for the object of his uncouth gallantries, and though his amorous toyings were something like the gentle caresses and endearments of a bear, yet it was whispered that she did not altogether discourage his hopes. Certain it is, his advances were signals for rival candidates to retire, who felt no inclination to cross a lion in his amours; insomuch, that when his horse was seen tied to Van Tassel's paling, of a Sunday night, a sure sign that his master was courting, or, as it is termed, "sparking," within, all other suitors passed by in despair, and carried the war into other quarters.

Such was the formidable rival with whom Ichabod Crane had to contend, and, considering all things, a stouter man than he would have shrunk from the competition, and a wiser man would have despaired. He had, however, a happy mixture of pliability and perseverance in his nature; he was in form and spirit like a supple jack—yielding, but tough; though he bent, he never broke; and though he bowed beneath the slightest pressure, yet, the moment it was away—jerk!—he was as erect, and carried his head as high as ever.

To have taken the field openly against his rival would have been madness; for he was not a man to be thwarted in his amours, any more than that stormy lover, Achilles. Ichabod, therefore, made his advances in a quiet and gently insinuating manner. Under cover of his character of singing-master, he made frequent visits at the farm house; not that he had any thing to apprehend from the meddlesome interference of parents, which is so often a stumbling block in the path of lovers. Balt Van Tassel was an easy indulgent soul; he loved his daughter better even than his pipe, and like a reasonable man, and an excellent father, let her have her way in every thing. His notable little wife too, had enough to do to attend to her housekeeping and manage her poultry, for, as she sagely observed, ducks and geese are foolish things, and must be looked after, but girls can take care of themselves. Thus while the busy dame bustled about the house, or plied her spinning wheel at one end of the piazza, honest Balt would sit smoking his evening pipe at the other, watching the achievements of a little wooden warrior, who, armed with a sword in each hand, was most valiantly fighting the wind on the pinnacle of the barn. In the mean time, Ichabod would carry on his suit with the daughter by the side of the spring under the great elm, or sauntering along in the twilight, that hour so favorable to the lover's eloquence.

I profess not to know how women's hearts are wooed and won. To me they have always been matters of riddle and admiration. Some seem to have but one vulnerable point, or door of access; while others have a thousand avenues, and may be captured in a thousand different ways. It is a great triumph of skill to gain the former, but a still greater proof of generalship to maintain possession of the latter, for a man must battle for his fortress at every door and window. He who wins a thousand common hearts is therefore entitled to some renown; but he who keeps undisputed sway over the heart of a coquette is indeed a hero. Certain it is, this was not the case with the redoubtable Brom Bones; and from the moment Ichabod Crane made his advances, the interests of the former evidently declined; his horse was no longer seen tied at the palings on Sunday nights, and a deadly feud gradually arose between him and the preceptor of Sleepy Hollow.

Brom, who had a degree of rough chivalry in his nature, would fain have carried matters to open warfare, and have settled their pretensions to the lady, according to the mode of those most concise and simple reasoners, the knights errant of yore—by single combat; but Ichabod was too conscious of the superior might of his adversary to enter the lists against him; he had overheard a boast of Bones, that he would "double the schoolmaster up, and lay him on a shelf of his own school house"; and he was too wary to give him an opportunity. There was something extremely provoking in this obstinately pacific system; it left Brom no alternative but to draw upon the funds of rustic waggery in his disposition, and to play off boorish practical jokes upon his rival. Ichabod became the object of whimsical persecution to Bones, and his gang of rough riders. They harried his hitherto peaceful domains; smoked out his singing school by stopping up the chimney; broke into the school house at night, in spite of its formidable fastenings of withe and window stakes, and turned every thing topsy-turvy, so that the poor schoolmaster began to think all the witches in the country held their meetings there. But what was still more annoying, Brom took all opportunities of turning him into ridicule in presence of his mistress, and had a scoundrel dog, whom he taught to whine in the most ludicrous manner, and introduced as a rival of Ichabod's, to instruct her in psalmody.

In this way, matters went on for some time, without producing any material effect on the relative situations of the contending powers. On a fine autumnal afternoon, Ichabod, in pensive mood, sat enthroned on the lofty stool from whence he usually watched all the concerns of his little literary realm. In his hand he swayed a ferule, that sceptre of despotic power; the birch of justice reposed on three nails, behind the throne, a constant terror to evil doers; while on the desk before him might be seen sundry contraband articles and prohibited weapons, detected upon the persons of idle urchins, such as half munched apples, popguns, whirligigs, fly cages, and whole legions of rampant little paper game cocks. Apparently there had been some appalling act of justice recently inflicted, for his scholars were all busily intent upon their books, or slyly whispering behind them with one eye kept upon the master; and a kind of buzzing stillness reigned throughout the school room. It was suddenly interrupted by the appearance of a negro in tow cloth jacket and trowsers, a round crowned fragment of a hat, like the cap of Mercury, and mounted on the back of a ragged, wild, half broken colt, which he managed with a rope by way of halter. He came clattering up to the school door with an invitation to Ichabod to attend a merry making or "quilting frolic," to be held that evening at Mynheer Van Tassel's, and having delivered his message with that air of importance, and effort at fine language, which a negro is apt to display on petty embassies of the kind, he dashed over the brook, and was seen scampering away up the hollow, full of the importance and hurry of his mission.

All was now bustle and hubbub in the late quiet school room. The scholars were hurried through their lessons without stopping at trifles; those who were nimble, skipped over half with impunity, and those who were tardy, had a smart application now and then in the rear, to quicken their speed, or help them over a tall word. Books were flung aside, without being put away on the shelves; inkstands were overturned, benches thrown down, and the whole school was turned loose an hour before the usual time, bursting forth like a legion of young imps, yelping and racketing about the green, in joy at their early emancipation.

The gallant Ichabod now spent at least an extra half hour at his toilet, brushing and furbishing up his best, and indeed only suit of rusty black, and arranging his locks by a bit of broken looking glass that hung up in the schoolhouse. That he might make his appearance before his mistress in the true style of a cavalier, he borrowed a horse from the farmer with whom he was domiciliated, a choleric old Dutchman, of the name of Hans Van Ripper, and thus gallantly mounted, issued forth like a knight errant in quest of adventures. But it is meet I should, in the true spirit of romantic story, give some account of the looks and equipments of my hero and his steed. The animal he bestrode was a broken down plough horse, that had outlived almost everything but his viciousness. He was gaunt and shagged, with a ewe neck and a head like a hammer; his rusty mane and tail were tangled and knotted with burrs; one eye had lost its pupil, and was glaring and spectral, but the other had the gleam of a genuine devil in it. Still he must have had fire and mettle in his day, if we may judge from the name he bore of Gunpowder. He had, in fact, been a favorite steed of his master's, the choleric Van Ripper, who was a furious rider, and had infused, very probably, some of his own spirit into the animal, for, old and broken down as he looked, there was more of the lurking devil in him than in any young filly in the country.

Ichabod was a suitable figure for such a steed. He rode with short stirrups, which brought his knees nearly up to the pommel of the saddle; his sharp elbows stuck out like grasshoppers'; he carried his whip perpendicularly in his hand, like a sceptre, and as his horse jogged on, the motion of his arms was not unlike the flapping of a pair of wings. A small wool hat rested on the top of his nose, for so his scanty strip of forehead might be called, and the skirts of his black coat fluttered out almost to the horse's tail. Such was the appearance of Ichabod and his steed, as they shambled out of the gate of Hans Van Ripper, and it was altogether such an apparition as is seldom to be met with in broad day light.

It was, as I have said, a fine autumnal day, the sky was clear and serene, and nature wore that rich and golden livery which we always associate with the idea of abundance. The forests had put on their sober brown and yellow, while some trees of the tenderer kind had been nipped by the frosts into brilliant dyes of orange, purple, and scarlet. Streaming files of wild ducks began to make their appearance high in the air; the bark of the squirrel might be heard from the groves of beech and hickory nuts, and the pensive whistle of the quail at intervals from the neighboring stubble field.

The small birds were taking their farewell banquets. In the fullness of their revelry, they fluttered, chirping and frolicking, from bush to bush, and tree to tree, capricious from the very profusion and variety around them. There was the honest cock robin, the favorite game of stripling sportsmen, with its loud querulous note; and the twittering blackbirds flying in sable clouds; and the golden winged woodpecker, with his crimson crest, his broad black gorget, and splendid plumage; and the cedar bird, with its red tipt wings and yellow tipt tail and its little monteiro cap of feathers; and the blue jay, that noisy coxcomb, in his gay light blue coat and white under clothes, screaming and chattering, nodding, and bobbing, and bowing, and pretending to be on good terms with every songster of the grove.

As Ichabod jogged slowly on his way, his eye, ever open to every symptom of culinary abundance, ranged with delight over the treasures of jolly autumn. On all sides he beheld vast store of apples, some hanging in oppressive opulence on the trees, some gathered into baskets and barrels for the market, others heaped up in rich piles for the cider press. Further on he beheld great fields of Indian corn, with its golden ears peeping from their leafy coverts, and holding out the promise of cakes and hasty pudding; and the yellow pumpkins lying beneath them, turning up their fair round bellies to the sun, and giving ample prospects of the most luxurious of pies; and anon he passed the fragrant buckwheat fields breathing the odor of the bee hive, and as he beheld them, soft anticipations stole over his mind of dainty slap jacks, well buttered, and garnished with honey or treacle, by the delicate little dimpled hand of Katrina Van Tassel.

Thus feeding his mind with many sweet thoughts and "sugared suppositions," he journeyed along the sides of a range of hills which look out upon some of the goodliest scenes of the mighty Hudson.

The sun gradually wheeled his broad disk down into the west. The wide bosom of the Tappaan Zee lay motionless and glassy, excepting that here and there a gentle undulation waved and prolonged the blue shadow of the distant mountain: a few amber clouds floated in the sky, without a breath of air to move them. The horizon was of a fine golden tint, changing gradually into a pure apple green, and from that into the deep blue of the mid-heaven. A slanting ray lingered on the woody crests of the precipices that overhung some parts of the river, giving greater depth to the dark grey and purple of their rocky sides. A sloop was loitering in the distance, dropping slowly down with the tide, her sail hanging uselessly against the mast, and as the reflection of the sky gleamed along the still water, it seemed as if the vessel was suspended in the air.

It was toward evening that Ichabod arrived at the castle of the Heer Van Tassel, which he found thronged with the pride and flower of the adjacent country. Old farmers, a spare, leathern-faced race, in home-spun coats and breeches, blue stockings, huge shoes and magnificent pewter buckles. Their brisk withered little dames in close crimped caps, long-waisted short gowns, homespun petticoats, with scissors and pincushions, and gay calico pockets, hanging on the outside. Buxom lasses, almost as antiquated as their mothers, excepting where a straw hat, a fine ribband, or perhaps a white frock, gave symptoms of city innovation. The sons, in short square-skirted coats with rows of stupendous brass buttons, and their hair generally queued in the fashion of the times, especially if they could procure an eel skin for the purpose, it being esteemed throughout the country as a potent nourisher and strengthener of the hair.

Brom Bones, however, was the hero of the scene, having come to the gathering on his favorite steed Daredevil, a creature, like himself, full of mettle and mischief, and which no one but himself could manage. He was in fact noted for preferring vicious animals, given to all kinds of tricks, which kept the rider in constant risk of his neck, for he held a tractable well broken horse as unworthy of a lad of spirit.

Fain would I pause to dwell upon the world of charms that burst upon the enraptured gaze of my hero, as he entered the state parlor of Van Tassel's mansion. Not those of the bevy of buxom lasses, with their luxurious display of red and white: but the ample charms of a genuine Dutch country tea table, in the sumptuous time of autumn. Such heaped up platters of cakes of various and almost indescribable kinds, known only to experienced Dutch housewives. There was the doughty dough nut, the tenderer oly koek, and the crisp and crumbling cruller; sweet cakes and short cakes, ginger cakes and honey cakes, and the whole family of cakes. And then there were apple pies and peach pies and pumpkin pies; besides slices of ham and smoked beef; and moreover delectable dishes of preserved plums, and peaches, and pears, and quinces; not to mention broiled shad and roasted chickens; together with bowls of milk and cream, all mingled higgledy-piggledy, pretty much as I have enumerated them, with the motherly tea pot sending up its clouds of vapor from the midst—Heaven bless the mark! I want breath and time to discuss this banquet as it deserves, and am too eager to get on with my story. Happily, Ichabod Crane was not in so great a hurry as his historian, but did ample justice to every dainty.

He was a kind and thankful creature, whose heart dilated in proportion as his skin was filled with good cheer, and whose spirits rose with eating, as some men's do with drink. He could not help, too, rolling his large eyes round him as he ate, and chuckling with the possibility that he might one day be lord of all this scene of almost unimaginable luxury and splendor. Then, he thought, how soon he'd turn his back upon the old school house; snap his fingers in the face of Hans Van Ripper, and every other niggardly patron, and kick any itinerant pedagogue out of doors that should dare to call him comrade!

Old Baltus Van Tassel moved about among his guests with a face dilated with content and good humor, round and jolly as the harvest moon. His hospitable attentions were brief, but expressive, being confined to a shake of the hand, a slap on the shoulder, a loud laugh, and a pressing invitation to "fall to, and help themselves."

And now the sound of the music from the common room or hall, summoned to the dance. The musician was an old grey headed negro, who had been the itinerant orchestra of the neighborhood for more than half a century. His instrument was as old and battered as himself. The greater part of the time he scraped away on two or three strings, accompanying every movement of the bow with a motion of the head; bowing almost to the ground, and stamping with his foot whenever a fresh couple were to start.

Ichabod prided himself upon his dancing as much as upon his vocal powers. Not a limb, not a fibre about him was idle, and to have seen his loosely hung frame in full motion, and clattering about the room, you would have thought Saint Vitus himself, that blessed patron of the dance, was figuring before you in person. He was the admiration of all the negroes, who, having gathered, of all ages and sizes, from the farm and the neighborhood, stood forming a pyramid of shining black faces at every door and window, gazing with delight at the scene, rolling their white eye balls, and showing grinning rows of ivory from ear to ear. How could the flogger of urchins be otherwise than animated and joyous; the lady of his heart was his partner in the dance; and smiling graciously in reply to all his amorous oglings, while Brom Bones, sorely smitten with love and jealousy, sat brooding by himself in one corner.

When the dance was at an end, Ichabod was attracted to a knot of the sager folks, who, with Old Van Tassel, sat smoking at one end of the piazza, gossiping over former times, and drawing out long stories about the war.

This neighborhood, at the time of which I am speaking, was one of those highly favored places which abound with chronicle and great men. The British and American line had run near it during the war; it had, therefore, been the scene of marauding, and infested with refugees, cow boys, and all kinds of border chivalry. Just sufficient time had elapsed to enable each story teller to dress up his tale with a little becoming fiction, and in the indistinctness of his recollection, to make himself the hero of every exploit.

There was the story of Doffue Martling, a large, blue bearded Dutchman, who had nearly taken a British frigate with an old iron nine pounder from a mud breastwork, only that his gun burst at the sixth discharge. And there was an old gentleman who shall be nameless, being too rich a mynheer to be lightly mentioned, who in the battle of White plains, being an excellent master of defence, parried a musket ball with a small sword, insomuch that he absolutely felt it whiz round the blade, and glance off at the hilt: in proof of which, he was ready at any time to show the sword, with the hilt a little bent. There were several more who had been equally great in the field, not one of whom but was persuaded that he had a considerable hand in bringing the war to a happy termination.

But all these were nothing to the tales of ghosts and apparitions that succeeded. The neighborhood is rich in legendary treasures of the kind. Local tales and superstitions thrive best in these sheltered, long settled retreats; but are trampled under foot, by the shifting throng that forms the population of most of our country places. Besides, there is no encouragement for ghosts in most of our villages, for they have scarcely had time to finish their first nap, and turn themselves in their graves, before their surviving friends have travelled away from the neighborhood; so that when they turn out of a night to walk the rounds, they have no acquaintance left to call upon. This is perhaps the reason why we so seldom hear of ghosts except in our long-established Dutch communities.

The immediate cause, however, of the prevalence of supernatural stories in these parts, was doubtless owing to the vicinity of Sleepy Hollow. There was a contagion in the very air that blew from that haunted region; it breathed forth an atmosphere of dreams and fancies infecting all the land. Several of the Sleepy Hollow people were present at Van Tassel's, and, as usual, were doling out their wild and wonderful legends. Many dismal tales were told about funeral trains, and mourning cries and wailings heard and seen about the great tree where the unfortunate Major André was taken, and which stood in the neighborhood. Some mention was made also of the woman in white, that haunted the dark glen at Raven Rock, and was often heard to shriek on winter nights before a storm, having perished there in the snow. The chief part of the stories, however, turned upon the favorite spectre of Sleepy Hollow, the headless horseman, who had been heard several times of late, patroling the country; and, it was said, tethered his horse nightly among the graves in the church yard.

The sequestered situation of this church seems always to have made it a favorite haunt of troubled spirits. It stands on a knoll, surrounded by locust trees and lofty elms, from among which its decent, white-washed walls shine modestly forth, like Christian purity, beaming through the shades of retirement. A gentle slope descends from it to a silver sheet of water, bordered by high trees, between which, peeps may be caught at the blue hills of the Hudson. To look upon its grass grown yard, where the sunbeams seem to sleep so quietly, one would think that there at least the dead might rest in peace. On one side of the church extends a wide woody dell, along which raves a large brook among broken rocks and trunks of fallen trees. Over a deep black part of the stream, not far from the church, was formerly thrown a wooden bridge; the road that led to it, and the bridge itself, were thickly shaded by overhanging trees, which cast a gloom about it, even in the day time; but occasioned a fearful darkness at night. Such was one of the favorite haunts of the headless horseman, and the place where he was most frequently encountered. The tale was told of old Brouwer, a most heretical disbeliever in ghosts, how he met the horseman returning from his foray into Sleepy Hollow, and was obliged to get up behind him; how they galloped over bush and brake, over hill and swamp, until they reached the bridge, when the horseman suddenly turned into a skeleton, threw old Brouwer into the brook, and sprang away over the tree tops with a clap of thunder.

This story was immediately matched by a thrice marvellous adventure of Brom Bones, who made light of the galloping Hessian as an arrant jockey. He affirmed that on returning one night from the neighboring village of Sing-Sing, he had been overtaken by this midnight trooper; that he had offered to race with him for a bowl of punch, and should have won it too, for Daredevil beat the goblin horse all hollow, but just as they came to the church bridge, the Hessian bolted, and vanished in a flash of fire.

All these tales, told in that drowsy undertone with which men talk in the dark, the countenances of the listeners only now and then receiving a casual gleam from the glare of a pipe, sunk deep in the mind of Ichabod. He repaid them in kind with large extracts from his invaluable author, Cotton Mather, and added many marvellous events that had taken place in his native state of Connecticut, and fearful sights which he had seen in his nightly walks about Sleepy Hollow.

The revel now gradually broke up. The old farmers gathered together their families in their wagons, and were heard for some time rattling along the hollow roads, and over the distant hills. Some of the damsels, mounted on pillions behind their favorite swains, and their light hearted laughter, mingling with the clatter of hoofs, echoed along the silent woodlands, sounding fainter and fainter until they gradually died away—and the late scene of noise and frolic was all silent and deserted. Ichabod only lingered behind, according to the custom of country lovers, to have a tête-à-tête with the heiress; fully convinced that he was now on the high road to success. What passed at this interview I will not pretend to say, for in fact I do not know. Something, however, I fear me, must have gone wrong, for he certainly sallied forth, after no very great interval, with an air quite desolate and chopfallen—Oh these women! these women! Could that girl have been playing off any of her coquettish tricks?—Was her encouragement of the poor pedagogue all a mere sham to secure her conquest of his rival?—Heaven only knows, not I!—Let it suffice to say, Ichabod stole forth with the air of one who had been sacking a hen roost, rather than a fair lady's heart. Without looking to the right or left to notice the scene of rural wealth, on which he had so often gloated, he went straight to the stable, and with several hearty cuffs and kicks, roused his steed most uncourteously from the comfortable quarters in which he was soundly sleeping, dreaming of mountains of corn and oats, and whole valleys of timothy and clover.

It was the very witching time of night that Ichabod, heavy-hearted and crest fallen, pursued his travel homewards, along the sides of the lofty hills which rise above Tarry Town, and which he had traversed so cheerily in the afternoon. The hour was as dismal as himself. Far below him the Tappaan Zee spread its dusky and indistinct waste of waters, with here and there the tall mast of a sloop, riding quietly at anchor under the land. In the dead hush of midnight, he could even hear the barking of the watch dog from the opposite shore of the Hudson; but it was so vague and faint as only to give an idea of his distance from this faithful companion of man. Now and then, too, the long drawn crowing of a cock, accidentally awakened, would sound far, far off, from some farm house away among the hills—but it was like a dreaming sound in his ear. No signs of life occurred near him, but occasionally the melancholy chirp of a cricket, or perhaps the guttural twang of a bull frog from a neighboring marsh, as if sleeping uncomfortably, and turning suddenly in his bed.

All the stories of ghosts and goblins that he had heard in the afternoon, now came crowding upon his recollection. The night grew darker and darker; the stars seemed to sink deeper in the sky, and driving clouds occasionally hid them from his sight. He had never felt so lonely and dismal. He was, moreover, approaching the very place where many of the scenes of the ghost stories had been laid. In the centre of the road stood an enormous tulip tree, which towered like a giant above all the other trees of the neighborhood, and formed a kind of land mark. Its limbs were gnarled, and fantastic, large enough to form trunks for ordinary trees, twisting down almost to the earth, and rising again into the air. It was connected with the tragical story of the unfortunate André, who had been taken prisoner hard by; and was universally known by the name of Major André's tree. The common people regarded it with a mixture of respect and superstition, partly out of sympathy for the fate of its ill starred namesake, and partly from the tales of strange sights, and doleful lamentations, told concerning it.

As Ichabod approached this fearful tree, he began to whistle; he thought his whistle was answered: it was but a blast sweeping sharply through the dry branches. As he approached a little nearer, he thought he saw something white, hanging in the midst of the tree: he paused and ceased whistling; but on looking more narrowly, perceived that it was a place where the tree had been scathed by lightning, and the white wood laid bare. Suddenly he heard a groan—his teeth chattered, and his knees smote against the saddle: it was but the rubbing of one huge bough upon another, as they were swayed about by the breeze. He passed the tree in safety, but new perils lay before him.

About two hundred yards from the tree, a small brook crossed the road, and ran into a marshy and thickly wooded glen, known by the name of Wiley's Swamp. A few rough logs, laid side by side, served for a bridge over this stream. On that side of the road where the brook entered the wood, a group of oaks and chestnuts, matted thick with wild grape vines, threw a cavernous gloom over it. To pass this bridge was the severest trial. It was at this identical spot that the unfortunate André was captured, and under the covert of those chestnuts and vines were the sturdy yeomen concealed who surprised him. This has ever since been considered a haunted stream, and fearful are the feelings of the schoolboy who has to pass it alone after dark.

As he approached the stream, his heart began to thump; he, however, summoned up all his resolution, gave his horse half a score of kicks in the ribs, and attempted to dash briskly across the bridge; but instead of starting forward, the perverse old animal made a lateral movement, and ran broadside against the fence. Ichabod, whose fears increased with the delay, jerked the reins on the other side, and kicked lustily with the contrary foot: it was all in vain; his steed started, it is true, but it was only to plunge to the opposite side of the road into a thicket of brambles and alder bushes. The schoolmaster now bestowed both whip and heel upon the starveling ribs of old Gunpowder, who dashed forward, snuffling and snorting, but came to a stand just by the bridge, with a suddenness that had nearly sent his rider sprawling over his head. Just at this moment a plashy tramp by the side of the bridge caught the sensitive ear of Ichabod. In the dark shadow of the grove, on the margin of the brook, he beheld something huge, mis-shapen, black and towering. It stirred not, but seemed gathered up in the gloom, like some gigantic monster ready to spring upon the traveller.

The hair of the affrighted pedagogue rose upon his head with ter-ror. What was to be done? To turn and fly was now too late; and besides, what chance was there of escaping ghost or goblin, if such it was, which could ride upon the wings of the wind? Summoning up, therefore, a show of courage, he demanded in stammering accents—"who are you?" He received no reply. He repeated his demand in a still more agitated voice.—Still there was no answer. Once more he cudgelled the sides of the inflexible Gunpowder, and shutting his eyes, broke forth with involuntary fervor into a psalm tune. Just then the shadowy object of alarm put itself in motion, and with a scramble and a bound, stood at once in the middle of the road. Though the night was dark and dismal, yet the form of the unknown might now in some degree be ascertained. He appeared to be a horseman of large dimensions, and mounted on a black horse of powerful frame. He made no offer of molestation or sociability, but kept aloof on one side of the road, jogging along on the blind side of old Gunpowder, who had now got over his fright and waywardness.

Ichabod, who had no relish for this strange midnight companion, and bethought himself of the adventure of Brom Bones with the gal-loping Hessian, now quickened his steed, in hopes of leaving him behind. The stranger, however, quickened his horse to an equal pace; Ichabod pulled up, and fell into a walk, thinking to lag behind—the other did the same. His heart began to sink within him; he endeavored to resume his psalm tune, but his parched tongue clove to the roof of his mouth, and he could not utter a stave. There was something in the moody and dogged silence of this pertinacious companion that was mysterious and appalling. It was soon fearfully accounted for. On mounting a rising ground, which brought the figure of his fellow traveller in relief against the sky, gigantic in height, and muffled in a cloak, Ichabod was horror struck, on perceiving that he was headless! but his horror was still more increased, on observing, that the head, which should have rested on his shoulders, was carried before him on the pommel of his saddle! His terror rose to desperation; he rained a shower of kicks and blows upon Gunpowder, hoping by a sudden movement, to give his companion the slip—but the spectre started full jump with him. Away, then, they dashed, through thick and thin; stones flying and sparks flashing, at every bound. Ichabod's flimsy garments fluttered in the air, as he stretched his long lank body away over his horse's head, in the eagerness of his flight.

They had now reached the road which turns off to Sleepy Hollow; but Gunpowder, who seemed possessed with a demon, instead of keeping up it, made an opposite turn, and plunged headlong down hill to the left. This road leads through a sandy hollow shaded by trees for about a quarter of a mile, where it crosses the bridge famous in goblin story, and just beyond swells the green knoll on which stands the whitewashed church.

As yet the panic of the steed had given his unskilful rider an apparent advantage in the chase, but just as he had got half way through the hollow, the girths of the saddle gave way, and he felt it slipping from under him; he seized it by the pommel, and endeavored to hold it firm, but in vain; and had just time to save himself by clasping old Gunpowder round the neck, when the saddle fell to the earth, and he heard it trampled under foot by his pursuer. For a moment the terror of Hans Van Ripper's wrath passed across his mind—for it was his Sunday saddle; but this was no time for petty fears: the goblin was hard on his haunches; and (unskilful rider that he was!) he had much ado to maintain his seat; sometimes slipping on one side, sometimes on another, and sometimes jolted on the high ridge of his horse's back bone, with a violence that he verily feared would cleave him asunder.

An opening in the trees now cheered him with the hopes that the Church Bridge was at hand. The wavering reflection of a silver star in the bosom of the brook told him that he was not mistaken. He saw the walls of the church dimly glaring under the trees beyond. He recollected the place where Brom Bones' ghostly competitor had disappeared. "If I can but reach that bridge," thought Ichabod, "I am safe." Just then he heard the black steed panting and blowing close behind him; he even fancied that he felt his hot breath. Another convulsive kick in the ribs, and old Gunpowder sprung upon the bridge;

he thundered over the resounding planks; he gained the opposite side, and now Ichabod cast a look behind to see if his pursuer should vanish, according to rule, in a flash of fire and brimstone. Just then he saw the goblin rising in his stirrups, and in the very act of hurling his head at him. Ichabod endeavored to dodge the horrible missile, but too late. It encountered his cranium with a tremendous crash—he was tumbled headlong into the dust, and Gunpowder, the black steed, and the goblin rider, passed by like a whirlwind.——

The next morning the old horse was found without his saddle, and with the bridle under his feet, soberly cropping the grass at his master's gate. Ichabod did not make his appearance at breakfast—dinner hour came, but no Ichabod. The boys assembled at the schoolhouse, and strolled idly about the banks of the brook; but no schoolmaster. Hans Van Ripper now began to feel some uneasiness about the fate of poor Ichabod, and his saddle. An inquiry was set on foot, and after diligent investigation they came upon his traces. In one part of the road leading to the church, was found the saddle trampled in the dirt; the tracks of horses' hoofs deeply dented in the road, and evidently at furious speed, were traced to the bridge, beyond which, on the bank of a broad part of the brook, where the water ran deep and black, was found the hat of the unfortunate Ichabod, and close beside it a shattered pumpkin.

The brook was searched, but the body of the schoolmaster was not to be discovered. Hans Van Ripper, as executor of his estate, examined the bundle which contained all his worldly effects. They consisted of two shirts and a half; two stocks for the neck; a pair or two of worsted stockings; an old pair of corduroy small clothes; a rusty razor; a book of psalm tunes full of dog's ears; and a broken pitch pipe. As to the books and furniture of the schoolhouse, they belonged to the community, excepting Cotton Mather's "History of Witchcraft," a "New England Almanac," and a book of dreams and fortune telling, in which last was a sheet of foolscap much scribbled and blotted, in several fruitless attempts to make a copy of verses in honor of the heiress of Van Tassel. These magic books and the poetic scrawl were forthwith consigned to the flames by Hans Van Ripper, who from that time forward determined to send his children no more to school, observing, that he never knew any good come of this same reading and writing. Whatever money the schoolmaster possessed, and he had received his quarter's pay but a day or two before, he must have had about his person at the time of his disappearance.

The mysterious event caused much speculation at the church on the following Sunday. Knots of gazers and gossips were collected in the church yard, at the bridge, and at the spot where the hat and pumpkin had been found. The stories of Brouwer, of Bones, and a whole budget of others, were called to mind; and when they had diligently considered them all, and compared them with the symptoms of the present case, they shook their heads, and came to the conclusion, that Ichabod had been carried off by the galloping Hessian. As he was a bachelor, and in nobody's debt, nobody troubled his head any more about him, the school was removed to a different quarter of the hollow, and another pedagogue reigned in his stead.

It is true, an old farmer, who had been down to New York on a visit several years after, and from whom this account of the ghostly adventure was received, brought home the intelligence that Ichabod Crane was still alive; that he had left the neighborhood partly through fear of the goblin and Hans Van Ripper, and partly in mortification at having been suddenly dismissed by the heiress; that he had changed his quarters to a distant part of the country; had kept school and studied law at the same time; had been admitted to the bar, turned politician, electioneered, written for the newspapers, and finally had been made a Justice of the Ten Pound Court. Brom Bones too, who, shortly after his rival's disappearance, conducted the blooming Katrina in triumph to the altar, was observed to look exceedingly knowing whenever the story of Ichabod was related, and always burst into a hearty laugh at the mention of the pumpkin; which led some to suspect that he knew more about the matter than he chose to tell.

The old country wives, however, who are the best judges of these matters, maintain to this day, that Ichabod was spirited away by supernatural means; and it is a favorite story often told about the neighborhood round the winter evening fire. The bridge became more than ever an object of superstitious awe, and that may be the reason why the road has been altered of late years, so as to approach the church by the border of the mill-pond. The schoolhouse being deserted, soon fell to decay, and was reported to be haunted by the ghost of the unfortunate pedagogue; and the plough boy, loitering homeward of a still summer evening, has often fancied his voice at a distance, chanting a melancholy psalm tune among the tranquil solitudes of Sleepy Hollow.

Postscript

Found in the Handwriting of Mr. Knickerbocker

The preceding Tale is given, almost in the precise words in which I heard it related at a corporation meeting of the ancient city of Manhattoes, at which were present many of its sagest and most illustrious burghers. The narrator was a pleasant, shabby, gentlemanly old fellow, in pepper and salt clothes, with a sadly humourous face, and one whom I strongly suspected of being poor, he made such efforts to be entertaining. When his story was concluded, there was much laughter and approbation, particularly from two or three deputy aldermen, who had been asleep the greater part of the time. There was, however, one tall, dry looking old gentleman, with beetling eye brows, who maintained a grave and rather severe face throughout; now and then folding his arms, inclining his head, and looking down upon the floor, as if turning a doubt over in his mind. He was one of your wary men, who never laugh but upon good grounds—when they have reason and the law on their side. When the mirth of the rest of the company had subsided, and silence was restored, he leaned one arm on the elbow of his chair, and sticking the other akimbo, demanded, with a slight, but exceedingly sage motion of the head, and contraction of the brow, what was the moral of the story, and what it went to prove.

The story teller, who was just putting a glass of wine to his lips, as a refreshment after his toils, paused for a moment, looked at his inquirer with an air of infinite deference, and lowering the glass slowly to the table, observed, that the story was intended most logically to prove,

"That there is no situation in life but has its advantages and pleasures, provided we will but take a joke as we find it:

"That, therefore, he that runs races with goblin troopers, is likely to have rough riding of it:

"Ergo, for a country schoolmaster to be refused the hand of a Dutch heiress, is a certain step to high preferment in the state."

The cautious old gentleman knit his brows tenfold closer after this explanation, being sorely puzzled by the ratiocination of the syllogism; while methought the one in pepper and salt eyed him with something of a triumphant leer. At length he observed, that all this was very well, but still he thought the story a little on the extravagant—there were one or two points on which he had his doubts.

"Faith, sir," replied the story teller, "as to that matter, I don't believe one half of it myself."

D.K.

RIP VAN WINKLE

INTRODUCTION

[The following Tale was found among the papers of the late Diedrich Knickerbocker, on old gentleman of New York, who was very curious in the Dutch history of the province, and the manners of the descendants from its primitive settlers. His historical researches, however, did not lie so much among books, as among men; for the former are lamentably scanty on his favorite topics; whereas he found the old burghers, and still more, their wives, rich in that legendary lore so invaluable to true history. Whenever, therefore, he happened upon a genuine Dutch family, snugly shut up in its low roofed farm house, under a spreading sycamore, he looked upon it as a little clasped volume of black letter, and studied it with the zeal of a bookworm.

The result of all these researches was a history of the province, during the reign of the Dutch governors, which he published some years since. There have been various opinions as to the literary character of his work and, to tell the truth, it is not a whit better than it should be. Its chief merit is its scrupulous accuracy, which indeed was a little questioned on its first appearance, but has since been completely established; and it is now admitted into all historical collections as a book of unquestionable authority.

The old gentleman died shortly after the publication of his work, and now that he is dead and gone, it cannot do much harm to his memory to say that his time might have been much better employed in weightier labors. He, however, was apt to ride his hobby his own way; and though it did now and then kick up the dust a little in the eyes of his neighbors, and grieve the spirit of some friends, for whom he felt the truest deference and affection; yet his errors and follies are remembered "more in sorrow than in anger," and it begins to be suspected that he never intended to injure or offend. But however his memory may be appreciated by critics, it is still held dear by many folk whose good opinion is well worth having; particularly by certain biscuit bakers, who have gone so far as to imprint his likeness on their new year cakes, and have thus given him a chance for immortality, almost equal to the being stamped on a Waterloo Medal, or a Queen Anne's Farthing.]

26

RIP VAN WINKLE

A Posthumous Writing of Diedrich Knickerbocker

By Woden, God of Saxons,
From whence comes Wensday, that is Wodensday,
Truth is a thing that ever I will keep
Unto thylke day in which I creep into
My sepulchre—

Cartwright

WHOEVER HAS MADE a voyage up the Hudson must remember the Kaatskill mountains. They are a dismembered branch of the great Appalachian family, and are seen away to the west of the river, swelling up to a noble height and lording it over the surrounding country. Every change of season, every change of weather, indeed, every hour of the day, produces some change in the magical hues and shapes of these mountains, and they are regarded by all the good wives far and near as perfect barometers. When the weather is fair and settled they are clothed in blue and purple, and print their bold outlines on the clear evening sky; but sometimes, when the rest of the landscape is cloudless, they will gather a hood of gray vapors about their summits, which, in the last rays of the setting sun, will glow and light up like a crown of glory.

At the foot of these fairy mountains the voyager may have descried the light smoke curling up from a village, whose shingle roofs gleam among the trees, just where the blue tints of the upland melt away into the fresh green of the nearer landscape. It is a little village of great antiquity, having been founded by some of the Dutch colonists in the early times of the province, just about the beginning of the government of the good Peter Stuyvesant, (may he rest in peace!) and there were some of the houses of the original settlers standing within a few years; built of small yellow bricks brought from Holland, having latticed windows and gable fronts, surmounted with weathercocks.

In that same village, and in one of these very houses (which to tell the precise truth, was sadly time worn and weather beaten) there lived many years since, while the country was yet a province of Great Britain, a simple good natured fellow of the name of Rip Van Winkle. He was a descendant of the Van Winkles who figured so gallantly in the chivalrous days of Peter Stuyvesant, and accompanied him to the siege of Fort Christina. He inherited, however, but little of the martial character of his ancestors. I have observed that he was a simple good natured man; he was moreover a kind neighbor, and an obedient henpecked husband. Indeed to the latter circumstance might be owing that meekness of spirit which gained him such universal popularity; for those men are most apt to be obsequious and conciliating abroad, who are under the discipline of shrews at home. Their tempers doubtless are rendered pliant and malleable in the fiery furnace of domestic tribulation, and a curtain lecture is worth all the sermons in the world for teaching the virtues of patience and long suffering. A termagant wife may therefore in some respects be considered a tolerable blessing—and if so, Rip Van Winkle was thrice blessed.

Certain it is that he was a great favorite among all the good wives of the village, who as usual with the amiable sex, took his part in all family squabbles, and never failed, whenever they talked those matters over in their evening gossipings, to lay all the blame on Dame Van Winkle. The children of the village too would shout with joy whenever he approached. He assisted at their sports, made their playthings, taught them to fly kites and shoot marbles, and told them long stories of ghosts, witches and Indians. Whenever he went dodging about the village, he was surrounded by a troop of them hanging on his skirts, clambering on his back and playing a thousand tricks on him with impunity; and not a dog would bark at him throughout the neighborhood.

The great error in Rip's composition was an insuperable aversion to all kinds of profitable labor. It could not be from the want of assiduity or perseverance; for he would sit on a wet rock, with a rod as long and heavy as a Tartar's lance, and fish all day without a murmur, even though he should not be encouraged by a single nibble. He would carry a fowling-piece on his shoulder for hours together, trudging through woods, and swamps and up hill and down dale, to shoot a few squirrels or wild pigeons; he would never refuse to assist a neighbor even in the roughest toil, and was a foremost man at all country frolics for husking Indian corn, or building stonefences; the women of the village too used to employ him to run their errands and to do such little odd jobs as their less obliging husbands would not do for them—in a word Rip was ready to attend to any body's business but his own; but as to doing family duty, and keeping his farm in order, he found it impossible.

In fact he declared it was of no use to work on his farm; it was the most pestilent little piece of ground in the whole country; every thing about it went wrong and would go wrong in spite of him. His fences were continually falling to pieces; his cow would either go astray or get among the cabbages, weeds were sure to grow quicker in his fields than any where else; the rain always made a point of setting in just as he had some outdoor work to do. So that though his patrimonial estate had dwindled away under his management, acre by acre until there was little more left than a mere patch of Indian corn and potatoes, yet it was the worst conditioned farm in the neighborhood.

His children too were as ragged and wild as if they belonged to nobody. His son Rip, an urchin begotten in his own likeness, promised to inherit the habits with the old clothes of his father. He was generally seen trooping like a colt at his mother's heels, equipped in a pair of his father's cast off galligaskins, which he had much ado to hold up with one hand, as a fine lady does her train in bad weather.

Rip Van Winkle, however, was one of those happy mortals of foolish, well oiled dispositions, who take the world easy, eat white bread or brown, whichever can be got with least thought or trouble, and would rather starve on a penny than work for a pound. If left to himself, he would have whistled life away in perfect contentment, but his wife kept continually dinning in his ears about his idleness, his carelessness and the ruin he was bringing on his family. Morning noon and night her tongue was incessantly going, and every thing he said or did was sure to produce a torrent of household eloquence. Rip had but one way of replying to all lectures of the kind, and that by frequent use had grown into a habit. He shrugged his shoulders, shook his head, cast up his eyes, but said nothing. This, however, always provoked a fresh volley from his wife, so that he was fain to draw off his forces, and take to the outside of the house—the only side which, in truth, belongs to a henpecked husband.

Rip's sole domestic adherent was his dog Wolf who was as much henpecked as his master, for Dame Van Winkle regarded them as companions in idleness, and even looked upon Wolf with an evil eye as the cause of his master's going so often astray. True it is, in all points of spirit befitting an honorable dog, he was as courageous an animal as ever scoured the woods—but what courage can withstand the ever during and all-besetting terrors of a woman's tongue? The moment Wolf entered the house his crest fell, his tail dropped to the ground, or curled between his legs, he sneaked about with a gallows air, casting many a sidelong glance at Dame Van Winkle, and at the least flourish of a broomstick or ladle he would fly to the door with yelping precipitation.

Times grew worse and worse with Rip Van Winkle as years of matrimony rolled on; a tart temper never mellows with age, and a sharp tongue is the only edged tool that grows keener with constant use. For a long while he used to console himself when driven from home, by frequenting a kind of perpetual club of the sages, philosophers and other idle personages of the village which held its sessions on a bench before a small inn, designated by a rubicund portrait of his majesty George the Third. Here they used to sit in the shade, through a long lazy summer's day, talking listlessly over village gossip, or telling endless sleepy stories about nothing. But it would have been worth any statesman's money to have heard the profound discussions that sometimes took place, when by chance an old newspaper fell into their hands from some passing traveller. How solemnly they would listen to the contents as drawled out by Derrick Van Bummel, the schoolmaster, a dapper, learned little man, who was not to be daunted by the most gigantic word in the dictionary; and how sagely they would deliberate upon public events some months after they had taken place.

The opinions of this junto were completely controlled by Nicholas Vedder, a patriarch of the village, and landlord of the inn, at the door of which he took his seat from morning till night, just moving sufficiently to avoid the sun and keep in the shade of a large tree; so that the neighbors could tell the hour by his movements as accurately as by a sun dial. It is true he was rarely heard to speak, but smoked his pipe incessantly. His adherents, however (for every great man has his adherents), perfectly understood him and knew how to gather his opinions. When any thing that was read or related displeased him, he was observed to smoke his pipe vehemently and to send forth short, frequent and angry puffs; but when pleased, he would inhale the smoke slowly and tranquilly and emit it in light and placid clouds, and sometimes taking the pipe from his mouth, and letting the fragrant vapor curl about his nose, would gravely nod his head in token of perfect approbation.

From even this stronghold the unlucky Rip was at length routed by his termagant wife who would suddenly break in upon the tranquility of the assemblage and call the members all to naught; nor was that august personage, Nicholas Vedder himself sacred from the daring tongue of this terrible virago, who charged him outright with encouraging her husband in habits of idleness.

Poor Rip was at last reduced almost to despair; and his only alternative, to escape from the labor of the farm and the clamor of his wife, was to take gun in hand and stroll away into the woods. Here he would sometimes seat himself at the foot of a tree and share the contents of his wallet with Wolf, with whom he sympathized as a fellow-sufferer in persecution. "Poor Wolf," he would say, "thy mistress leads thee a dog's life of it, but never mind my lad, whilst I live thou shalt never want a friend to stand by thee!" Wolf would wag his tail, look wistfully in his master's face, and if dogs can feel pity I verily believe he reciprocated the sentiment with all his heart.

In a long ramble of the kind on a fine autumnal day, Rip had unconsciously scrambled to one of the highest parts of the Kaatskill mountains. He was after his favorite sport of squirrel shooting, and the still solitudes had echoed and reechoed with the reports of his gun. Panting and fatigued, he threw himself, late in the afternoon, on a green knoll, covered with mountain herbage, that crowned the brow of a precipice. From an opening between the trees he could overlook all the lower country for many a mile of rich woodland. He saw at a distance the lordly Hudson, far, far below him, moving on its silent but majestic course, with the reflection of a purple cloud, or the sail of a lagging bark here and there sleeping on its glassy bosom, and at last losing itself in the blue highlands.

On the other side he looked down into a deep mountain glen, wild, lonely and shagged, the bottom filled with fragments from the impending cliffs and scarcely lighted by the reflected rays of the setting sun. For some time Rip lay musing on this scene, evening was gradually advancing, the mountains began to throw their long blue shadows over the valleys, he saw that it would be dark, long before he could reach the village, and he heaved a heavy sigh when he thought of encountering the terrors of Dame Van Winkle.

As he was about to descend he heard a voice from a distance hallooing, "Rip Van Winkle! Rip Van Winkle!" He looked around, but could see nothing but a crow winging its solitary flight across the mountain. He thought his fancy must have deceived him and turned again to descend, when he heard the same cry ring through the still evening air: "Rip Van Winkle! Rip Van Winkle!"—at the same time Wolf bristled up his back and giving a low growl, skulked to his master's side, looking fearfully down into the glen. Rip now felt a vague apprehension stealing over him; he looked anxiously in the same direction, and perceived a strange figure slowly toiling up the rocks and bending under the weight of something he carried on his back. He was surprised to see any human being in this lonely and unfrequented place, but supposing it to be some one of the neighborhood in need of his assistance, he hastened down to yield it.

On nearer approach he was still more surprised at the singularity of the stranger's appearance. He was a short square built old fellow, with thick bushy hair and a grizzled beard. His dress was of the antique Dutch fashion—a cloth jerkin strapped round the waist—several pair of breeches, the outer one of ample volume decorated with rows of buttons down the sides and bunches at the knees. He bore on his shoulder a stout keg that seemed full of liquor, and made signs for Rip to approach and assist him with the load. Though rather shy and distrustful of this new acquaintance Rip complied with his usual alacrity, and mutually relieving each other, they clambered up a narrow gully apparently the dry bed of a mountain torrent. As they ascended Rip every now and then heard long rolling peals like distant thunder that seemed to issue out of a deep ravine or rather cleft between lofty rocks, toward which their rugged path conducted. He paused for an instant, but supposing it to be the muttering of one of those transient thunder showers which often take place in mountain heights, he proceeded. Passing through the ravine they came to a hollow like a small amphitheatre, surrounded by perpendicular precipices, over the brinks of which impending trees shot their branches, so that you only caught glimpses of the azure sky and the bright evening cloud. During the whole time Rip and his companion had labored on in silence, for though the former marvelled greatly what could be the object of carrying a keg of liquor up this wild mountain, yet there was something strange and incomprehensible about the unknown, that inspired awe and checked familiarity.

On entering the amphitheatre new objects of wonder presented themselves. On a level spot in the centre was a company of odd looking personages playing at ninepins. They were dressed in a quaint outlandish fashion—some wore short doublets, others jerkins with long knives in their belts and most of them had enormous breeches of similar style with that of the guide's. Their visages too were peculiar. One had a large head, broad face and small piggish eyes. The face of another seemed to consist entirely of nose, and was surmounted by a white sugarloaf hat, set off with a little red cock's tail. They all had beards of various shapes and colors. There was one who seemed to be the Commander. He was a stout old gentleman, with a weather-beaten countenance. He wore a laced doublet, broad belt and hanger, high crowned hat and feather, red stockings and high heel'd shoes with roses in them. The whole group reminded Rip of the figures in an old Flemish painting, in the parlor of Dominie Van Shaick, the village parson, and which had been brought over from Holland at the time of the settlement.

What seemed particularly odd to Rip was, that though these folks were evidently amusing themselves, yet they maintained the gravest faces, the most mysterious silence, and were, withal, the most melancholy party of pleasure he had ever witnessed. Nothing interrupted the stillness of the scene, but the noise of the balls, which, whenever they were rolled, echoed along the mountains like rumbling peals of thunder.

As Rip and his companion approached them they suddenly desisted from their play and stared at him with such fixed statue like gaze, and such strange uncouth, lacklustre countenances, that his heart turned within him, and his knees smote together. His companion now emptied the contents of the keg into large flagons and made signs to him to wait upon the company. He obeyed with fear and trembling; they quaffed the liquor in profound silence and then returned to their game.

By degrees Rip's awe and apprehension subsided. He even ventured, when no eye was fixed upon him, to taste the beverage, which he found had much of the flavor of excellent hollands. He was naturally a thirsty soul and was soon tempted to repeat the draught. One taste provoked another, and he reiterated his visits to the flagon so often that at length his senses were overpowered, his eyes swam in his head—his head gradually declined, and he fell into a deep sleep.

On awaking he found himself on the green knoll from whence he had first seen the old man of the glen. He rubbed his eyes—it was a bright, sunny morning. The birds were hopping and twittering among the bushes, and the eagle was wheeling aloft and breasting the pure mountain breeze. "Surely," thought Rip, "I have not slept here all night." He recalled the occurences before he fell asleep. The strange man with a keg of liquor—the mountain ravine—the wild retreat among the rocks—the woebegone party at ninepins—the flagon—"ah! that flagon! that wicked flagon!" thought Rip—"what excuse shall I make to Dame Van Winkle?"

He looked round for his gun, but in place of the clean well oiled fowling piece he found an old firelock lying by him, the barrel encrusted with rust; the lock falling off and the stock worm eaten. He now suspected that the grave roysters of the mountain had put a trick upon him, and having dosed him with liquor, had robbed him of his gun. Wolf too had disappeared but he might have strayed away after a squirrel or partridge. He whistled after him and shouted his name—but all in vain; the echoes repeated his whistle and shout, but no dog was to be seen.

He determined to revisit the scene of the last evening's gambol, and if he met with any of the party, to demand his dog and gun. As he arose to walk, he found himself stiff in the joints and wanting in his usual activity. "These mountain beds do not agree with me," thought Rip, "and if this frolic should lay me up with a fit of the rheumatism, I shall have a blessed time with Dame Van Winkle." With some difficulty he got down into the glen; he found the gully up which he and his companion had ascended the preceding evening, but to his astonishment a mountain stream was now foaming down it; leaping from rock to rock, and filling the glen with babbling murmurs. He, however, made shift to scramble up its sides working his toilsome way through thickets of birch, sassafras and witch hazel, and sometimes tripped up or entangled by the wild grape vines that twisted their coils or tendrils from tree to tree, and spread a kind of net work in his path.

At length he reached to where the ravine had opened through the cliffs, to the amphitheatre—but no traces of such opening remained. The rocks presented a high impenetrable wall over which the torrent came tumbling in a sheet of feathery foam, and fell into a broad deep basin black from the shadows of the surrounding forest. Here then poor Rip was brought to a stand. He again called and whistled after his dog—he was only answered by the cawing of a flock of idle crows, sporting high in air about a dry tree that overhung a sunny precipice; and who, secure in their elevation, seemed to look down and scoff at the poor man's perplexities.

What was to be done? The morning was passing away and Rip felt famished for want of his breakfast. He grieved to give up his dog and gun; he dreaded to meet his wife; but it would not do to starve among the mountains. He shook his head, shouldered the rusty fire lock and with a heart full of trouble and anxiety, turned his steps homeward.

As he approached the village he met a number of people, but none whom he knew which somewhat surprised him, for he had thought himself acquainted with every one in the country round. Their dress too was of a different fashion from that to which he was accustomed. They all stared at him with equal marks of surprise, and whenever they cast their eyes upon him, invariably stroked their chins. The constant recurrence of this gesture induced Rip involuntarily to do the same, when to his astonishment he found his beard had grown a foot long!

He had now entered the skirts of the village. A troop of strange children ran at his heels, hooting after him and pointing at his gray beard. The dogs too, not one of which he recognized for an old acquaintance, barked at him as he passed. The very village was altered—it was larger and more populous. There were rows of houses which he had never seen before, and those which had been his familiar haunts had disappeared. Strange names were over the doors—strange faces at the windows—every thing was strange. His mind now misgave him; he began to doubt whether both he and the world around him were not bewitched. Surely this was his native village which he had left but the day before. There stood the Kaatskill mountains—there ran the silver Hudson at a distance—there was every hill and

dale precisely as it had always been—Rip was sorely perplexed—
"That flagon last night," thought he, "has addled my poor head
sadly!"

It was with some difficulty that he found the way to his own house,
which he approached with silent awe, expecting every moment to
hear the shrill voice of Dame Van Winkle. He found the house gone
to decay—the roof fallen in, the windows shattered, and the doors off
the hinges. A half starved dog that looked like Wolf was sulking about
it. Rip called him by name but the cur snarled, shewed his teeth and
passed on. This was an unkind cut indeed—"My very dog," sighed
poor Rip, "has forgotten me!"

He entered the house, which, to tell the truth, Dame Van Winkle
had always kept in neat order. It was empty, forlorn, and apparently
abandoned. This desolateness overcame all his connubial fears—he
called loudly for his wife and children—the lonely chambers rang for
a moment with his voice, and then all again was silence.

He now hurried forth and hastened to his old resort, the village
inn—but it too was gone. A large, rickety wooden building stood in
its place, with great gaping windows, some of them broken and
mended with old hats and petticoats, and over the door was printed,
"The Union Hotel, by Jonathan Doolittle." Instead of the great tree,
that used to shelter the quiet little Dutch inn of yore, there now was
reared a tall naked pole with something on the top that looked like a
red night cap, and from it was fluttering a flag on which was a singular assemblage of stars and stripes—all this was strange and incomprehensible. He recognized on the sign, however, the ruby face of King
George under which he had smoked so many a peaceful pipe, but
even this was singularly metamorphosed. The red coat was changed
for one of blue and buff; a sword was held in the hand instead of a
sceptre, the head was decorated with a cocked hat, and underneath
was painted in large characters, GENERAL WASHINGTON.

There was as usual a crowd of folk about the door; but none that
Rip recollected. The very character of the people seemed changed.
There was a busy, bustling, disputatious tone about it, instead of the
accustomed phlegm and drowsy tranquility. He looked in vain for the
sage Nicholas Vedder with his broad face, double chin and fair long
pipe, uttering clouds of tobacco smoke instead of idle speeches. Or
Van Bummel the schoolmaster doling forth the contents of an ancient
newspaper. In place of these a lean bilious looking fellow with his
pockets full of hand bills, was haranguing vehemently about rights of
citizens—elections—members of Congress—liberty—Bunker's
Hill—heroes of seventy-six—and other words which were a perfect
babylonish jargon to the bewildered Van Winkle.

The appearance of Rip with his long grizzled beard, his rusty fowling piece, his uncouth dress and an army of women and children at his heels soon attracted the attention of the tavern politicians. They crowded around him eyeing him from head to foot, with great curiosity. The orator bustled up to him, and drawing him partly aside, inquired "on which side he voted?"—Rip stared in vacant stupidity. Another short but busy little fellow pulled him by the arm and inquired in his ear, "whether he was Federal or Democrat?"—Rip was equally at a loss to comprehend the question—when a knowing, self important old gentleman, in a sharp cocked hat, made his way through the crowd, putting them to the right and left with his elbows as he passed, and planting himself before Van Winkle, with one arm akimbo, the other resting on his cane, his keen eyes and sharp hat penetrating as it were into his very soul, demanded in an austere tone—"what brought him to the election with a gun on his shoulder and a mob at his heels, and whether he meant to breed a riot in the village?"—"Alas! gentlemen," cried Rip, somewhat dismayed, "I am a poor quiet man, a native of the place, and a loyal subject of the King—God bless him!"

Here a general shout burst from the byestanders—"A tory! a tory! a spy! a Refugee! hustle him! away with him!"—It was with great difficulty that the self important man in the cocked hat restored order; and having assumed a ten fold austerity of brow demanded again of the unknown culprit, what he came there for and whom he was seeking. The poor man humbly assured him that he meant no harm; but merely came there in search of some of his neighbors, who used to keep about the tavern.

"—Well—who are they?—name them."

Rip bethought himself a moment, and inquired, "Where's Nicholas Vedder?"

There was a silence for a little while, when an old man replied, in a thin piping voice, "Nicholas Vedder? why he is dead and gone these eighteen years! There was a wooden tombstone in the church yard that used to tell all about him, but that's rotted and gone too."

"Where's Brom Dutcher?"

"Oh he went off to the army in the beginning of the war; some say he was killed at the storming of Stoney Point—others say he was drowned in a squall at the foot of Antony's Nose—I don't know—he never came back again."

"Where's Van Bummel, the schoolmaster?"

"He went off to the wars too—was a great militia general, and is now in Congress."

Rip's heart died away at hearing of these sad changes in his home and friends, and finding himself thus alone in the world—every answer puzzled him too by treating of such enormous lapses of time and of matters which he could not understand—war—Congress, Stoney Point—he had no courage to ask after any more friends, but cried out in despair, "Does nobody here know Rip Van Winkle?"

"Oh. Rip Van Winkle?" exclaimed two or three—"oh to be sure—that's Rip Van Winkle—yonder—leaning against the tree."

Rip looked and beheld a precise counterpart of himself, as he went up to the mountain: apparently as lazy and certainly as ragged! The poor fellow was now completely confounded. He doubted his own identity, and whether he was himself or another man. In the midst of his bewilderment the man in the cocked hat demanded who he was,—what was his name?

"God knows," exclaimed he, at his wit's end, "I'm not myself.—I'm somebody else—that's me yonder—no—that's somebody else got into my shoes—I was myself last night; but I fell asleep on the mountain, and they've changed my gun, and every thing's changed—and I'm changed, and I can't tell what's my name, or who I am!"

The byestanders began now to look at each other, nod, wink significantly and tap their fingers against their foreheads. There was a whisper also about securing the gun, and keeping the old fellow from doing mischief—at the very suggestion of which, the self important man in the cocked hat retired with some precipitation. At this critical moment a fresh likely looking woman pressed through the throng to get a peep at the graybearded man. She had a chubby child in her arms, which frightened at his looks began to cry. "Hush Rip," cried she, "hush you little fool, the old man won't hurt you." The name of the child, the air of the mother, the tone of her voice all awakened a train of recollections in his mind. "What is your name my good woman?" asked he.

"Judith Gardenier."

"And your father's name?"

"Ah, poor man, Rip Van Winkle was his name, but it's twenty years since he went away from home with his gun and never has been heard of since—his dog came home without him; but whether he shot himself, or was carried away by the Indians no body can tell. I was then but a little girl."

Rip had but one question more to ask, but he put it with a faltering voice—

"Where's your mother?"—

Oh she too had died but a short time since—she broke a blood vessel in a fit of passion at a New England peddler.—

There was a drop of comfort at least in this intelligence. The

honest man could contain himself no longer—he caught his daughter
and her child in his arms.—"I am your father!" cried he—"Young
Rip Van Winkle once—old Rip Van Winkle now!—does nobody
know poor Rip Van Winkle?"

All stood amazed, until an old woman tottering out from among
the crowd put her hand to her brow and peering under it in his face
for a moment exclaimed—"Sure enough!—it is Rip Van Winkle—it
is himself—welcome home again old neighbor—why, where have
you been these twenty long years?"

Rip's story was soon told, for the whole twenty years had been to
him but as one night. The neighbors stared when they heard it; some
were seen to wink at each other and put their tongues in their cheeks,
and the self important man in the cocked hat, who when the alarm
was over had returned to the field, screwed down the corners of his
mouth and shook his head—upon which there was a general shaking
of the head throughout the assemblage.

It was determined, however, to take the opinion of old Peter
Vanderdonk, who was seen slowly advancing up the road. He was a
descendant of the historian of that name, who wrote one of the earli-
est accounts of the province. Peter was the most ancient inhabitant of
the village and well versed in all the wonderful events and traditions
of the neighborhood. He recollected Rip at once, and corroborated
his story in the most satisfactory manner. He assured the company
that it was a fact handed down from his ancestor the historian, that
the Kaatskill mountains had always been haunted by strange beings.
That it was affirmed that the great Hendrick Hudson, the first discov-
erer of the river and country, kept a kind of vigil there every twenty
years, with his crew of the Half Moon—being permitted in this way
to revisit the scenes of his enterprise and keep a guardian eye upon
the river and the great city called by his name. That his father had
once seen them in their old Dutch dresses playing at nine pins in a
hollow of the mountain; and that he himself had heard one summer
afternoon the sound of their balls, like distant peals of thunder.

To make a long story short—the company broke up, and returned
to the more important concerns of the election. Rip's daughter took
him home to live with her; she had a snug well furnished house, and
a stout cheery farmer for a husband whom Rip recollected for one of
the urchins that used to climb upon his back. As to Rip's son and
heir, who was the ditto of himself seen leaning against the tree; he was
employed to work on the farm; but evinced an hereditary disposition
to attend to any thing else but his business.

Rip now resumed his old walks and habits; he soon found many of
his former cronies, though all rather the worse for the wear and tear

of time; and preferred making friends among the rising generation, with whom he soon grew into great favor. Having nothing to do at home, and being arrived at that happy age when a man can be idle with impunity, he took his place once more on the bench at the inn door and was reverenced as one of the patriarchs of the village, and a chronicle of the old times "before the war." It was some time before he could get into the regular track of gossip, or could be made to comprehend the strange events that had taken place during his torpor. How that there had been a revolutionary war—that the country had thrown off the yoke of Old England and that instead of being a sub-ject of his majesty George the Third, he was now a free citizen of the United States. Rip in fact was no politician; the changes of states and empires made but little impression on him; but there was one species of despotism under which he had long groaned, and that was petticoat government. Happily that was at an end—he had got his neck out of the yoke of matrimony, and could go in and out whenever he pleased without dreading the tyranny of Dame Van Winkle. Whenever her name was mentioned, however, he shook his head, shrugged his shoulders and cast up his eyes; which might pass either for an expres-sion of resignation to his fate or joy at his deliverance.

He used to tell his story to every stranger that arrived at Mr. Doolittle's hotel. He was observed at first to vary on some points, every time he told it, which was doubtless owing to his having so recently awaked. It at last settled down precisely to the tale I have related and not a man woman or child in the neighborhood but knew it by heart. Some always pretended to doubt the reality of it, and insisted that Rip had been out of his head, and that this was one point on which he always remained flighty. The old Dutch inhabitants, however, almost universally gave it full credit—Even to this day they never hear a thunder storm of a summer afternoon about the Kaatskill, but they say Hendrick Hudson and his crew are at their game of nine pins; and it is a common wish of all henpecked husbands in the neigh-borhood, when life hangs heavy on their hands, that they might have a quieting draught out of Rip Van Winkle's flagon.

Note

The foregoing tale, one would suspect, had been suggested to Mr. Knickerbocker by a little German superstition about the emperor Frederick *der Rothbart* and the Kypphauser Mountain; the subjoined note, however, which he had appended to the tale, shows that it is an absolute fact, narrated with his usual fidelity.—

"The story of Rip Van Winkle may seem incredible to many, but nevertheless I give it my full belief, for I know the vicinity of our old Dutch settlements to have been very subject to marvellous events and appearances. Indeed I have heard many stranger stories than this, in the villages along the Hudson; all of which were too well authenticated to admit of a doubt. I have even talked with Rip Van Winkle myself, who when last I saw him was a very venerable old man and so perfectly rational and consistent on every other point, that I think no conscientious person could refuse to take this into the bargain— nay I have seen a certificate on the subject taken before a country justice and signed with a cross in the justice's own hand writing. The story therefore is beyond the possibility of doubt.

D.K."

Postscript

The following are travelling notes from a memorandum book of Mr. Knickerbocker.

The Kaatsberg or Catskill mountains have always been a region full of fable. The Indians considered them the abode of spirits who influenced the weather, spreading sunshine or clouds over the landscape and sending good or bad hunting seasons. They were ruled by an old squaw spirit, said to be their mother. She dwelt on the highest peak of the Catskills and had charge of the doors of day and night to open and shut them at the proper hour. She hung up the new moons in the skies and cut up the old ones into stars. In times of drought, if properly propitiated, she would spin light summer clouds out of cobwebs and morning dew, and send them off, from the crest of the mountain, flake after flake, like flakes of carded cotton to float in the air: until, dissolved by the heat of the sun, they would fall in gentle showers, causing the grass to spring, the fruits to ripen and the corn to grow an inch an hour. If displeased, however, she would brew up clouds black as ink, sitting in the midst of them like a bottle bellied spider in the midst of its web; and when these clouds broke—woe betide the valleys!

In old times say the Indian traditions, there was a kind of Manitou or Spirit, who kept about the wildest recesses of the Catskill mountains, and took a mischievous pleasure in wreaking all kinds of evils and vexations upon the red men. Sometimes he would assume the form of a bear a panther or a deer, lead the bewildered hunter a weary chase through tangled forests and among rugged rocks; and then spring off with a loud ho! ho! leaving him aghast on the brink of a beetling precipice or raging torrent.

The favorite abode of this Manitou is still shown. It is a great rock or cliff in the loneliest part of the mountains, and, from the flowering vines which clamber about it, and the wild flowers which abound in its neighborhood, is known by the name of the Garden Rock. Near the foot of it is a small lake the haunt of the solitary bittern, with water snakes basking in the sun on the leaves of the pond lillies which lie on the surface. This place was held in great awe by the Indians, insomuch that the boldest hunter would not pursue his game within its precincts. Once upon a time, however, a hunter who had lost his way, penetrated to the garden rock where he beheld a number of gourds placed in the crotches of trees. One of these he seized and made off with it, but in the hurry of his retreat he let it fall among the rocks, when a great stream gushed forth which washed him away and swept him down precipices where he was dashed to pieces, and the stream made its way to the Hudson and continues to flow to the present day; being the identical stream known by the name of the Kaaters-kill.

THE SPECTRE BRIDEGROOM

A Traveller's Tale

> He that supper for is dight,
> He lyes full cold, I trow, this night!
> Yestreen to chamber I him led,
> This night Gray-steel has made his bed!
> *Sir Eger, Sir Grahame, and Sir Gray-steel*

ON THE SUMMIT of one of the heights of the Odenwald, a wild and romantic tract of Upper Germany, that lies not far from the confluence of the Main and the Rhine, there stood, many, many years since, the Castle of the Baron Von Landshort. It is now quite fallen to decay, and almost buried among beech trees and dark firs, above which, however, its old watch tower may still be seen struggling, like the former possessor I have mentioned, to carry a high head, and look down upon the neighboring country.

The Baron was a dry branch of the great family of Katzenellenbogen, and inherited the relics of the property, and all the pride of his ancestors. Though the warlike disposition of his predecessors had much impaired the family possessions, yet the Baron still endeavored to keep up some show of former state. The times were peaceable, and the German nobles, in general, had abandoned their inconvenient old castles, perched like eagles' nests among the mountains, and had built more convenient residences in the valleys: still the Baron remained proudly drawn up in his little fortress, cherishing with hereditary inveteracy, all the old family feuds; so that he was on ill terms with some of his nearest neighbors, on account of disputes that had happened between their great great grandfathers.

The Baron had but one child, a daughter; but nature, when she grants but one child, always compensates by making it a prodigy; and so it was with the daughter of the Baron. All the nurses, gossips, and country cousins, assured her father that she had not her equal for beauty in all Germany; and who should know better than they. She had, moreover, been brought up with great care under the superintendence of two maiden aunts, who had spent some years of their early life at one of the little German courts, and were skilled in all the branches of knowledge necessary to the education of a fine lady. Under their instructions, she became a miracle of accomplishments. By the time she was eighteen she could embroider to admiration, and had worked whole histories of the saints in tapestry, with such strength of expression in their countenances, that they looked like so many souls in purgatory. She could read without great difficulty, and had spelled her way through several church legends, and almost all the chivalric wonders of the Heldenbuch. She had even made considerable proficiency in writing, could sign her own name without missing a letter, and so legibly, that her aunts could read it without spectacles. She excelled in making little elegant good for nothing lady like nicknacks of all kinds; was versed in the most abstruse dancing of the day; played a number of airs on the harp and guitar; and knew all the tender ballads of the Minne-lieders by heart.

Her aunts, too, having been great flirts and coquettes in their younger days, were admirably calculated to be vigilant guardians and strict censors of the conduct of their niece; for there is no duenna so rigidly prudent, and inexorably decorous, as a superannuated coquette. She was rarely suffered out of their sight; never went beyond the domains of the castle, unless well attended, or rather, well watched; had continual lectures read to her about strict decorum and implicit obedience; and, as to the men—pah!—she was taught to hold them at such a distance and in such absolute distrust, that, unless properly authorized, she would not have cast a glance upon the handsomest cavalier in the world—no, not if he were even dying at her feet!

The good effects of this system were wonderfully apparent. The young lady was a pattern of docility and correctness. While others were wasting their sweetness in the glare of the world, and liable to be plucked and thrown aside by every hand, she was coyly blooming into fresh and lovely womanhood under the protection of those immaculate spinsters, like a rose bud blushing forth among guardian thorns. Her aunts looked upon her with pride and exultation, and vaunted that though all the other young ladies in the world might go astray, yet thank heaven, nothing of the kind could happen to the heiress of Katzenellenbogen.

But, however scantily the Baron Von Landshort might be provided with children, his household was by no means a small one, for providence had enriched him with abundance of poor relations. They, one and all, possessed the affectionate disposition common to humble relatives: were wonderfully attached to the Baron, and took every possible occasion to come in swarms and enliven the castle. All family

festivals were commemorated by these good people at the Baron's
expense; and when they were filled with good cheer, they would
declare that there was nothing on earth so delightful as these family
meetings, these jubilees of the heart.

The Baron, though a small man, had a large soul, and it swelled
with satisfaction at the consciousness of being the greatest man in the
little world about him. He loved to tell long stories about the stark
old warriors whose portraits looked grimly down from the walls
around, and he found no listeners equal to those who fed at his expense. He was much given to the marvellous, and a firm believer in
all those supernatural tales with which every mountain and valley in
Germany abounds. The faith of his guests exceeded even his own:
they listened to every tale of wonder with open eyes and mouth, and
never failed to be astonished, even though repeated for the hundredth
time. Thus lived the Baron Von Landshort, the oracle of his table, the
absolute monarch of his little territory, and happy above all things, in
the persuasion that he was the wisest man of the age.

At the time of which my story treats, there was a great family gathering at the Castle on an affair of the utmost importance: it was to
receive the destined bridegroom of the Baron's daughter. A negotia-
tion had been carried on between the father and an old nobleman of
Bavaria to unite the dignity of their houses by the marriage of their
children. The preliminaries had been conducted with proper punc-
tilio. The young people were betrothed without seeing each other,
and the time was appointed for the marriage ceremony. The young
Count Von Altenburg had been recalled from the army for the purpose, and was actually on his way to the Baron's to receive his bride.
Missives had even been received from him, from Wurtzburg, where
he was accidentally detained, mentioning the day and hour when he
might be expected to arrive.

The castle was in a tumult of preparation to give him a suitable
welcome. The fair bride had been decked out with uncommon care.
The two aunts had superintended her toilet, and quarrelled the whole
morning about every article of her dress. The young lady had taken
advantage of their contest to follow the bent of her own taste; and
fortunately it was a good one. She looked as lovely as youthful bridegroom could desire; and the flutter of expectation heightened the
lustre of her charms.

The suffusions that mantled her face and neck, the gentle heaving
of the bosom, the eye now and then lost in reverie, all betrayed the
soft tumult that was going on in her little heart. The aunts were continually hovering around her; for maiden aunts are apt to take great
interest in affairs of this nature. They were giving her a world of staid

counsel how to deport herself, what to say, and in what manner to receive the expected lover.

The Baron was no less busied in preparations. He had, in truth, nothing exactly to do; but he was naturally a fuming, bustling little man, and could not remain passive when all the world was in a hurry. He worried from top to bottom of the castle, with an air of infinite anxiety; he continually called the servants from their work to exhort them to be diligent, and buzzed about every hall and chamber, as idly restless and importunate as a blue bottle fly of a warm summer's day.

In the mean time, the fatted calf had been killed; the forests had rung with the clamor of the huntsmen; the kitchen was crowded with good cheer; the cellars had yielded up whole oceans of *Rhein-wein* and *Ferne-wein,* and even the great Heidelberg tun had been laid under contribution. Every thing was ready to receive the distinguished guest with *Saus und Braus* in the true spirit of German hospitality—but the guest delayed to make his appearance. Hour rolled after hour. The sun that had poured his downward rays upon the rich forests of the Odenwald, now just gleamed along the summits of the mountains. The Baron mounted the highest tower, and strained his eyes in hopes of catching a distant sight of the Count and his attendants. Once he thought he beheld them; the sound of horns came floating from the valley, prolonged by the mountain echoes. A number of horsemen were seen far below, slowly advancing along the road; but when they had nearly reached the foot of the mountain, they suddenly struck off in a different direction. The last ray of sunshine departed— the bats began to flit by in the twilight—the road grew dimmer and dimmer to the view; and nothing appeared stirring in it, but now and then a peasant lagging homeward from his labor.

While the old castle of Landshort was in this state of perplexity, a very interesting scene was transacting in a different part of the Odenwald.

The young Count Von Altenburg was tranquilly pursuing his route in that sober jog trot way in which a man travels towards matrimony, when his friends have taken all the trouble and uncertainty of courtship off his hands, and a bride is waiting for him, as—certainly as a dinner, at the end of his journey. He had encountered, at Wurtzburg, a youthful companion in arms—with whom he had seen some service on the frontiers; Herman Von Starkenfaust, one of the stoutest hands, and worthiest hearts, of German chivalry, who was now returning from the army. His father's castle was not far distant from the old fortress of Landshort, although an hereditary feud rendered the families hostile, and strangers to each other.

In the warm hearted moment of recognition, the young friends related all their past adventures and fortunes, and the count gave the whole history of his intended nuptials with a young lady whom he had never seen, but of whose charms he had received the most enrapturing descriptions.

As the route of the friends lay in the same direction, they agreed to perform the rest of their journey together; and that they might do it the more leisurely, set off from Wurtzburg at an early hour, the count having given directions for his retinue to follow and overtake him.

They beguiled their wayfaring with recollections of their military scenes and adventures; but the count was apt to be a little tedious, now and then, about the reputed charms of his bride, and the felicity that awaited him.

In this way they had entered among the mountains of the Odenwald, and were traversing one of its most lonely and thickly wooded passes. It is well known that the forests of Germany have always been as much infested by robbers as its castles by spectres; and, at this time, the former were particularly numerous from the hordes of disbanded soldiers wandering about the country. It will not appear extraordinary, therefore, that the cavaliers were attacked by a gang of these stragglers, in the midst of the forest. They defended themselves with bravery, but were nearly overpowered, when the count's retinue arrived to their assistance. At sight of them the robbers fled, but not until the count had received a mortal wound. He was slowly and carefully conveyed back to the city of Wurtzburg, and a friar summoned from a neighboring convent, who was famous for his skill in administering to both soul and body. But half of his skill was superfluous; the moments of the unfortunate count were numbered.

With his dying breath he entreated his friend to repair instantly to the castle of Landshort, and explain the fatal cause of his not keeping his appointment with his bride. Though not the most ardent of lovers, he was one of the most punctilious of men; and appeared earnestly solicitous that this mission should be speedily and courteously executed. "Unless this is done," said he, "I shall not sleep quietly in my grave!" He repeated these last words with peculiar solemnity. A request, at a moment so impressive, admitted no hesitation. Starkenfaust endeavored to soothe him to calmness, promised faithfully to execute his wish, and gave him his hand in solemn pledge. The dying man pressed it in acknowledgment, but soon lapsed into delirium—raved about his bride—his engagement—his plighted word; ordered his horse, that he might ride to the castle of Landshort, and expired in the fancied act of vaulting into the saddle.

Starkenfaust bestowed a sigh, and a soldier's tear, on the untimely fate of his comrade; and then pondered on the awkward mission he had undertaken. His heart was heavy, and his head perplexed; for he was to present himself an unbidden guest among hostile people, and to damp their festivity with tidings fatal to their hopes. Still there were certain whisperings of curiosity in his bosom to see this far-famed beauty of Katzenellenbogen, so cautiously shut up from the world; for he was a passionate admirer of the sex, and there was a dash of eccentricity and enterprise in his character that made him fond of all singular adventure.

Previous to his departure, he made all due arrangements with the holy fraternity of the convent for the funeral solemnities of his friend, who was to be buried in the cathedral of Wurtzburg, near some of his illustrious relatives; and the mourning retinue of the count took charge of his remains.

It is now high time that we should return to the ancient family of Katzenellenbogen, who were impatient for their guest, and still more for their dinner; and to the worthy little Baron, whom we left airing himself on the watch tower.

Night closed in, but still no guest arrived. The Baron descended from the tower in despair. The banquet, which had been delayed from hour to hour could no longer be postponed. The meats were already overdone; the cook in an agony; and the whole household had the look of a garrison that had been reduced by famine. The Baron was obliged reluctantly to give orders for the feast without the presence of the guest. All were seated at table, and just on the point of commencing, when the sound of a horn from without the gate gave notice of the approach of a stranger. Another long blast filled the old courts of the castle with its echoes, and was answered by the warder from the walls. The Baron hastened to receive his future son in law.

The drawbridge had been let down, and the stranger was before the gate. He was a tall gallant cavalier, mounted on a black steed. His countenance was pale, but he had a beaming, romantic eye, and an air of stately melancholy. The Baron was a little mortified that he should have come in this simple, solitary style. His dignity for a moment was ruffled, and he felt disposed to consider it a want of proper respect for the important occasion, and the important family with which he was to be connected. He, however, pacified himself with the conclusion that it must have been youthful impatience which had induced him thus to spur on sooner than his attendants.

"I am sorry," said the stranger, "to break in upon you thus unseasonably—"

Here the Baron interrupted him with a world of compliments and greetings; for, to tell the truth, he prided himself upon his courtesy and eloquence. The stranger attempted, once or twice, to stem the torrent of words, but in vain, so he bowed his head and suffered it to flow on. By the time the Baron had come to a pause, they had reached the inner court of the castle; and the stranger was again about to speak, when he was once more interrupted by the appearance of the female part of the family, leading forth the shrinking and blushing bride. He gazed on her for a moment as one entranced; it seemed as if his whole soul beamed forth in the gaze, and rested upon that lovely form. One of the maiden aunts whispered something in her ear; she made an effort to speak; her moist blue eye was timidly raised, gave a shy glance of inquiry on the stranger, and was cast again to the ground. The words died away; but there was a sweet smile playing about her lips, and a soft dimpling of the cheek, that showed her glance had not been unsatisfactory. It was impossible for a girl of the fond age of eighteen, highly predisposed for love and matrimony, not to be pleased with so gallant a cavalier.

The late hour at which the guest had arrived left no time for parley. The Baron was peremptory, and deferred all particular conversation until the morning, and led the way to the untasted banquet.

It was served up in the great hall of the castle. Around the walls hung the hard favored portraits of the heroes of the house of Katzenellenbogen, and the trophies which they had gained in the field and in the chase. Hacked corselets, splintered jousting spears, and tattered banners, were mingled with the spoils of sylvan warfare: the jaws of the wolf, and the tusks of the boar, grinned horribly among cross bows and battle axes, and a huge pair of antlers branched immediately over the head of the youthful bridegroom.

The cavalier took but little notice of the company, or the entertainment. He scarcely tasted the banquet, but seemed absorbed in admiration of his bride. He conversed in a low tone that could not be overheard—for the language of love is never loud; but where is the female ear so dull that it cannot catch the softest whisper of the lover? There was a mingled tenderness and gravity in his manner, that appeared to have a powerful effect upon the young lady. Her color came and went as she listened with deep attention. Now and then she made some blushing reply, and when his eye was turned away, she would steal a side long glance at his romantic countenance, and heave a gentle sigh of tender happiness. It was evident that the young couple were completely enamored. The aunts, who were deeply versed in the mysteries of the heart, declared that they had fallen in love with each other at first sight.

The feast went on merrily, or at least noisily, for the guests were all blessed with those keen appetites that attend upon light purses and mountain air. The Baron told his best and longest stories, and never had he told them so well, or with such great effect. If there was any thing marvellous, his auditors were lost in astonishment; and if any thing facetious, they were sure to laugh exactly in the right place. The Baron, it is true, like most great men, was too dignified to utter any joke but a dull one; it was always enforced, however, by a bumper of excellent Hoch-heimer; and even a dull joke at one's own table, served up with jolly old wine, is irresistible. Many good things were said by poorer and keener wits, that would not bear repeating, except on similar occasions; many sly speeches whispered in ladies' ears, that almost convulsed them with suppressed laughter; and a song or two roared out by a poor, but merry and broad faced cousin of the Baron that absolutely made the maiden aunts hold up their fans.

Amidst all this revelry, the stranger guest maintained a most singular and unseasonable gravity. His countenance assumed a deeper cast of dejection as the evening advanced, and, strange as it may appear, even the Baron's jokes seemed only to render him the more melancholy. At times he was lost in thought, and at times there was a perturbed and restless wandering of the eye that bespoke a mind but ill at ease. His conversations with the bride became more and more earnest and mysterious. Lowering clouds began to steal over the fair serenity of her brow, and tremors to run through her tender frame.

All this could not escape the notice of the company. Their gayety was chilled by the unaccountable gloom of the bridegroom; their spirits were infected; whispers and glances were interchanged, accompanied by shrugs and dubious shakes of the head. The song and the laugh grew less and less frequent; there were dreary pauses in the conversation, which were at length succeeded by wild tales, and supernatural legends. One dismal story produced another still more dismal, and the Baron nearly frightened some of the ladies into hysterics with the history of the goblin horseman that carried away the fair Leonora; a dreadful, but true story, which has since been put into excellent verse, and is read and believed by all the world.

The bridegroom listened to this tale with profound attention. He kept his eyes steadily fixed on the Baron, and as the story drew to a close, began gradually to rise from his seat, growing taller and taller, until, in the Baron's entranced eye, he seemed almost to tower into a giant. The moment the tale was finished, he heaved a deep sigh, and took a solemn farewell of the company. They were all amazement. The Baron was perfectly thunderstruck.

"What! going to leave the castle at midnight? why, every thing was prepared for his reception: a chamber was ready for him if he wished to retire."

The stranger shook his head mournfully, and mysteriously; "I must lay my head in a different chamber tonight!"

There was something in this reply, and the tone in which it was uttered that made the Baron's heart misgive him; but he rallied his forces and repeated his hospitable entreaties.

The stranger shook his head silently, but positively, at every offer, and waving his farewell to the company, stalked slowly out of the hall. The maiden aunts were absolutely petrified—the bride hung her head, and a tear stole to her eye.

The Baron followed the stranger to the great court of the castle, where the black charger stood pawing the earth, and snorting with impatience. When they had reached the portal, whose deep archway was dimly lighted by a cresset, the stranger paused, and addressed the Baron in a hollow tone of voice, which the vaulted roof rendered still more sepulchral.

"Now that we are alone," said he, "I will impart to you the reason of my going. I have a solemn, an indispensable engagement—"

"Why," said the Baron, "cannot you send some one in your place?"

"It admits of no substitute—I must attend it in person—I must away to Wurtzburg cathedral—"

"Aye," said the Baron, plucking up spirit, "but not until tomorrow—tomorrow you shall take your bride there."

"No! no!" replied the stranger, with tenfold solemnity, "my engagement is with no bride—the worms! the worms expect me! I am a dead man—I have been slain by robbers—my body lies at Wurtzburg—at midnight I am to be buried—the grave is waiting for me—I must keep my appointment!"

He sprang on his black charger, dashed over the drawbridge, and the clattering of his horse's hoofs was lost in the whistling of the night blast.

The Baron returned to the hall in the utmost consternation, and related what had passed. Two ladies fainted outright, others sickened at the idea of having banqueted with a spectre. It was the opinion of some, that this might be the wild huntsman famous in German legend. Some talked of mountain sprites, of wood demons, and of other supernatural beings, with which the good people of Germany have been so grievously harassed since time immemorial. One of the poor relations ventured to suggest that it might be some sportive evasion of the young cavalier, and that the very gloominess of the caprice seemed to accord with so melancholy a personage. This, however, drew on him the indignation of the whole company, and especially of the Baron, who looked upon him as little better than an infidel; so that he was fain to abjure his heresy as speedily as possible, and come into the faith of the true believers.

But, whatever may have been the doubts entertained, they were completely put to an end by the arrival, next day, of regular missives, confirming the intelligence of the young Count's murder, and his interment in Wurtzburg cathedral.

The dismay at the castle may well be imagined. The Baron shut himself up in his chamber. The guests, who had come to rejoice with him, could not think of abandoning him in his distress. They wandered about the courts, or collected in groups in the hall, shaking their heads and shrugging their shoulders, at the troubles of so good a man; and sat longer than ever at table, and ate and drank more stoutly than ever, by way of keeping up their spirits. But the situation of the widowed bride was the most pitiable. To have lost a husband before she had even embraced him—and such a husband! if the very spectre could be so gracious and noble, what must have been the living man! She filled the house with lamentations.

On the night of the second day of her widowhood she had retired to her chamber, accompanied by one of her aunts, who insisted on sleeping with her. The aunt, who was one of the best tellers of ghost stories in all Germany, had just been recounting one of her longest, and had fallen asleep in the very midst of it. The chamber was remote, and overlooked a small garden. The niece lay pensively gazing at the beams of the rising moon, as they trembled on the leaves of an aspen tree before the lattice. The castle clock had just tolled midnight when a soft strain of music stole up from the garden. She rose hastily from her bed, and stepped lightly to the window. A tall figure stood among the shadows of the trees. As it raised its head, a beam of moonlight fell upon the countenance. Heaven and earth! she beheld the Spectre Bridegroom! A loud shriek at that moment burst upon her ear, and her aunt, who had been awakened by the music, and had followed her silently to the window, fell into her arms. When she looked again, the spectre had disappeared.

Of the two females, the aunt now required the most soothing, for she was perfectly beside herself with terror. As to the young lady, there was something, even in the spectre of her lover, that seemed endearing. There was still the semblance of manly beauty; and though the shadow of a man is but little calculated to satisfy the affections of a love sick girl, yet, where the substance is not to be had, even that is consoling. The aunt declared she would never sleep in that chamber again; the niece, for once, was refractory, and declared as strongly that she would sleep in no other in the castle: the consequence was, that she had to sleep in it alone; but she drew a promise from her aunt not to relate the story of the spectre, lest she should be denied the only melancholy pleasure left her on earth—that of inhabiting the chamber over which the guardian shade of her lover kept its nightly vigils.

How long the good old lady would have observed this promise is uncertain, for she dearly loved to talk of the marvellous, and there is a triumph in being the first to tell a frightful story; it is, however, still quoted in the neighborhood, as a memorable instance of female secrecy that she kept it to herself for a whole week, when she was suddenly absolved from all further restraint, by intelligence brought to the breakfast table one morning, that the young lady was not to be found. Her room was empty—the bed had not been slept in—the window was open, and the bird had flown!

The astonishment and concern with which the intelligence was received, can only be imagined by those who have witnessed the agitation which the mishaps of a great man cause among his friends. Even the poor relations paused for a moment from the indefatigable labors of the trencher; when the aunt, who had at first been struck speechless, wrung her hands, and shrieked out, "the goblin" the goblin! she's carried away by the goblin!"

In a few words, she related the fearful scene of the garden, and concluded that the spectre must have carried off his bride. Two of the domestics corroborated the opinion, for they had heard the clattering of a horse's hoofs down the mountain about midnight, and had no doubt that it was the spectre on his black charger, bearing her away to the tomb. All present were struck with the direful probability; for events of the kind are extremely common in Germany, as many well authenticated histories bear witness.

What a lamentable situation was that of the poor Baron! What a heartrending dilemma for a fond father, and a member of the great family of Katzenellenbogen! His only daughter had either been rapt away to the grave, or he was to have some wood demon for a son in law, and, perchance, a troop of goblin grand children. As usual, he was completely bewildered, and all the castle in an uproar. The men were ordered to take horse, and, scour every road, and path, and glen of the Odenwald. The Baron himself had just drawn on his jack boots, girded on his sword, and was about to mount his steed to sally forth on the doubtful quest, when he was brought to a pause by a new apparition. A lady was seen approaching the castle, mounted on a palfrey, attended by a cavalier on horseback. She galloped up to the gate, sprang from her horse, and falling at the Baron's feet, embraced his knees. It was his lost daughter, and her companion—the Spectre Bridegroom! The Baron was astounded. He looked at his daughter, then at the Spectre, and almost doubted the evidence of his senses.

The latter, too, was wonderfully improved in his appearance, since his visit to the world of spirits. His dress was splendid, and set off a noble figure of manly symmetry. He was no longer pale and melancholy. His fine countenance was flushed with the glow of youth, and joy rioted in his large dark eye.

The mystery was soon cleared up. The cavalier (for in truth, as you must have known all the while, he was no goblin) announced himself as Sir Herman Von Starkenfaust. He related his adventure with the young Count. He told how he had hastened to the castle to deliver the unwelcome tidings, but that the eloquence of the Baron had interrupted him in every attempt to tell his tale. How the sight of the bride had completely captivated him, and that to pass a few hours near her, he had tacitly suffered the mistake to continue. How he had been sorely perplexed in what way to make a decent retreat, until the Baron's goblin stories had suggested his eccentric exit. How, fearing the feudal hostility of the family, he had repeated his visits by stealth— had haunted the garden beneath the young lady's window—had wooed—had won—had borne away in triumph—and, in a word, had wedded the fair.

Under any other circumstances, the Baron would have been inflexible, for he was tenacious of paternal authority, and devoutly obstinate in all family feuds; but he loved his daughter; he had lamented her as lost; he rejoiced to find her still alive; and, though her husband was of a hostile house, yet, thank heaven, he was not a goblin. There was something, it must be acknowledged, that did not exactly accord with his notions of strict veracity, in the joke the knight had passed upon him of his being a dead man; but several old friends present, who had served in the wars, assured him that every stratagem was excusable in love, and that the cavalier was entitled to especial privilege, having lately served as a trooper.

Matters, therefore, were happily arranged. The Baron pardoned the young couple on the spot. The revels at the castle were resumed. The poor relations overwhelmed this new member of the family with loving kindness; he was so gallant, so generous, and so rich. The aunts, it is true, were somewhat scandalized that their system of strict seclusion and passive obedience, should be so badly exemplified, but attributed it all to their negligence in not having the windows grated. One of them was particularly mortified at having her marvellous story marred, and that the only spectre she had ever seen should turn out a counterfeit; but the niece seemed perfectly happy at having found him substantial flesh and blood—and so the story ends.

THE MUTABILITY OF LITERATURE

A Colloquy in Westminster Abbey

I know that all beneath the moon decays,
And what by mortals in this world is brought,
In time's great period shall return to nought.
I know that all the muses' heavenly layes,
With toil of sprite which are so dearly bought,
As idle sounds of few or none are sought,
That there is nothing lighter than mere praise.
Drummond of Hawthornden

THERE ARE CERTAIN half-dreaming moods of mind, in which we naturally steal away from noise and glare, and seek some quiet haunt, where we may indulge our reveries and build our air castles undisturbed. In such a mood I was loitering about the old gray cloisters of Westminster Abbey, enjoying that luxury of wandering thought which one is apt to dignify with the name of reflection, when suddenly an irruption of madcap boys from Westminster school playing at football broke in upon the monastic stillness of the place, making the vaulted passages and mouldering tombs echo with their merriment. I sought to take refuge from their noise by penetrating still deeper into the solitudes of the pile, and applied to one of the vergers for admission to the library. He conducted me through a portal rich with the crumbling sculpture of former ages, which opened upon a gloomy passage leading to the chapter house and the chamber in which doomsday book is deposited. Just within the passage is a small door on the left. To this the verger applied a key; it was double locked, and opened with some difficulty, as if seldom used. We now ascended a dark narrow staircase, and passing through a second door, entered the library.

I found myself in a lofty antique hall, the roof supported by massive joists of old English oak. It was soberly lighted by a row of Gothic windows at a considerable height from the floor, and which apparently opened upon the roofs of the cloisters. An ancient picture of

54

some reverend dignitary of the church in his robes hung over the fire place. Around the hall and in a small gallery were the books, arranged in carved oaken cases. They consisted principally of old polemical writers, and were much more worn by time than use. In the centre of the library was a solitary table with two or three books on it; an inkstand without ink, and a few pens parched by long disuse. The place seemed fitted for quiet study and profound meditation. It was buried deep among the massive walls of the abbey, and shut up from the tumult of the world. I could only hear now and then the shouts of the school boys faintly swelling from the cloisters, and the sound of a bell tolling for prayers, echoing soberly along the roofs of the abbey. By degrees the shouts of merriment grew fainter and fainter, and at length died away. The bell ceased to toll, and a profound silence reigned through the dusky hall.

I had taken down a little thick quarto, curiously bound in parchment, with brass clasps, and seated myself at the table in a venerable elbow chair. Instead of reading, however, I was beguiled by the solemn monastic air, and lifeless quiet of the place, into a train of musing. As I looked around upon the old volumes in their mouldering covers, thus ranged on the shelves, and apparently never disturbed in their repose, I could not but consider the library a kind of literary catacomb, where authors, like mummies, are piously entombed, and left to blacken and moulder in dusty oblivion.

How much, thought I, has each of these volumes, now thrust aside with such indifference, cost some aching head; how many weary days—how many sleepless nights. How have their authors buried themselves in the solitude of cells and cloisters; shut themselves up from the face of man, and the still more blessed face of nature, and devoted themselves to painful research and intense reflection. And all for what! to occupy an inch of dusty shelf—to have the title of their works read now and then in a future age, by some drowsy churchman, or casual straggler like myself; and in another age to be lost, even to remembrance. Such is the amount of this boasted immortality.—A mere temporary rumor, a local sound, like the tone of that bell which has just tolled among these towers, filling the ear for a moment—lingering transiently in echo—and then passing away, like a thing that was not!

While I sat half murmuring, half meditating these unprofitable speculations, with my head resting on my hand, I was thrumming with the other hand upon the quarto, until I accidentally loosened the clasps, when, to my utter astonishment, the little book gave two or three yawns, like one awaking from a deep sleep; then a husky hem, and at length began to talk. At first its voice was very hoarse and

broken, being much troubled by a cobweb which some studious spider had woven across it; and having probably contracted a cold from
long exposure to the chills and damps of the abbey. In a short time,
however, it became more distinct, and I soon found it an exceedingly
fluent conversable little tome. Its language, to be sure, was rather
quaint and obsolete, and its pronunciation, what, in the present day,
would be deemed barbarous; but I shall endeavor, as far as I am able,
to render it in modern parlance.

It began with railings about the neglect of the world—about merit
being suffered to languish in obscurity, and other such common place
topics of literary repining, and complained bitterly that it had not
been opened for more than two centuries. That the Dean only looked
now and then into the library, sometimes took down a volume or
two, trifled with them for a few moments, and then returned them to
their shelves. "What a plague do they mean," said the little quarto,
which I began to perceive was somewhat choleric, "what a plague do
they mean by keeping several thousand volumes of us shut up here,
and watched by a set of old vergers, like so many beauties in a harem,
merely to be looked at now and then by the Dean? Books were written to give pleasure and to be enjoyed; and I would have a rule passed
that the Dean should pay each of us a visit at least once a year; or if
he is not equal to the task, let them once in a while turn loose the
whole school of Westminster among us, that at any rate we may now
and then have an airing."

"Softly, my worthy friend," replied I, "you are not aware how
much better you are off than most books of your generation. By
being stored away in this ancient library, you are like the treasured
remains of those saints and monarchs which lie enshrined in the adjoining chapels, while the remains of your contemporary mortals, left
to the ordinary course of nature, have long since returned to dust."

"Sir," said the little tome, ruffling his leaves and looking big, "I was
written for all the world, not for the bookworms of an abbey. I was
intended to circulate from hand to hand, like other great contemporary works; but here have I been clasped up for more than two centuries, and might have silently fallen a prey to these worms that are
playing the very vengeance with my intestines, if you had not by
chance given me an opportunity of uttering a few last words before I
go to pieces."

"My good friend," rejoined I, "had you been left to the circulation
of which you speak, you would long ere this have been no more. To
judge from your physiognomy, you are now well stricken in years:
very few of your contemporaries can be at present in existence; and
those few owe their longevity to being immured like yourself in old

libraries; which, suffer me to add, instead of likening to harems, you might more properly and gratefully have compared to those infirmaries attached to religious establishments, for the benefit of the old and decrepit, and where, by quiet fostering and no employment, they often endure to an amazingly good for nothing old age. You talk of your contemporaries as if in circulation—where do we meet with their works? what do we hear of Robert Groteste of Lincoln? No one could have toiled harder than he for immortality. He is said to have written nearly two hundred volumes. He built, as it were, a pyramid of books to perpetuate his name: but, alas! the pyramid has long since fallen, and only a few fragments are scattered in various libraries, where they are scarcely disturbed even by the antiquarian. What do we hear of Giraldus Cambrensis, the historian, antiquary, philosopher, theologian, and poet? He declined two bishoprics that he might shut himself up and write for posterity; but posterity never inquires after his labors. What of Henry of Huntingdon, who, besides a learned history of England, wrote a treatise on the contempt of the world, which the world has revenged by forgetting him. What is quoted of Joseph of Exeter, styled the miracle of his age in classical composition? Of his three great heroic poems one is lost forever, excepting a mere fragment; the others are known only to a few of the curious in literature, and as to his love verses and epigrams, they have entirely disappeared. What is in current use of John Wallis, the Franciscan, who acquired the name of the tree of life? Of William of Malmsbury;—of Simeon of Durham; of Benedict of Peterborough; of John Hanvill of St. Albans; of——"

"Prithee, friend," cried the quarto, in a testy tone, "how old do you think me? You are talking of authors that lived long before my time, and wrote either in Latin or French, so that they in a manner expatriated themselves, and deserved to be forgotten; but I, sir, was ushered into the world from the press of the renowned Wynkyn de Worde. I was written in my own native tongue at a time when the language had become fixed, and indeed I was considered a model of pure and elegant English."

(I should observe that these remarks were couched in such intolerably antiquated terms, that I have had infinite difficulty in rendering them into modern phraseology.)

"I cry your mercy," said I, "for mistaking your age; but it matters little; almost all the writers of your time have likewise passed into forgetfulness; and De Worde's publications are mere literary rarities among book collectors. The purity and stability of language, too, on which you found your claims to perpetuity, have been the fallacious dependence of authors of every age, even back to the times of the

worthy Robert of Gloucester, who wrote his history in rhymes of
mongrel Saxon. Even now, many talk of Spenser's 'well of pure
English undefiled,' as if the language ever sprang from a well or
fountain-head, and was not rather a mere confluence of various
tongues, perpetually subject to changes and intermixtures. It is this
which has made English literature so extremely mutable, and the
reputation built upon it so fleeting. Unless thought can be committed
to something more permanent and unchangeable than such a medium, even thought must share the fate of every thing else, and fall
into decay. This should serve as a check upon the vanity and exultation of the most popular writer. He finds the language in which he
has embarked his fame gradually altering, and subject to the dilapidations of time and the caprice of fashion. He looks back and beholds
the early authors of his country, once the favorites of their day, supplanted by modern writers. A few short ages have covered them with
obscurity, and their merits can only be relished by the quaint taste of
the bookworm. And such, he anticipates, will be the fate of his own
work, which, however it may be admired in its day, and held up as a
model of purity, will in the course of years grow antiquated and obsolete, until it shall become almost as unintelligible in its native land
as an Egyptian obelisk, or one of those Runic inscriptions said to exist
in the deserts of Tartary. I declare," added I with some emotion,
"when I contemplate a modern library, filled with new works in all
the bravery of rich gilding and binding, I feel disposed to sit down
and weep, like the good Xerxes when he surveyed his army, pranked
out in all the splendor of military array, and reflected that in one
hundred years not one of them would be in existence!"

"Ah," said the little quarto, with a heavy sigh, "I see how it is;
these modern scribblers have superseded all the good old authors. I
suppose nothing is read now-a-days but Sir Philip Sydney's Arcadia,
Sackville's stately plays, and Mirror for Magistrates, or the fine spun
euphuisms of the 'unparalleled John Lyly'."

"There you are again mistaken," said I, "the writers whom you
suppose in vogue, because they happened to be so when you were
last in circulation, have long since had their day. Sir Philip Sydney's
Arcadia, the immortality of which was so fondly predicted by his
admirers, and which, in truth, is full of noble thoughts, delicate images, and graceful turns of language, is now scarcely ever mentioned.
Sackville has strutted into obscurity; and even Lyly, though his writings were once the delight of a court, and apparently perpetuated by
a proverb, is now scarcely known even by name. A whole crowd of
authors who wrote and wrangled at the time, have likewise gone
down with all their writings and their controversies. Wave after wave

of succeeding literature has rolled over them, until they are buried so deep, that it is only now and then that some industrious diver after fragments of antiquity brings up a specimen for the gratification of the curious.

"For my part," I continued, "I consider this mutability of language a wise precaution of Providence for the benefit of the world at large, and of authors in particular. To reason from analogy, we daily behold the varied and beautiful tribes of vegetables springing up, flourishing, adorning the fields for a short time, and then fading into dust, to make way for their successors. Were not this the case, the fecundity of nature would be a grievance instead of a blessing. The earth would groan with rank and excessive vegetation, and its surface become a tangled wilderness. In like manner, the works of genius and learning decline and make way for subsequent productions. Language gradually varies, and with it fade away the writings of authors who have flourished their allotted time; otherwise the creative powers of genius would overstock the world, and the mind would be completely bewildered in the endless mazes of literature. Formerly there were some restraints on this excessive multiplication. Works had to be transcribed by hand, which was a slow and laborious operation; they were written either on parchment, which was expensive, so that one work was often erased to make way for another; or on papyrus, which was fragile and extremely perishable. Authorship was a limited and unprofitable craft, and pursued chiefly by monks in the leisure and solitude of their cloisters. The accumulation of manuscripts was slow and costly, and confined almost entirely to monasteries. To these circumstances it may in some measure be owing that we have not been inundated by the intellect of antiquity; that the fountains of thought have not been broken up, and modern genius drowned in the deluge. But the inventions of paper and the press have put an end to all these restraints. They have made every one a writer, and enabled every mind to pour itself into print, and diffuse itself over the whole intellectual world. The consequences are alarming. The stream of literature has swollen into a torrent—augmented into a river—expanded into a sea. A few centuries since, five or six hundred manuscripts constituted a great library; but what would you say to libraries, such as actually exist, containing three and four hundred thousand volumes; legions of authors at the same time busy, and the press going on with fearfully increasing activity, to double and quadruple the number? Unless some unforseen mortality should break out among the progeny of the muse, now that she has become so prolific, I tremble for posterity. I fear the mere fluctuation of language will not be sufficient. Criticism may do much; it increases with the increase of literature, and resembles one of those salutary checks on population spoken of by economists. All possible encouragement, therefore, should be given to the growth of critics, good or bad. But I fear all will be in vain; let criticism do what it may, writers will write, printers will print, and the world will inevitably be overstocked with good books. It will soon be the employment of a life time merely to learn their names. Many a man of passable information at the present day reads scarcely any thing but reviews, and before long a man of erudition will be little better than a mere walking catalogue."

"My very good sir," said the little quarto, yawning most drearily in my face, "excuse my interrupting you, but I perceive you are rather given to prose. I would ask the fate of an author who was making some noise just as I left the world. His reputation, however, was considered quite temporary. The learned shook their heads at him, for he was a poor half educated varlet, that knew little of Latin, and nothing of Greek, and had been obliged to run the country for deer stealing. I think his name was Shakspeare. I presume he soon sunk into oblivion."

"On the contrary," said I, "it is owing to that very man that the literature of his period has experienced a duration beyond the ordinary term of English literature. There arise authors now and then, who seem proof against the mutability of language, because they have rooted themselves in the unchanging principles of human nature. They are like gigantic trees that we sometimes see on the banks of a stream; which, by their vast and deep roots, penetrating through the mere surface, and laying hold on the very foundations of the earth, preserve the soil around them from being swept away by the ever-flowing current, and hold up many a neighboring plant, and, perhaps, worthless weed, to perpetuity. Such is the case with Shakspeare, whom we behold, defying the encroachments of time, retaining in modern use the language and literature of his day, and giving duration to many an indifferent author, merely from having flourished in his vicinity. But even he, I grieve to say, is gradually assuming the tint of age, and his whole form is overrun by a profusion of commentators, who, like clambering vines and creepers, almost bury the noble plant that upholds them."

Here the little quarto began to heave his sides and chuckle, until at length he broke out in a plethoric fit of laughter that had well nigh choked him, by reason of his excessive corpulency. "Mighty well!" cried he, as soon as he could recover breath, "mighty well! and so you would persuade me that the literature of an age is to be perpetuated by a vagabond deer stealer! by a man without learning! by a poet, forsooth—a poet!" And here he wheezed forth another fit of laughter.

I confess that I felt somewhat nettled at this rudeness, which, however, I pardoned on account of his having flourished in a less polished age. I determined, nevertheless, not to give up my point.

"Yes," resumed I positively, "a poet; for of all writers he has the best chance for immortality. Others may write from the head, but he writes from the heart, and the heart will always understand him. He is the faithful portrayer of nature, whose features are always the same, and always interesting. Prose writers are voluminous and unwieldy; their pages are crowded with common places, and their thoughts expanded into tediousness. But with the true poet every thing is terse, touching, or brilliant. He gives the choicest thoughts in the choicest language. He illustrates them by every thing that he sees most striking in nature and art. He enriches them by pictures of human life, such as it is passing before him. His writings, therefore, contain the spirit, the aroma, if I may use the phrase, of the age in which he lives. They are caskets which inclose within a small compass the wealth of the language—its family jewels, which are thus transmitted in a portable form to posterity. The setting may occasionally be antiquated, and require now and then to be renewed, as in the case of Chaucer; but the brilliancy and intrinsic value of the gems continue unaltered. Cast a look back over the long reach of literary history. What vast valleys of dulness, filled with monkish legends and academical controversies. What bogs of theological speculations; what dreary wastes of metaphysics! Here and there only do we behold the heaven-illuminated bards, elevated like beacons on their widely separated heights, to transmit the pure light of poetical intelligence from age to age."

I was just about to launch forth into eulogiums upon the poets of the day, when the sudden opening of the door caused me to turn my head. It was the verger, who came to inform me that it was time to close the library. I sought to have a parting word with the quarto, but the worthy little tome was silent; the clasps were closed, and it looked perfectly unconscious of all that had passed. I have been to the library two or three times since, and have endeavored to draw it into farther conversation, but in vain. And whether all this rambling colloquy actually took place, or whether it was another of those odd day dreams to which I am subject, I have never, to this moment, been able to discover.

WESTMINSTER ABBEY

When I behold, with deepe astonishment,
To famous Westminster how there resorte,
Living in brasse or stoney monyment,
The princes and the worthies of all sorte:
Doe not I see reformde nobilitie,
Without contempt, or pride, or ostentation,
And looke upon offenselesse majesty,
Naked of pompe or earthly domination?
And how a play-game of a painted stone,
Contents the quiet now and silent sprites,
Whome all the world which late they stood upon,
Could not content nor quench their appetites.
    Life is a frost of cold felicitie
    And death the thaw of all our vanitie.
        Christolero's Epigrams, by T. B. 1598

ON ONE OF THOSE sober and rather melancholy days, in the latter part of Autumn, when the shadows of morning and evening almost mingle together, and throw a gloom over the decline of the year, I passed several hours in rambling about Westminster Abbey. There was something congenial to the season in the mournful magnificence of the old pile; and as I passed its threshold, it seemed like stepping back into the regions of antiquity, and losing myself among the shades of former ages.

I entered from the inner court of Westminster School, through a long, low, vaulted passage, that had an almost subterranean look, being dimly lighted in one part by circular perforations in the massive walls. Through this dark avenue I had a distant view of the cloisters, with the figure of an old verger, in his black gown, moving along their shadowy vaults, and seeming like a spectre from one of the neighboring tombs. The approach to the abbey through these gloomy monastic remains prepares the mind for its solemn contemplation. The cloisters still retain something of the quiet and seclusion of former days. The gray walls are discolored by damps, and crumbling with age; a coat of hoary moss has gathered over the inscriptions of the mural monuments, and obscured the death's heads, and other funereal emblems. The sharp touches of the chisel are gone from the rich tracery of the arches; the roses which adorned the key stones have lost their leafy beauty; every thing bears marks of the gradual dilapidations of time, which yet has something touching and pleasing in its very decay.

The sun was pouring down a yellow autumnal ray into the square of the cloisters; beaming upon a scanty plot of grass in the centre, and lighting up an angle of the vaulted passage with a kind of dusty splendor. From between the arcades the eye glanced up to a bit of blue sky or a passing cloud, and beheld the sun-gilt pinnacles of the abbey towering into the azure heaven.

As I paced the cloisters, sometimes contemplating this mingled picture of glory and decay, and sometimes endeavoring to decipher the inscriptions on the tombstones, which formed the pavement beneath my feet, my eye was attracted to three figures, rudely carved in relief, but nearly worn away by the footsteps of many generations. They were the effigies of three of the early abbots; the epitaphs were entirely effaced; the names alone remained, having no doubt been renewed in later times (Vitalis. Abbas. 1082, and Gislebertus Crispinus. Abbas. 1114, and Laurentius. Abbas. 1176). I remained some little while, musing over these casual relics of antiquity, thus left like wrecks upon this distant shore of time, telling no tale but that such beings had been, and had perished; teaching no moral but the futility of that pride which hopes still to exact homage in its ashes, and to live in an inscription. A little longer and even these faint records will be obliterated and the monument will cease to be a memorial. Whilst I was yet looking down upon the gravestones, I was roused by the sound of the abbey clock, reverberating from buttress to buttress, and echoing among the cloisters. It is almost startling to hear this warning of departed time sounding among the tombs, and telling the lapse of the hour, which like a billow has rolled us onward towards the grave.

I pursued my walk to an arched door opening to the interior of the abbey. On entering here, the magnitude of the building breaks fully upon the mind, contrasted with the vaults of the cloisters. The eye gazes with wonder at clustered columns of gigantic dimensions, with arches springing from them to such an amazing height; and man wandering about their bases, shrunk into insignificance in comparison with his own handywork. The spaciousness and gloom of this vast edifice produce a profound and mysterious awe. We step cautiously and softly about, as if fearful of disturbing the hallowed silence of the tomb; while every footfall whispers along the walls, and chatters among the sepulchres, making us more sensible of the quiet we have interrupted.

It seems as if the awful nature of the place presses down upon the soul, and hushes the beholder into noiseless reverence. We feel that we are surrounded by the congregated bones of the great men of past times; who have filled history with their deeds, and the earth with their renown. And yet it almost provokes a smile at the vanity of human ambition, to see how they are crowded together and justled in the dust: what parsimony is observed in doling out a scanty nook; a gloomy corner; a little portion of earth, to those, whom, when alive, kingdoms could not satisfy: and how many shapes, and forms and artifices are devised to catch the casual notice of the passenger, and save from forgetfulness, for a few short years, a name which once aspired to occupy ages of the world's thought and admiration.

I passed some time in Poet's Corner, which occupies an end of one of the transepts or cross aisles of the Abbey. The monuments are generally simple; for the lives of literary men afford no striking themes for the sculptor. Shakespeare and Addison have statues erected to their memories; but the greater part have busts, medallions, and sometimes mere inscriptions. Notwithstanding the simplicity of these memorials, I have always observed that the visitors to the abbey remain longest about them. A kinder and fonder feeling takes place of that cold curiosity or vague admiration with which they gaze on the splendid monuments of the great and the heroic. They linger about these as about the tombs of friends and companions; for indeed there is something of companionship between the author and the reader. Other men are known to posterity only through the medium of history, which is continually growing faint and obscure; but the intercourse between the author and his fellow men is ever new, active and immediate. He has lived for them more than for himself; he has sacrificed surrounding enjoyments, and shut himself up from the delights of social life, that he might the more intimately commune with distant minds and distant ages. Well may the world cherish his renown, for it has been purchased, not by deeds of violence and blood, but by the diligent dispensation of pleasure. Well may posterity be grateful to his memory; for he has left it an inheritance, not of empty names and sounding actions, but whole treasures of wisdom, bright gems of thought, and golden veins of language.

From Poets' Corner I continued my stroll towards that part of the abbey which contains the sepulchres of the kings. I wandered among what once were chapels, but which are now occupied by the tombs and monuments of the great. At every turn I met with some illustrious name; or the cognizance of some powerful house renowned in history. As the eye darts into these dusky chambers of death, it catches glimpses of quaint effigies; some kneeling in niches, as if in devotion; others stretched upon the tombs, with hands piously pressed together; warriors in armor, as if reposing after battle; prelates, with croziers and mitres; and nobles in robes and coronets, lying as it were in state. In glancing over this scene, so strangely populous, yet where every form is so still and silent, it seems almost as if we were treading a mansion of that fabled city, where every being had been suddenly transmuted into stone.

I paused to contemplate a tomb on which lay the effigy of a knight in complete armor. A large buckler was on one arm; the hands were pressed together in supplication upon the breast; the face was almost covered by the morion; the legs were crossed in token of the warrior's having been engaged in the holy war. It was the tomb of a crusader; of one of those military enthusiasts, who so strangely mingled religion and romance, and whose exploits form the connecting link between fact and fiction; between the history and the fairy tale. There is something extremely picturesque in the tombs of these adventurers, decorated as they are with rude armorial bearings and gothic sculpture. They comport with the antiquated chapels in which they are generally found; and in considering them, the imagination is apt to kindle with the legendary associations, the romantic fictions, the chivalrous pomp and pageantry which poetry has spread over the wars for the Sepulchre of Christ. They are the relics of times utterly gone by, of beings passed from recollection, of customs and manners with which ours have no affinity. They are like objects from some strange and distant land, of which we have no certain knowledge, and about which all our conceptions are vague and visionary. There is something extremely solemn and awful in those effigies on Gothic tombs, extended as if in the sleep of death, or in the supplication of the dying hour. They have an effect infinitely more impressive on my feelings than the fanciful attitudes, the overwrought conceits, and allegorical groups, which abound on modern monuments. I have been struck, also, with the superiority of many of the old sepulchral inscriptions. There was a noble way, in former times of saying things simply, and yet saying them proudly; and I do not know an epitaph that breathes a loftier consciousness of family worth and honorable lineage than one which affirms, of a noble house, that "all the brothers were brave, and all the sisters virtuous."

In the opposite transept to Poets' Corner stands a monument which is among the most renowned achievements of modern art; but which, to me, appears horrible rather than sublime. It is the tomb of

Mrs. Nightingale, by Roubillac. The bottom of the monument is represented as throwing open its marble doors, and a sheeted skeleton is starting forth. The shroud is falling from his fleshless frame as he launches his dart at his victim. She is sinking into her affrighted husband's arms, who strives, with vain and frantic effort, to avert the blow. The whole is executed with terrible truth and spirit; we almost fancy we hear the gibbering yell of triumph, bursting from the distended jaws of the spectre.—But why should we thus seek to clothe death with unnecessary terrors, and to spread horrors round the tomb of those we love? The grave should be surrounded by every thing that might inspire tenderness and veneration for the dead; or that might win the living to virtue. It is the place, not of disgust and dismay, but of sorrow and meditation.

While wandering about these gloomy vaults and silent aisles, studying the records of the dead, the sound of busy existence from without occasionally reaches the ear;—the rumbling of the passing equipage; the murmur of the multitude, or perhaps the light laugh of pleasure. The contrast is striking with the deathlike repose around: and it has a strange effect upon the feelings, thus to hear the surges of active life hurrying along and beating against the very walls of the sepulchre.

I continued in this way to move from tomb to tomb, and from chapel to chapel. The day was gradually wearing away; the distant tread of loiterers about the abbey grew less and less frequent; the sweet tongued bell was summoning to evening prayers; and I saw at a distance the choristers, in their white surplices crossing the aisle and entering the choir. I stood before the entrance to Henry the Seventh's chapel. A flight of steps leads up to it, through a deep and gloomy, but magnificent arch. Great gates of brass, richly and delicately wrought, turn heavily upon their hinges, as if proudly reluctant to admit the feet of common mortals into this most gorgeous of sepulchres.

On entering, the eye is astonished by the pomp of architecture, and the elaborate beauty of sculptured detail. The very walls are wrought into universal ornament, encrusted with tracery, and scooped into niches, crowded with the statues of saints and martyrs. Stone seems, by the cunning labor of the chisel, to have been robbed of its weight and density, suspended aloft as if by magic, and the fretted roof achieved with the wonderful minuteness and airy security of a cobweb.

Along the sides of the chapel are the lofty stalls of the Knights of the Bath, richly carved of oak, though with the grotesque decorations of Gothic architecture. On the pinnacles of the stalls are affixed the helmets and crests of the knights, with their scarfs and swords; and above them are suspended their banners, emblazoned with armorial bearings, and contrasting the splendor of gold and purple and crimson, with the cold gray fretwork of the roof. In the midst of this grand mausoleum stands the sepulchre of its founder,—his effigy, with that of his queen, extended on a sumptuous tomb—and the whole surrounded by a superbly wrought brazen railing.

There is a sad dreariness in this magnificence; this strange mixture of tombs and trophies; these emblems of living and aspiring ambition, close beside mementos which show the dust and oblivion in which all must sooner or later terminate. Nothing impresses the mind with a deeper feeling of loneliness, than to tread the silent and deserted scene of former throng and pageant. On looking round on the vacant stalls of the knights and their esquires; and on the rows of dusty but gorgeous banners that were once borne before them, my imagination conjured up the scene when this hall was bright with the valor and beauty of the land; glittering with the splendor of jewelled rank and military array; alive with the tread of many feet and the hum of an admiring multitude. All had passed away: the silence of death had settled again upon the place; interrupted only by the casual chirping of birds, which had found their way into the chapel and built their nests among its friezes and pendants—sure signs of solitariness and desertion.

When I read the names inscribed on the banners, they were those of men scattered far and wide about the world; some tossing upon distant seas; some under arms in distant lands; some mingling in the busy intrigues of courts and cabinets; all seeking to deserve one more distinction in this mansion of shadowy honors; the melancholy reward of a monument.

Two small aisles on each side of this chapel present a touching instance of the equality of the grave; which brings down the oppressor to a level with the oppressed, and mingles the dust of the bitterest enemies together. In one is the sepulchre of the haughty Elizabeth, in the other is that of her victim, the lovely and unfortunate Mary. Not an hour in the day but some ejaculation of pity is uttered over the fate of the latter, mingled with indignation at her oppressor. The walls of Elizabeth's sepulchre continually echo with the sighs of sympathy heaved at the grave of her rival.

A peculiar melancholy reigns over the aisle where Mary lies buried. The light struggles dimly through windows darkened by dust. The greater part of the place is in deep shadow, and the walls are stained and tinted by time and weather. A marble figure of Mary is stretched upon the tomb, round which is an iron railing, much corroded, bearing her national emblem the thistle. I was weary with wandering, and sat down to rest myself by the monument, revolving in my mind the chequered and disastrous story of poor Mary.

The sound of casual footsteps had ceased from the abbey. I could only hear, now and then, the distant voice of the priest repeating the evening service, and the faint responses of the choir; these paused for a time, and all was hushed. The stillness, the desertion and obscurity that were gradually prevailing around, gave a deeper and more solemn interest to the place:

> For in the silent grave no conversation,
> No joyful tread of friends, no voice of lovers,
> No careful father's counsel—nothing's heard,
> For nothing is, but all oblivion,
> Dust and an endless darkness.

Suddenly the notes of the deep laboring organ burst upon the ear, falling with doubled and redoubled intensity, and rolling, as it were, huge billows of sound. How well do their volume and grandeur accord with this mighty building! With what pomp do they swell through its vast vaults, and breathe their awful harmony through these caves of death, and make the silent sepulchre vocal!—And now they rise in triumphant acclamation, heaving higher and higher their accordant notes, and piling sound on sound.—And now they pause, and the soft voices of the choir break out into sweet gushes of melody; they soar aloft, and warble along the roof, and seem to play about these lofty vaults like the pure airs of heaven. Again the pealing organ heaves its thrilling thunders, compressing air into music, and rolling it forth upon the soul. What long drawn cadences! What solemn sweeping concords! It grows more and more dense and powerful—it fills the vast pile, and seems to jar the very walls—the ear is stunned—the senses are overwhelmed. And now it is winding up in full jubilee—it is rising from the earth to heaven—the very soul seems rapt away and floated upwards on this swelling tide of harmony!

I sat for some time lost in that kind of reverie which a strain of music is apt sometimes to inspire: the shadows of evening were gradually thickening around me; the monuments began to cast deeper and deeper gloom; and the distant clock again gave token of the slowly waning day.

I rose and prepared to leave the abbey. As I descended the flight of steps which lead into the body of the building, my eye was caught by the shrine of Edward the Confessor, and I ascended the small staircase that conducts to it, to take from thence a general survey of this wilderness of tombs. The shrine is elevated upon a kind of platform, and close around it are the sepulchres of various kings and queens. From this eminence the eye looks down between pillars and funeral trophies to the chapels and chambers below, crowded with tombs; where warriors, prelates, courtiers and statesmen lie mouldering in their "beds of darkness." Close by me stood the great chair of coronation, rudely carved of oak, in the barbarous taste of a remote and gothic age. The scene seemed almost as if contrived with theatrical artifice, to produce an effect upon the beholder. Here was a type of the beginning and the end of human pomp and power; here it was literally but a step from the throne to the sepulchre. Would not one think that these incongruous mementos had been gathered together as a lesson to living greatness?—to show it, even in the moment of its proudest exaltation, the neglect and dishonor to which it must soon arrive; how soon that crown which encircles its brow must pass away; and it must lie down in the dust and disgraces of the tomb, and be trampled upon by the feet of the meanest of the multitude. For, strange to tell, even the grave is here no longer a sanctuary. There is a shocking levity in some natures, which leads them to sport with awful and hallowed things; and there are base minds, which delight to revenge on the illustrious dead the abject homage and grovelling servility which they pay to the living. The coffin of Edward the Confessor has been broken open, and his remains despoiled of their funereal ornaments; the sceptre has been stolen from the hand of the imperious Elizabeth; and the effigy of Henry the Fifth lies headless. Not a royal monument but bears some proof how false and fugitive is the homage of mankind. Some are plundered; some mutilated; some covered with ribaldry and insult—all more or less outraged and dishonored!

The last beams of day were now faintly streaming through the painted windows in the high vaults above me: the lower parts of the abbey were already wrapped in the obscurity of twilight. The chapels and aisles grew darker and darker. The effigies of the kings faded into shadows; the marble figures of the monuments assumed strange shapes in the uncertain light; the evening breeze crept through the aisles like the cold breath of the grave; and even the distant footfall of a verger, traversing the Poets' Corner, had something strange and dreary in its sound. I slowly retraced my morning's walk, and as I passed out at the portal of the cloisters, the door, closing with a jarring noise behind me, filled the whole building with echoes.

I endeavored to form some arrangement in my mind of the objects I had been contemplating, but found they were already falling into indistinctness and confusion. Names, inscriptions, trophies, had all become confounded in my recollection, though I had scarcely taken my foot from off the threshold. What, thought I, is this vast assemblage of sepulchres but a treasury of humiliation; a huge pile of reiterated homilies on the emptiness of renown, and the certainty of oblivion! It is, indeed, the empire of death; his great shadowy palace;

where he sits in state, mocking at the relics of human glory, and spreading dust and forgetfulness on the monuments of princes. How idle a boast, after all, is the immortality of a name! Time is ever silently turning over his pages; we are too much engrossed by the story of the present, to think of the characters and anecdotes that gave interest to the past; and each age is a volume thrown aside to be speedily forgotten. The idol of today pushes the hero of yesterday out of our recollection; and will, in turn, be supplanted by his successor of tomorrow. "Our fathers," says Sir Thomas Brown, "find their graves in our short memories, and sadly tell us how we may be buried in our survivors." History fades into fable; fact becomes clouded with doubt and controversy; the inscription moulders from the tablet; the statue falls from the pedestal. Columns, arches, pyramids, what are they but heaps of sand; and their epitaphs, but characters written in the dust? What is the security of a tomb, or the perpetuity of an embalmment? The remains of Alexander the Great have been scattered to the wind, and his empty sarcophagus is now the mere curiosity of a museum. "The Egyptian mummies, which Cambyses or time hath spared, avarice now consumeth; Mizraim cures wounds, and Pharaoh is sold for balsams."

What then is to ensure this pile which now towers above me from sharing the fate of mightier mausoleums? The time must come when its gilded vaults, which now spring so loftily, shall lie in rubbish beneath the feet; when, instead of the sound of melody and praise, the wind shall whistle through the broken arches and the owl hoot from the shattered tower—when the garish sun beam shall break into those gloomy mansions of death, and the ivy twine round the fallen column; and the fox glove hang its blossoms about the nameless urn, as if in mockery of the dead. Thus man passes away; his name perishes from record and recollection; his history is as a tale that is told, and his very monument becomes a ruin.

Notes Concerning Westminster Abbey

Toward the end of the sixth century when Britain, under the dominion of the Saxons, was in a state of barbarism and idolatry Pope Gregory the Great, struck with the beauty of some Anglo Saxon youths, exposed for sale in the Market place at Rome, conceived a fancy for the race and determined to send missionaries to preach the Gospel among these comely but benighted islanders. He was encouraged to this by learning that Ethelbert King of Kent and the most potent of the Anglo Saxon princes, had married Bertha a Christian princess, only daughter of the King of Paris, and that she was allowed by stipulation, the full exercise of her religion.

The shrewd Pontiff knew the influence of the sex in matters of religious faith. He forthwith dispatched Augustine a Roman Monk with forty associates to the Court of Ethelbert at Canterbury, to effect the conversion of the King and to obtain through him a foothold in the island.

Ethelbert received them warily and held a conference in the open air; being distrustful of foreign priest craft, and fearful of spells and magic. They ultimately succeeded in making him as good a christian as his wife; the conversion of the King of course produced the conversion of his loyal subjects. The zeal and success of Augustine were rewarded by his being made archbishop of Canterbury and being endowed with authority over all the British churches.

One of the most prominent converts was Segebert or Sebert, King of the East Saxons a nephew of Ethelbert. He reigned at London, of which Mellitus, one of the Roman Monks who had come over with Augustine was made bishop.

Sebert, in 605, in his religious zeal founded a monastery by the river side to the west of the city on the ruins of a temple of Apollo, being in fact the origin of the present pile of Westminster Abbey. Great preparations were made for the consecration of the church which was to be dedicated to St. Peter. On the morning of the appointed day Mellitus the bishop proceeded with great pomp and solemnity to perform the ceremony. On approaching the edifice he was met by a fisherman who informed him that it was needless to proceed as the ceremony was over. The bishop stared with surprise when the fisherman went on to relate that the night before, as he was in his boat on the Thames St. Peter appeared to him and told him that he intended to consecrate the church himself that very night. The Apostle accordingly went into the church which suddenly became illuminated. The ceremony was performed in sumptuous style accompanied by strains of heavenly music and clouds of fragrant incense. After this the Apostle came onto the boat and ordered the fisherman to cast his net. He did so and had a miraculous draft of fishes; one of which he was commanded to present to the Bishop, and to signify to him that the Apostle had relieved him from the necessity of consecrating the church.

Mellitus was a wary man, slow of belief, and required confirmation of the fisherman's tale. He opened the church doors and beheld wax candles, crosses, holy water; oil sprinkled in various places and various other traces of a grand ceremonial. If he had still any lingering doubts they were completely removed on the fisherman's producing the identical fish which he had been ordered by the Apostle to present to him. To resist this would have been to resist ocular demonstration.

The good bishop accordingly was convinced that the church had actually been consecrated by St. Peter in person; so he reverently abstained from proceeding further in the business.

The foregoing tradition is said to be the reason why King Edward the Confessor chose this place as the scite of a religious house which he meant to endow. He pulled down the old church and built another in its place in 1045. In this his remains were deposited in a magnificent shrine.

The sacred edifice again underwent modifications if not a reconstruction by Henry III in 1220 and began to assume its present appearance.

Under Henry VIII it lost its conventual character, that monarch turning the monks away and seizing upon the revenues.

Relics of Edward the Confessor

A curious narrative was printed in 1688 by one of the choiristers of the Cathedral, who appears to have been the Paul Pry of the sacred edifice, giving an account of his rummaging among the bones of Edward the Confessor, after they had quietly reposed in their sepulchre upwards of six hundred years, and of his drawing forth the crucifix and golden chain of the deceased monarch. During eighteen years that he had officiated in the choir it had been a common tradition, he says, among his brother choiristers and the grey headed servants of the abbey that the body of King Edward was deposited in a kind of chest or coffin which was indistinctly seen in the upper part of the shrine erected to his memory. None of the abbey gossips, however, had ventured upon a nearer inspection, until the worthy narrator to gratify his curiosity mounted to the coffin by the aid of a ladder and found it to be made of wood, apparently very strong and firm, being secured by bands of iron.

Subsequently, in 1685, on taking down the scaffolding used in the coronation of James II, the coffin was found to be broken, a hole appearing in the lid, probably made through accident, by the workmen. No one ventured, however, to meddle with the sacred depository of royal rest, until, several weeks afterwards, the circumstance came to the knowledge of the aforesaid choirister. He forthwith repaired to the abbey in company with two friends of congenial tastes who were desirous of inspecting the tombs. Procuring a ladder he again mounted to the coffin and found, as had been represented, a hole in the lid about six inches long and four inches broad, just in front of the left breast. Thrusting in his hand and groping among the bones he drew from underneath the shoulder a crucifix, richly adorned and enamelled affixed to a gold chain twenty four inches long. These he showed to his inquisitive friends, who were equally surprised with himself.

"At the time," says he, "when I took the cross and chain out of the coffin, *I drew the head to the hole and viewed it,* being very sound and firm with the upper and nether jaws whole and full of teeth, and a list of gold above an inch broad, in the nature of a coronet, surrounding the temples. There was also in the coffin, white linen and gold coloured flowered silk, that looked indifferent fresh but the least stress put thereto showed it was well nigh perished. There were all his bones and much dust likewise which I left as I found." It is difficult to conceive a more grotesque lesson to human pride than the scull of Edward the Confessor thus irreverently pulled about in its coffin by a prying choirister, and brought to grin face to face with him through a hole in the lid!

Having satisfied his curiosity the choirister put the crucifix and chain back again into the coffin and sought the Dean, to apprize him of his discovery. The Dean not being accessible at the time; and fearing that the "holy treasure" might be taken away by other hands, he got a brother choirister to accompany him to the shrine about two or three hours afterwards and in his presence again drew forth the reliques. These he afterwards delivered on his knees to King James. The King subsequently had the old coffin enclosed in a new one of great strength: "each plank being two inches thick and cramped together with large iron wedges, where it now remains (1688) as a testimony of his pious care that no abuse might be offered to the sacred ashes therein reposited."

As the story of this shrine is full of moral I subjoin a description of it in modern times. "The solitary and forlorn shrine," says a British writer, "now stands a mere skeleton of what it was. A few faint traces of its sparkling decorations inlaid on solid mortar catch the rays of the sun, forever set on its splendor ★ ★ ★ ★ Only two of the spiral pillars remain. The wooden Ionic top is much broken and covered with dust. The mosaic is picked away in every part within reach, only the lozenges of about a foot square and five circular pieces of the rich marble remain."

Malcolm. Lond. Rediv.

Inscription on a monument alluded to in the Sketch.

Here lyes the Loyal Duke of Newcastle, and his Dutchess his second wife, by whom he had no issue. Her name was Margaret Lucas, youngest sister to the Lord Lucas of Colchester, a noble Family; for all the brothers were valiant and all the sisters virtuous. This Dutchess was a wise, witty, and learned Lady, which her many Bookes do well testify: she was a most virtuous, and loving and careful wife, and was with her lord all the time of his banishment and miseries, and when he came home, never parted from him in his solitary retirements.

In the winter time, when the days are short, the service in the afternoon is performed by the light of tapers. The effect is fine of the choir partially lighted up; while the main body of the cathedral and the transepts are in profound and cavernous darkness. The white dresses of the choiristers gleam amidst the deep brown of the oaken slatts and canopies; the partial illumination makes enormous shadows from columns and screens, and darting into the surrounding gloom catches here and there upon a sepulchral decoration, or monumental effigy. The swelling notes of the organ accord well with the scene.

When the service is over the Dean is lighted to his dwelling, in the old conventual part of othe pile, by the boys of the choir in their white dresses, bearing tapers, and the procession passes through the abbey and along the shadowy cloisters, lighting up angles and arches and grim sepulchral monuments and leaving all behind in darkness.

On entering the cloisters at night from what is called the Dean's Yard the eye ranging through a dark vaulted passage catches a distant view of a white marble figure reclining on a tomb, on which a strong glare thrown by a gas light, has quite a spectral effect. It is a mural monument of one of the Pultneys.

The cloisters are well worth visiting by moonlight, when the moon is in the full.

THE WIFE

The treasures of the deep are not so precious
As are the conceal'd comforts of a man
Locked up in woman's love. I scent the air
Of blessings, when I come but near the house.
What a delicious breath marriage sends forth,
The violet bed's not sweeter.

Middleton

I HAVE OFTEN had occasion to remark the fortitude with which
women sustain the most overwhelming reverses of fortune. Those
disasters which break down the spirit of a man, and prostrate him in
the dust, seem to call forth all the energies of the softer sex, and give
such intrepidity and elevation to their character, that at times it ap-
proaches to sublimity. Nothing can be more touching than to behold
a soft and tender female, who had been all weakness and dependence,
and alive to every trivial roughness while treading the prosperous
paths of life, suddenly rising in mental force, to be the comforter and
support of her husband under misfortune, and abiding, with un-
shrinking firmness, the bitterest blasts of adversity.

As the vine which has long twined its graceful foliage about the
oak, and been lifted by it into sunshine, will, when the hardy plant is
rifted by the thunderbolt, cling round it with its caressing tendrils and
bind up its shattered boughs; so is it beautifully ordered by providence, that woman, who is the mere dependent and ornament of man
in his happier hours, should be his stay and solace when smitten with
sudden calamity, winding herself into the rugged recesses of his nature; tenderly supporting the drooping head, and binding up the
broken heart.

I was once congratulating a friend, who had around him a blooming family knit together in the strongest affection. "I can wish you no
better lot," said he, with enthusiasm, "than to have a wife and children. If you are prosperous, there they are to share your prosperity; if
otherwise, there they are to comfort you.—" And indeed I have
observed that a married man falling into misfortune, is more apt to

75

retrieve his situation in the world than a single one; partly because he is more stimulated to exertion by the necessities of the helpless and beloved beings who depend upon him for subsistence; but chiefly because his spirits are soothed and relieved by domestic endearments, and his self-respect kept alive by finding, that though all abroad is darkness and humiliation, yet there is still a little world of love at home, of which he is the monarch. Whereas a single man is apt to run to waste and self-neglect; to fancy himself lonely and abandoned, and his heart to fall to ruin like some deserted mansion, for want of an inhabitant.

These observations call to mind a little domestic story, of which I was once a witness. My intimate friend Leslie had married a beautiful and accomplished girl, who had been brought up in the midst of fashionable life. She had, it is true, no fortune, but that of my friend was ample and he delighted in the anticipation of indulging her in every elegant pursuit; and administering to those delicate tastes and fancies that spread a kind of witchery about the sex—"her life," said he, "shall be like a fairy tale."

The very difference in their characters produced an harmonious combination. He was of a romantic and somewhat serious cast; she was all life and gladness. I have often noticed the mute rapture with which he would gaze upon her in company, of which her sprightly powers made her the delight; and how, in the midst of applause, her eye would still turn to him, as if there alone she sought favor and acceptance. When leaning on his arm her slender form contrasted finely with his tall, manly person. The fond confiding air with which she looked up to him, seemed to call forth a flush of triumphant pride and cherishing tenderness; as if he doted on his lovely burden for its very helplessness.—Never did a couple set forward on the flowery path of early and well-suited marriage with a fairer prospect of felicity.

It was the misfortune of my friend, however, to have embarked his property in large speculations, and he had not been married many months, when, by a succession of sudden disasters, it was swept from him, and he found himself reduced almost to penury. For a time he kept his situation to himself and went about with a haggard countenance and a breaking heart. His life was but a protracted agony, and what rendered it more insupportable was the necessity of keeping up a smile in the presence of his wife; for he could not bring himself to overwhelm her with the news. She saw, however, with the quick eyes of affection, that all was not well with him. She marked his altered looks and stifled sighs, and was not to be deceived by his sickly and vapid attempts at cheerfulness. She tasked all her sprightly powers and tender blandishments to win him back to happiness; but she only drove the arrow deeper into his soul—the more he saw cause to love her the more torturing was the thought that he was soon to make her wretched. A little while, thought he, and the smile will vanish from that cheek—the song will die away from those lips—the lustre of those eyes will be quenched with sorrow; and the happy heart which now beats lightly in that bosom, will be weighed down like mine by the cares and miseries of the world.

At length he came to me, one day, and related his whole situation in a tone of the deepest despair. When I heard him through I inquired, "Does your wife know all this?"—at the question he burst into an agony of tears—"For God's sake!" cried he, "if you have any pity on me, don't mention my wife—it is the thought of her that drives me almost to madness!"

"And why not?" said I, "she must know it sooner or later: you cannot keep it long from her, and the intelligence may break upon her in a more startling manner than if imparted by yourself; for the accents of those we love soften the harshest tidings. Besides you are depriving yourself of the comforts of her sympathy and not merely that, but also endangering the only bond that can keep hearts together, an unreserved community of thought and feeling. She will soon perceive that something is secretly preying upon your mind, and true love will not brook reserve: it feels undervalued and outraged when even the sorrows of those it loves are concealed from it."

"Oh but my friend! to think what a blow I am to give to all her future prospects—how I am to strike her very soul to the earth, by telling her that her husband is a beggar!—That she is to forego all the elegancies of life—all the pleasures of society—to shrink with me into indigence and obscurity!—To tell her that I have dragged her down from the sphere in which she might have continued to move in constant brightness—the light of every eye—the admiration of every heart!—How can she bear poverty!—she has been brought up in all the refinements of opulence.—How can she bear neglect!—she has been the idol of society.—oh, it will break her heart!—it will break her heart!—"

I saw his grief was eloquent and I let it have its flow, for sorrow relieves itself by words. When his paroxysm had subsided and he had relapsed into moody silence, I resumed the subject gently, and urged him to break his situation at once to his wife. He shook his head mournfully, but positively.

"But how are you to keep it from her? It is necessary she should know it, that you may take the steps proper to the alteration of your circumstances. You must change your style of living—nay," observing a pang to pass across his countenance—"don't let that afflict you.

I am sure you have never placed your happiness in outward show—you have yet friends, warm friends, who will not think the worse of you for being less splendidly lodged;—and surely it does not require a palace to be happy with Mary—"

"I could be happy with her," cried he, convulsively, "in a hovel!—I could go down with her into poverty and the dust!—I could—I could—God bless her!—God bless her!—" cried he, bursting into a transport of grief and tenderness.

"And believe me my friend," said I stepping up and grasping him warmly by the hand—"believe me she can be the same with you. Aye, more—it will be a source of pride and triumph to her—it will call forth all the latent energies and fervent sympathies of her nature; for she will rejoice to prove that she loves you for yourself. There is in every true woman's heart a spark of heavenly fire which lies dormant in the broad daylight of prosperity; but which kindles up, and beams and blazes in the dark hour of adversity. No man knows what the wife of his bosom is—no man knows what a ministering angel she is—until he has gone with her through the fiery trials of this world."

There was something in the earnestness of my manner, and the figurative style of my language that caught the excited imagination of Leslie. I knew the auditor I had to deal with; and following up the impression I had made, I finished by persuading him to go home and unburden his sad heart to his wife.

I must confess, notwithstanding all I had said, I felt some little solicitude for the result. Who can calculate on the fortitude of one whose life has been a round of pleasures?—Her gay spirits might revolt at the dark downward path of low humility suddenly pointed out before her, and might cling to the sunny regions in which they had hitherto revelled. Besides, ruin in fashionable life is accompanied by so many galling mortifications to which in other ranks it is a stranger—in short, I could not meet Leslie the next morning without trepidation. He had made the disclosure.

—"And how did she bear it?"

"Like an angel! It seemed rather to be a relief to her mind, for she threw her arms round my neck, and asked if this was all that had lately made me unhappy—but, poor girl,"—added he, "she cannot realize the change we must undergo. She has no idea of poverty but in the abstract—she has only read of it in poetry, where it is allied to love. She feels as yet no privation—she suffers no loss of accustomed conveniences nor elegancies. When we come practically to experience its sordid cares, its paltry wants, its petty humiliations—then will be the real trial."

"But," said I, "now that you have got over the severest task, that of breaking it to her, the sooner you let the world into the secret the better. The disclosure may be mortifying, but then it is a single misery and soon over, whereas you otherwise suffer it in anticipation, every hour in the day. It is not poverty so much as pretence, that harasses a ruined man. The struggle between a proud mind and an empty purse—the keeping up a hollow show that must soon come to an end. Have the courage to appear poor and you disarm poverty of its sharpest sting."—On this point I found Leslie perfectly prepared. He had no false pride himself, and as to his wife, she was only anxious to conform to their altered fortunes.

Some days afterwards he called upon me in the evening. He had disposed of his dwelling house and taken a small cottage in the country, a few miles from town. He had been busied all day in sending out furniture. The new establishment required few articles, and those of the simplest kind. All the splendid furniture of his late residence had been sold, excepting his wife's Harp. That, he said, was too closely associated with the idea of herself—it belonged to the little story of their loves—for some of the sweetest moments of their courtship were those when he had leant over that instrument and listened to the melting tones of her voice.—I could not but smile at this instance of romantic gallantry in a doting husband.

He was now going out to the cottage, where his wife had been all day, superintending its arrangement. My feelings had become strongly interested in the progress of this family story and as it was a fine evening I offered to accompany him.

He was wearied with the fatigues of the day, and as we walked out, fell into a fit of gloomy musing.

"Poor Mary!" at length broke, with a heavy sigh from his lips.

"And what of her?" asked I: "has anything happened to her?"

"What," said he, darting an impatient glance, "is it nothing to be reduced to this paltry situation—to be caged in a miserable cottage—to be obliged to toil almost in the menial concerns of her wretched habitation?"

"Has she then repined at the change?"

"Repined!—she has been nothing but sweetness and good humor. Indeed, she seems in better spirits than I have ever known her—she has been to me all love and tenderness and comfort!"

"Admirable girl!" exclaimed I. "You call yourself poor my friend; you never were so rich—you never knew the boundless treasures of excellence you possessed in that woman."

"Oh! but, my friend—if this first meeting at the cottage were over—I think I could then be comfortable. But this is her first day of real experience. She has been introduced into a humble dwelling. She has been employed all day in arranging its miserable equipments. She has for the first time known the fatigues of domestic employment—She has for the first time looked around her on a home destitute of every thing elegant,—almost of every thing convenient, and may now be sitting down exhausted and spiritless, brooding over a prospect of future poverty."

There was a degree of probability in this picture that I could not gainsay—so we walked on in silence.

After turning from the main road up a narrow lane so thickly shaded with forest trees as to give it a complete air of seclusion, we came in sight of the cottage. It was humble enough in its appearance for the most pastoral poet; and yet it had a pleasing rural look. A wild vine had over run one end with a profusion of foliage—a few trees threw their branches gracefully over it, and I observed several pots of flowers tastefully disposed about the door and on the grass plot in front. A small wicket gate opened upon a foot path that wound through some shrubbery to the door. Just as we approached we heard the sound of music.—Leslie grasped my arm—we paused and listened. It was Mary's voice singing, in a style of the most touching simplicity, a little air of which her husband was peculiarly fond.

I felt Leslie's hand tremble on my arm. He stepped forward to hear more distinctly—His step made a noise on the gravel walk—a bright beautiful face glanced out at the window and vanished—a light footstep was heard, and Mary came tripping forth to meet us. She was in a pretty, rural dress of white; a few wild flowers were twisted in her fine hair; a fresh bloom was on her cheek; her whole countenance beamed with smiles—I had never seen her look so lovely.

"My dear George," cried she, "I am so glad you are come—I have been watching and watching for you; and running down the lane, and looking out for you. I've set out a table under a beautiful tree behind the cottage—and I've been gathering some of the most delicious strawberries, for I know you are fond of them—and we have such excellent cream—and every thing is so sweet and still here—Oh!" said she, putting her arm within his, and looking up brightly in his face—"oh, we shall be so happy!"

Poor Leslie was overcome—He caught her to his bosom—he folded his arms round her—he kissed her again and again—he could not speak, but the tears gushed into his eyes—And he has often assured me that though the world has since gone prosperously with him, and his life has, indeed, been a happy one; yet never has he experienced a moment of more exquisite felicity.

MOUNTJOY;

or, Some Passages Out of the Life of a Castle-builder

I WAS BORN among romantic scenery, in one of the wildest parts of the Hudson, which at that time was not so thickly settled as at present. My father was descended from one of the old Huguenot families, that came over to this country on the revocation of the Edict of Nantz. He lived in a style of easy, rural independence, on a patrimonial estate that had been for two or three generations in the family. He was an indolent, good-natured man, who took the world as it went, and had a kind of laughing philosophy, that parried all rubs and mishaps, and served him in the place of wisdom. This was the part of his character least to my taste; for I was of an enthusiastic, excitable temperament, prone to kindle up with new schemes and projects, and he was apt to dash my sallying enthusiasm by some unlucky joke; so that whenever I was in a glow with any sudden excitement, I stood in mortal dread of his good-humor.

Yet he indulged me in every vagary; for I was an only son, and of course a personage of importance in the household. I had two sisters older than myself, and one younger. The former were educated at New York, under the eye of a maiden aunt; the latter remained at home, and was my cherished playmate, the companion of my thoughts. We were two imaginative little beings, of quick susceptibility, and prone to see wonders and mysteries in everything around us. Scarce had we learned to read, when our mother made us holiday presents of all the nursery literature of the day, which at that time consisted of little books covered with gilt paper, adorned with "cuts," and filled with tales of fairies, giants, and enchanters. What draughts of delightful fiction did we then inhale! My sister Sophy was of a soft and tender nature. She would weep over the woes of the Children in the Wood, or quake at the dark romance of Blue-Beard, and the terrible mysteries of the blue chamber. But I was all for enterprise and adventure. I burned to emulate the deeds of that heroic prince who delivered the white cat from her enchantment; or he of no less royal

81

blood, and doughty enterprise, who broke the charmed slumber of the Beauty in the Wood!

The house in which we lived was just the kind of place to foster such propensities. It was a venerable mansion, half villa, half farmhouse. The oldest part was of stone, with loopholes for musketry, having served as a family fortress in the time of the Indians. To this there had been made various additions, some of brick, some of wood, according to the exigencies of the moment; so that it was full of nooks and crooks, and chambers of all sorts and sizes. It was buried among willows, elms, and cherry trees, and surrounded with roses and hollyhocks, with honeysuckle and sweetbrier clambering about every window. A brood of hereditary pigeons sunned themselves upon the roof; hereditary swallows and martins built about the eaves and chimneys; and hereditary bees hummed about the flower-beds.

Under the influence of our story-books every object around us now assumed a new character, and a charmed interest. The wild flowers were no longer the mere ornaments of the fields, or the resorts of the toilful bee; they were the lurking-places of fairies. We would watch the humming-bird, as it hovered around the trumpet-creeper at our porch, and the butterfly as it flitted up into the blue air, above the sunny tree-tops, and fancy them some of the tiny beings from fairy land. I would call to mind all that I had read of Robin Goodfellow, and his power of transformation. Oh, how I envied him that power! How I longed to be able to compress my form into utter littleness, to ride the bold dragon-fly, swing on the tall bearded grass, follow the ant into his subterraneous habitation, or dive into the cavernous depths of the honeysuckle!

While I was yet a mere child, I was sent to a daily school, about two miles distant. The schoolhouse was on the edge of a wood, close by a brook overhung with birches, alders, and dwarf-willows. We of the school who lived at some distance came with our dinners put up in little baskets. In the intervals of school hours, we would gather round a spring, under a tuft of hazel-bushes, and have a kind of picnic; interchanging the rustic dainties with which our provident mothers had fitted us out. Then, when our joyous repast was over, and my companions were disposed for play, I would draw forth one of my cherished story-books, stretch myself on the greensward, and soon lose myself in its bewitching contents.

I became an oracle among my schoolmates, on account of my superior erudition, and soon imparted to them the contagion of my infected fancy. Often in the evening, after school hours, we would sit on the trunk of some fallen tree in the woods, and vie with each other in telling extravagant stories, until the whip-poor-will began his nightly moaning, and the fire-flies sparkled in the gloom. Then came the perilous journey homeward. What delight we would take in getting up wanton panics, in some dusky part of the wood; scampering like frightened deer, pausing to take breath, renewing the panic, and scampering off again, wild with fictitious terror!

Our greatest trial was to pass a dark, lonely pool, covered with pond-lilies, peopled with bull-frogs and water-snakes, and haunted by two white cranes. Oh! the terrors of that pond! How our little hearts would beat, as we approached it; what fearful glances we would throw around! And if by chance a plash of a wild duck, or the guttural twang of a bull-frog, struck our ears as we stole quietly by—away we sped, nor paused until completely out of the woods. Then, when I reached home, what a world of adventures and imaginary terrors would I have to relate to my sister Sophy!

As I advanced in years, this turn of mind increased upon me, and became more confirmed. I abandoned myself to the impulses of a romantic imagination, which controlled my studies, and gave a bias to all my habits. My father observed me continually with a book in my hand, and satisfied himself that I was a profound student; but what were my studies? Works of fiction, tales of chivalry, voyages of discovery, travels in the East; everything, in short, that partook of adventure and romance. I well remember with what zest I entered upon that part of my studies which treated of the heathen mythology, and particularly of the sylvan deities. Then indeed my school-books became dear to me. The neighborhood was well calculated to foster the reveries of a mind like mine. It abounded with solitary retreats, wild streams, solemn forests, and silent valleys. I would ramble about for a whole day, with a volume of Ovid's *Metamorphoses* in my pocket, and work myself into a kind of self-delusion, so as to identify the surrounding scenes with those of which I had just been reading. I would loiter about a brook that glided through the shadowy depths of the forest, picturing it to myself the haunt of Naiades. I would steal round some bushy copse that opened upon a glade, as if I expected to come suddenly upon Diana and her nymphs; or to behold Pan and his satyrs bounding, with whoop and halloo, through the woodland. I would throw myself, during the panting heats of a summer noon, under the shade of some widespreading tree, and muse and dream away the hours, in a state of mental intoxication. I drank in the very light of day, as nectar, and my soul seemed to bathe with ecstasy in the deep blue of a summer sky.

In these wanderings nothing occurred to jar my feelings, or bring me back to the realities of life. There is a repose in our mighty forests that gives full scope to the imagination. Now and then I would hear the distant sound of the wood-cutter's axe, or the crash of some tree which he had laid low; but these noises, echoing along the quiet landscape, could easily be wrought by fancy into harmony with its illusions. In general, however, the woody recesses of the neighborhood were peculiarly wild and unfrequented. I could ramble for a whole day, without coming upon any traces of cultivation. The partridge of the wood scarcely seemed to shun my path, and the squirrel, from his nut-tree, would gaze at me for an instant, with sparkling eye, as if wondering at the unwonted intrusion.

I cannot help dwelling on this delicious period of my life; when as yet I had known no sorrow, nor experienced any worldly care. I have since studied much, both of books and men, and of course have grown too wise to be so easily pleased; yet with all my wisdom, I must confess I look back with a secret feeling of regret to the days of happy ignorance, before I had begun to be a philosopher.

It must be evident that I was in a hopeful training, for one who was to descend into the arena of life, and wrestle with the world. The tutor, also, who superintended my studies, in the more advanced stage of my education, was just fitted to complete the *fata morgana* which was forming in my mind. His name was Glencoe. He was a pale, melancholy-looking man, about forty years of age; a native of Scotland, liberally educated, and who had devoted himself to the instruction of youth, from taste rather than necessity; for, as he said, he loved the human heart, and delighted to study it in its earlier impulses. My two elder sisters, having returned home from a city boarding-school, were likewise placed under his care, to direct their reading in history and belles-lettres.

We all soon became attached to Glencoe. It is true we were at first somewhat prepossessed against him. His meagre, pallid countenance, his broad pronunciation, his inattention to the little forms of society, and an awkward and embarrassed manner, on first acquaintance, were much against him; but we soon discovered that under this unpromising exterior existed the kindest urbanity the warmest sympathies, the most enthusiastic benevolence. His mind was ingenious and acute. His reading had been various, but more abstruse than profound; his memory was stored, on all subjects, with facts, theories, and quotations, and crowded with crude materials for thinking. These, in a moment of excitement, would be, as it were, melted down and poured forth in the lava of a heated imagination. At such moments, the change in the whole man was wonderful. His meagre form would acquire a dignity and grace; his long, pale visage would flash with a hectic glow; his eyes would beam with intense speculation; and there would be pathetic tones and deep modulations in his voice, that delighted the ear, and spoke movingly to the heart.

But what most endeared him to us, was the kindness and sympathy with which he entered into all our interests and wishes. Instead of curbing and checking our young imaginations with the reins of sober reason, he was a little too apt to catch the impulse, and be hurried away with us. He could not withstand the excitement of any sally of feeling or fancy, and was prone to lend heightening tints to the illusive coloring of youthful anticipation.

Under his guidance my sisters and myself soon entered upon a more extended range of studies; but while they wandered, with delighted minds, through the wide field of history and belles-lettres, a nobler walk was opened to my superior intellect.

The mind of Glencoe presented a singular mixture of philosophy and poetry. He was fond of metaphysics, and prone to indulge in abstract speculations, though his metaphysics were somewhat fine-spun and fanciful, and his speculations were apt to partake of what my father most irreverently termed "humbug." For my part, I delighted in them, and the more especially because they set my father to sleep, and completely confounded my sisters. I entered, with my accustomed eagerness, into this new branch of study. Metaphysics were now my passion. My sisters attempted to accompany me, but they soon faltered, and gave out before they had got half way through *Smith's Theory of the Moral Sentiments*. I, however, went on, exulting in my strength. Glencoe supplied me with books, and I devoured them with appetite, if not digestion. We walked and talked together under the trees before the house, or sat apart, like Milton's angels, and held high converse upon themes beyond the grasp of ordinary intellects. Glencoe possessed a kind of philosophic chivalry, in imitation of the old peripatetic sages, and was continually dreaming of romantic enterprises in morals, and splendid systems for the improvement of society. He had a fanciful mode of illustrating abstract subjects, peculiarly to my taste; clothing them with the language of poetry, and throwing round them almost the magic hues of fiction. "How charming," thought I, "is divine philosophy";

> "Not harsh and crabbed, as dull fools suppose,
>   But musical as is Apollo's lute;
>   And a perpetual feast of nectar'd sweets,
>   Where no crude surfeit reigns."

I felt a wonderful self-complacency at being on such excellent terms with a man whom I considered on a parallel with the sages of antiquity, and looked down with a sentiment of pity on the feebler intellects of my sisters, who could comprehend nothing of metaphysics. It is true, when I attempted to study them by myself I was apt to get in a fog; but when Glencoe came to my aid, everything was soon as clear to me as day. My ear drank in the beauty of his words; my imagination was dazzled with the splendor of his illustrations. It caught up the sparkling sands of poetry that glittered through his speculations, and mistook them for the golden ore of wisdom. Struck with the facility with which I seemed to imbibe and relish the most abstract doctrines, I conceived a still higher opinion of my mental powers, and was convinced that I also was a philosopher.

I was now verging toward man's estate, and though my education had been extremely irregular,—following the caprices of my humor, which I mistook for the impulses of my genius,—yet I was regarded with wonder and delight by my mother and sisters, who considered me almost as wise and infallible as I considered myself. This high opinion of me was strengthened by a declamatory habit, which made me an oracle and orator at the domestic board. The time was now at hand, however, that was to put my philosophy to the test.

We had passed through a long winter, and the spring at length opened upon us, with unusual sweetness. The soft serenity of the weather; the beauty of the surrounding country, the joyous notes of the birds, the balmy breath of flower and blossom, all combined to fill my bosom with indistinct sensations, and nameless wishes. Amid the soft seductions of the season I lapsed into a state of utter indolence, both of body and mind. Philosophy had lost its charms for me. Metaphysics—faugh! I tried to study; took down volume after volume, ran my eye vacantly over a few pages, and threw them by with distaste. I loitered about the house, with my hands in my pockets, and an air of complete vacancy. Something was necessary to make me happy; but what was that something? I sauntered to the apartments of my sisters, hoping their conversation might amuse me. They had walked out, and the room was vacant. On the table lay a volume which they had been reading. It was a novel. I had never read a novel, having conceived a contempt for works of the kind, from hearing them universally condemned. It is true, I had remarked that they were universally read; but I considered them beneath the attention of a philosopher, and never would venture to read them, lest I should lessen my mental superiority in the eyes of my sisters. Nay, I had taken up a work of the kind, now and then, when I knew my sisters were observing me, looked into it for a moment, and then laid it down, with a slight supercilious smile. On the present occasion, out of mere listlessness, I took up the volume, and turned over a few of the first pages. I thought I heard some one coming, and laid it down. I was mistaken; no one was near, and what I had read, tempted my curiosity to read a little farther. I leaned against a window-frame, and in a few minutes was completely lost in the story. How long I stood there reading I know not, but I believe for nearly two hours. Suddenly I heard my sisters on the stairs, when I thrust the book into my bosom, and the two other volumes, which lay near, into my pockets, and hurried out of the house to my beloved woods. Here I remained all day beneath the trees, bewildered, bewitched; devouring the contents of these delicious volumes; and only returned to the house when it was too dark to peruse their pages.

This novel finished, I replaced it in my sisters' apartment, and looked for others. Their stock was ample, for they had brought home all that were current in the city; but my appetite demanded an immense supply. All this course of reading was carried on clandestinely, for I was a little ashamed of it, and fearful that my wisdom might be called in question; but this very privacy gave it additional zest. It was "bread eaten in secret"; it had the charm of a private amour.

But think what must have been the effect of such a course of reading on a youth of my temperament and turn of mind; indulged, too, amidst romantic scenery, and in the romantic season of the year. It seemed as if I had entered upon a new scene of existence. A train of combustible feelings were lighted up in me, and my soul was all tenderness and passion. Never was youth more completely love-sick, though as yet it was a mere general sentiment, and wanted a definite object. Unfortunately, our neighborhood was particularly deficient in female society, and I languished in vain for some divinity, to whom I might offer up this most uneasy burden of affections. I was at one time seriously enamored of a lady whom I saw occasionally in my rides reading at the window of a country-seat, and actually serenaded her with my flute; when, to my confusion, I discovered that she was old enough to be my mother. It was a sad damper to my romance; especially as my father heard of it, and made it the subject of one of those household jokes, which he was apt to serve up at every meal-time.

I soon recovered from this check, however, but it was only to relapse into a state of amorous excitement. I passed whole days in the fields, and along the brooks; for there is something in the tender passion that makes us alive to the beauties of Nature. A soft sunshine morning infused a sort of rapture into my breast; I flung open my arms, like the Grecian youth in Ovid, as if I would take in and embrace the balmy atmosphere. The song of the birds melted me to tenderness. I would lie by the side of some rivulet for hours, and form garlands of the flowers on its banks, and muse on ideal beauties, and sigh from the crowd of undefined emotions that swelled my bosom.

In this state of amorous delirium, I was strolling one morning along a beautiful wild brook which I had discovered in a glen. There was one place where a small waterfall, leaping from among rocks into a natural basin, made a scene such as a poet might have chosen as the haunt of some shy Naiad. It was here I usually retired to banquet on my novels. In visiting the place this morning, I traced distinctly, on the margin of the basin, which was of fine clear sand, the prints of a female foot, of the most slender and delicate proportions. This was sufficient for an imagination like mine. Robinson Crusoe himself, when he discovered the print of a savage foot on the beach of his lonely island, could not have been more suddenly assailed with thick-coming fancies.

I endeavored to track the steps, but they only passed for a few paces along the fine sand, and then were lost among the herbage. I remained gazing in reverie upon this passing trace of loveliness. It evidently was not made by any of my sisters, for they knew nothing of this haunt; besides, the foot was smaller than theirs; it was remarkable for its beautiful delicacy.

My eye accidentally caught two or three half withered wildflowers lying on the ground. The unknown nymph had doubtless dropped them from her bosom! Here was a new document of taste and sentiment. I treasured them up as invaluable relics. The place, too, where I found them, was remarkably picturesque, and the most beautiful part of the brook. It was overhung with a fine elm, entwined with grapevines. She who could select such a spot, who could delight in wild brooks, and wild-flowers, and silent solitudes, must have fancy, and feeling, and tenderness; and, with all these qualities, she must be beautiful!

But who could be this Unknown, that had thus passed by, as in a morning dream, leaving merely flowers and fairy footsteps to tell of her loveliness! There was a mystery in it that bewildered me. It was so vague and disembodied, like those "airy tongues that syllable men's names" in solitude. Every attempt to solve the mystery was vain. I could hear of no being in the neighborhood to whom this trace could be ascribed. I haunted the spot, and became more and more enamored. Never, surely, was passion more pure and spiritual, and never lover in more dubious situation. My case could only be compared with that of the amorous prince, in the fairy tale of *Cinderella;* but he had a glass slipper on which to lavish his tenderness. I, alas! was in love with a footstep!

The imagination is alternately a cheat and a dupe; nay, more, it is the most subtle of cheats, for it cheats itself, and becomes the dupe of its own delusions. It conjures up "airy nothings," gives to them a "local habitation and a name," and then bows to their control as implicitly as if they were realities. Such was now my case. The good Numa could not more thoroughly have persuaded himself that the nymph Egeria hovered about her sacred fountain, and communed with him in spirit, than I had deceived myself into a kind of visionary intercourse with the airy phantom fabricated in my brain. I constructed a rustic seat at the foot of the tree where I had discovered the footsteps. I made a kind of bower there, where I used to pass my mornings, reading poetry and romances. I carved hearts and darts on the tree, and hung it with garlands. My heart was full to overflowing, and wanted some faithful bosom into which it might relieve itself. What is a lover without a confidante? I thought at once of my sister Sophy, my early playmate, the sister of my affections. She was so reasonable, too, and of such correct feelings, always listening to my words as oracular sayings, and admiring my scraps of poetry, as the very inspirations of the Muse. From such a devoted, such a rational being, what secrets could I have?

I accordingly took her one morning to my favorite retreat. She looked around, with delighted surprise, upon the rustic seat, the bower, the tree carved with emblems of the tender passion. She turned her eyes upon me to inquire the meaning.

"O, Sophy," exclaimed I, clasping both her hands in mine, and looking earnestly in her face, "I am in love!"

She started with surprise.

"Sit down," said I, "and I will tell you all."

She seated herself upon the rustic bench, and I went into a full history of the footstep, with all the associations of idea that had been conjured up by my imagination.

Sophy was enchanted; it was like a fairy tale: she had read of such mysterious visitations in books, and the loves thus conceived were always for beings of superior order, and were always happy. She caught the illusion in all its force; her cheek glowed; her eye brightened.

"I dare say she's pretty," said Sophy.

"Pretty!" echoed I, "she is beautiful!" I went through all the reasoning by which I had logically proved the fact to my own satisfaction. I dwelt upon the evidences of her taste, her sensibility to the beauties of Nature; her soft meditative habit, that delighted in solitude; "Oh," said I, clasping my hands, "to have such a companion to wander through these scenes; to sit with her by this murmuring stream; to wreathe garlands round her brow; to hear the music of her voice mingling with the whisperings of these groves——"

"Delightful! delightful!" cried Sophy; "what a sweet creature she must be! She is just the friend I want. How I shall dote upon her! Oh, my dear brother! you must not keep her all to yourself. You must let *me* have some share of her!"

I caught her to my bosom: "You shall—you shall!" cried I, "my dear Sophy; we will all live for each other!"

The conversation with Sophy heightened the illusions of my mind; and the manner in which she had treated my daydream, identified it with facts and persons, and gave it still more the stamp of reality. I walked about as one in a trance, heedless of the world around, and lapped in an elysium of the fancy.

In this mood I met, one morning, with Glencoe. He accosted me with his usual smile, and was proceeding with some general observations, but paused and fixed on me an inquiring eye.

"What is the matter with you?" said he; "you seem agitated; has anything in particular happened?"

"Nothing," said I, hesitating; "at least nothing worth communicating to you."

"Nay, my dear young friend," said he, "whatever is of sufficient importance to agitate you, is worthy of being communicated to me."

"Well—but my thoughts are running on what you would think a frivolous subject."

"No subject is frivolous that has the power to awaken strong feelings."

"What think you," said I, hesitating, "what think you of love?"

Glencoe almost started at the question. "Do you call that a frivolous subject?" replied he. "Believe me, there is none fraught with such deep, such vital interest. If you talk, indeed, of the capricious inclination awakened by the mere charm of perishable beauty, I grant it to be idle in the extreme; but that love which springs from the concordant sympathies of virtuous hearts; that love which is awakened by the perception of moral excellence, and fed by meditation on intellectual as well as personal beauty; that is a passion which refines and enobles the human heart. Oh, where is there a sight more nearly approaching to the intercourse of angels, than that of two young beings, free from the sins and follies of the world, mingling pure thoughts, and looks, and feelings, and becoming as it were soul of one soul, and heart of one heart! How exquisite the silent converse that they hold; the soft devotion of the eye, that needs no words to make it eloquent! Yes, my friend, if there be anything in this weary world worthy of heaven, it is the pure bliss of such a mutual affection!"

The words of my worthy tutor overcame all farther reserve. "Mr. Glencoe," cried I, blushing still deeper, "I am in love!"

"And is that what you were ashamed to tell me? Oh, never seek to conceal from your friend so important a secret. If your passion be unworthy, it is for the steady hand of friendship to pluck it forth: if honorable, none but an enemy would seek to stifle it. On nothing does the character and happiness so much depend, as on the first affection of the heart. Were you caught by some fleeting or superficial charm—a bright eye, a blooming cheek, a soft voice, or a voluptuous form—I would warn you to beware; I would tell you that beauty is but a passing gleam of the morning, a perishable flower; that accident may becloud and blight it, and that at best it must soon pass away. But were you in love with such a one as I could describe; young in years, but still younger in feelings; lovely in person, but as a type of the mind's beauty; soft in voice, in token of gentleness of spirit; blooming in countenance, like the rosy tints of morning kindling with the promise of a genial day; an eye beaming with the benignity of a happy heart; a cheerful temper, alive to all kind impulses, and frankly diffusing its own felicity; a self-poised mind, that needs not lean on others for support; an elegant taste, that can embellish solitude, and furnish out its own enjoyments—"

"My dear sir," cried I, for I could contain myself no longer, "you have described the very person!"

"Why then, my dear young friend," said he, affectionately pressing my hand, "in God's name, love on!"

For the remainder of the day I was in some such state of dreamy beatitude as a Turk is said to enjoy when under the influence of opium. It must be already manifest how prone I was to bewilder myself with picturings of the fancy, so as to confound them with existing realities. In the present instance, Sophy and Glencoe had contributed to promote the transient delusion. Sophy, dear girl, had as usual joined with me in my castle-building, and indulged in the same train of imaginings, while Glencoe, duped by my enthusiasm, firmly believed that I spoke of a being I had seen and known. By their sympathy with my feelings, they in a manner became associated with the Unknown in my mind, and thus linked her with the circle of my intimacy.

In the evening our family party was assembled in the hall, to enjoy the refreshing breeze. Sophy was playing some favorite Scotch airs on the piano, while Glencoe, seated apart, with his forehead resting on his hand, was buried in one of those pensive reveries that made him so interesting to me.

"What a fortunate being I am!" thought I, "blessed with such a sister and such a friend! I have only to find out this amiable Unknown, to wed her, and be happy! What a paradise will be my home, graced with a partner of such exquisite refinement! It will be a perfect fairy bower, buried among sweets and roses. Sophy shall live with us, and be the companion of all our enjoyments. Glencoe, too, shall no more be the solitary being that he now appears. He shall have a home with us. He shall have his study, where, when he pleases, he may shut himself up from the world, and bury himself in his own reflections. His retreat shall be sacred; no one shall intrude there; no one but myself, who will visit him now and then, in his seclusion, where we will devise grand schemes together for the improvement of mankind. How delightfully our days will pass, in a round of rational pleasures and elegant employments! Sometimes we will have music; sometimes we will read; sometimes we will wander through the flower garden, when I will smile with complacency on every flower my wife has planted; while in the long winter evenings, the ladies will sit at their work and listen, with hushed attention to Glencoe and myself, as we discuss the abstruse doctrines of metaphysics."

From this delectable reverie I was startled by my father's slapping me on the shoulder. "What possesses the lad?" cried he; "here have I been speaking to you half a dozen times, without receiving an answer."

"Pardon me, sir," replied I; "I was so completely lost in thought, that I did not hear you."

"Lost in thought! And pray what were you thinking of? Some of your philosophy, I suppose."

"Upon my word," said my sister Charlotte, with an arch laugh, "I suspect Harry's in love again."

"And if I were in love, Charlotte," said I, somewhat nettled, and recollecting Glencoe's enthusiastic eulogy of the passion, "if I were in love, is that a matter of jest and laughter? Is the tenderest and most fervid affection that can animate the human breast to be made a matter of cold-hearted ridicule?"

My sister colored. "Certainly not, brother! nor did I mean to make it so, or to say anything that should wound your feelings. Had I really suspected that you had formed some genuine attachment, it would have been sacred in my eyes; but—but," said she, smiling, as if at some whimsical recollection, "I thought that you—you might be indulging in another little freak of the imagination."

"I'll wager any money," cried my father, "he has fallen in love again with some old lady at a window!"

"Oh, no!" cried my dear sister Sophy, with the most gracious warmth; "she is young and beautiful."

"From what I understand," said Glencoe, rousing himself, "she must be lovely in mind as in person."

I found my friends were getting me into a fine scrape. I began to perspire at every pore, and felt my ears tingle.

"Well, but," cried my father, "who is she?—what is she? Let us hear something about her."

This was no time to explain so delicate a matter. I caught up my hat and vanished out of the house.

The moment I was in the open air, and alone, my heart upbraided me. Was this respectful treatment to my father—to *such* a father too—who had always regarded me as the pride of his age—the staff of his hopes? It is true, he was apt sometimes, to laugh at my enthusiastic flights, and did not treat my philosophy with due respect; but when had he ever thwarted a wish of my heart? Was I then to act with reserve toward him, in a matter which might affect the whole current of my future life? "I have done wrong," thought I; "but it is not too late to remedy it. I will hasten back, and open my whole heart to my father!"

I returned accordingly, and was just on the point of entering the house, with my heart full of filial piety, and a contrite speech upon my lips, when I heard a burst of obstreperous laughter from my father, and a loud titter from my two elder sisters.

"A footstep!" shouted he, as soon as he could recover himself; "in love with a footstep! why, this beats the old lady at the window!" And then there was another appalling burst of laughter. Had it been a clap of thunder, it could hardly have astounded me more completely. Sophy, in the simplicity of her heart, had told all, and had set my father's risible propensities in full action.

Never was poor mortal so thoroughly crest-fallen as myself. The whole delusion was at an end. I drew off silently from the house, shrinking smaller and smaller at every fresh peal of laughter; and, wandering about until the family had retired, stole quietly to my bed. Scarce any sleep, however, visited my eyes that night. I lay overwhelmed with mortification, and meditating how I might meet the family in the morning. The idea of ridicule was always intolerable to me: but to endure it on a subject by which my feelings had been so much excited, seemed worse than death. I almost determined, at one time, to get up, saddle my horse, and ride off, I knew not whither.

At length I came to a resolution. Before going down to breakfast I sent for Sophy, and employed her as an ambassador to treat formally in the matter. I insisted that the subject should be buried in oblivion; otherwise I would not show my face at table. It was readily agreed to; for not one of the family would have given me pain for the world. They faithfully kept their promise. Not a word was said of the matter; but there were wry faces, and suppressed titters, that went to my soul;

and whenever my father looked me in the face, it was with such a tragic-comical leer—such an attempt to pull down a serious brow upon a whimsical mouth—that I had a thousand times rather he had laughed outright.

For a day or two after the mortifying occurrence mentioned, I kept as much as possible out of the way of the family, and wandered about the fields and woods by myself. I was sadly out of tune: my feelings were all jarred and unstrung. The birds sang from every grove, but I took no pleasure in their melody; and the flowers of the field bloomed unheeded around me. To be crossed in love is bad enough; but then one can fly to poetry for relief, and turn one's woes to account in soul-subduing stanzas. But to have one's whole passion, object and all, annihilated, dispelled, proved to be such stuff as dreams are made of, or, worse than all, to be turned into a proverb and a jest—what consolation is there in such a case?

I avoided the fatal brook where I had seen the footstep. My favorite resort was now the banks of the Hudson, where I sat upon the rocks and mused upon the current that dimpled by, or the waves that laved the shore; or watched the bright mutations of the clouds, and the shifting lights and shadows of the distant mountain. By degrees a returning serenity stole over my feelings; and a sigh now and then, gentle and easy, and unattended by pain, showed that my heart was recovering its susceptibility.

As I was sitting in this musing mood, my eye became gradually fixed upon an object that was borne along by the tide. It proved to be a little pinnace, beautifully modelled, and gayly painted and decorated. It was an unusual sight in this neighborhood, which was rather lonely; indeed it was rare to see any pleasure barks in this part of the river. As it drew nearer, I perceived that there was no one on board: it had apparently drifted from its anchorage. There was not a breath of air; the little bark came floating along on the glassy stream, wheeling about with the eddies. At length it ran aground, almost at the foot of the rock on which I was seated. I descended to the margin of the river, and drawing the bark to shore, admired its light and elegant proportions, and taste with which it was fitted up. The benches were covered with cushions, and its long streamer was of silk. On one of the cushion's lay a lady's glove, of delicate size and shape, with beautifully tapered fingers. I instantly seized it and thrust it in my bosom: it seemed a match for the fairy footstep that had so fascinated me.

In a moment all the romance of my bosom was again in a glow. Here was one of the very incidents of fairy tale; a bark sent by some invisible power, some good genius, or benevolent fairy, to waft me to some delectable adventure. I recollected something of an enchanted bark, drawn by white swans, that conveyed a knight down the current of the Rhine, on some enterprise connected with love and beauty. The glove, too, showed that there was a lady fair concerned in the present adventure. It might be a gauntlet of defiance, to dare me to the enterprise.

In the spirit of romance, and the whim of the moment, I sprang on board, hoisted the light sail, and pushed from shore. As if breathed by some presiding power, a light breeze at that moment sprang up, swelled out the sail, and dallied with the silken streamer. For a time I glided along under steep umbrageous banks, or across deep sequestered bays; and then stood out over a wide expansion of the river, toward a high rocky promontory. It was a lovely evening: the sun was setting in a congregation of clouds that threw the whole heavens in a glow, and were reflected in the river. I delighted myself with all kinds of fantastic fancies, as to what enchanted island, or mystic bower, or necromantic palace, I was to be conveyed by the fairy bark.

In the revel of my fancy, I had not noticed that the gorgeous congregation of clouds which had so much delighted me, was, in fact, a gathering thunder-gust. I perceived the truth too late. The clouds came hurrying on, darkening as they advanced. The whole face of Nature was suddenly changed, and assumed that baleful and livid tint, predictive of a storm. I tried to gain the shore; but, before I could reach it, a blast of wind struck the water and lashed it at once into foam. The next moment it overtook the boat. Alas! I was nothing of a sailor; and my protecting fairy forsook me in the moment of peril. I endeavored to lower the sail, but in so doing I had to quit the helm; the bark was overturned in an instant, and I was thrown into the water. I endeavored to cling to the wreck, but missed my hold: being a poor swimmer, I soon found myself sinking, but grasped a light oar that was floating by me. It was not sufficient for my support: I again sank beneath the surface; there was a rushing and bubbling sound in my ears, and all sense forsook me.

How long I remained insensible, I know not. I had a confused notion of being moved and tossed about, and of hearing strange beings and strange voices around me; but all was like a hideous dream. When I at length recovered full consciousness and perception, I found myself in bed, in a spacious chamber, furnished with more taste than I had been accustomed to. The bright rays of a morning sun were intercepted by curtains of a delicate rose color, that gave a soft, voluptuous tinge to every object. Not far from my bed, on a classic tripod, was a basket of beautiful exotic flowers, breathing the sweetest fragrance.

"Where am I? How came I here?"

I tasked my mind to catch at some previous event, from which I might trace up the thread of existence to the present moment. By degrees I called to mind the fairy pinnace, my daring embarkation, my adventurous voyage, and my disastrous shipwreck. Beyond that all was chaos. How came I here? What unknown region had I landed upon? The people that inhabited it must be gentle and amiable, and of elegant tastes, for they loved downy beds, fragrant flowers, and rose-colored curtains.

While I lay thus musing, the tones of a harp reached my ear. Presently they were accompanied by a female voice. It came from the room below; but in the profound stillness of my chamber not a modulation was lost. My sisters were all considered good musicians, and sang very tolerably; but I had never heard a voice like this. There was no attempt at difficult execution, or striking effect; but there were exquisite inflexions, and tender turns, which art could not reach. Nothing but feeling and sentiment could produce them. It was soul breathed forth in sound. I was always alive to the influence of music; indeed I was susceptible of voluptuous influences of every kind,—sounds, colors, shapes, and fragrant odors. I was the very slave of sensation.

I lay mute and breathless, and drank in every note of this siren strain. It thrilled through my whole frame, and filled my soul with melody and love. I pictured to myself, with curious logic, the form of the unseen musician. Such melodious sounds and exquisite inflexions could only be produced by organs of the most delicate flexibility. Such organs do not belong to coarse, vulgar forms; they are the harmonious results of fair proportions and admirable symmetry. A being so organized must be lovely.

Again my busy imagination was at work. I called to mind the Arabian story of a prince, borne away during sleep by a good genius, to the distant abode of a princess of ravishing beauty. I do not pretend to say that I believed in having experienced a similar transportation; but it was my inveterate habit to cheat myself with fancies of the kind, and to give the tinge of illusion to surrounding realities.

The witching sound had ceased, but its vibrations still played round my heart, and filled it with a tumult of soft emotions. At this moment a self-upbraiding pang shot through my bosom. "Ah, recreant!" a voice seemed to exclaim, "is this the stability of thine affections? What! hast thou so soon forgotten the nymph of the fountain? Has one song, idly piped in thine ear, been sufficient to charm away the cherished tenderness of a whole summer?"

The wise may smile; but I am in a confiding mood, and must confess my weakness. I felt a degree of compunction at this sudden infidelity, yet I could not resist the power of present fascination. My peace of mind was destroyed by conflicting claims. The nymph of the fountain came over my memory, with all the associations of fairy footsteps, shady groves, soft echoes, and wild streamlets; but this new passion was produced by a strain of soul-subduing melody, still lingering in my ear, aided by a downy bed, fragrant flowers, and rose-colored curtains. "Unhappy youth!" sighed I to myself, "distracted by such rival passions, and the empire of thy heart thus violently contested by the sound of a voice and the print of a footstep!"

I had not remained long in this mood, when I heard the door of the room gently opened. I turned my head to see what inhabitant of this enchanted palace should appear; whether page in green, hideous dwarf, or haggard fairy. It was my own man Scipio. He advanced with cautious step, and was delighted, as he said, to find me so much myself again. My first questions were as to where I was, and how I came there? Scipio told me a long story of his having been fishing in a canoe, at the time of my hare-brained cruise; of his noticing the gathering squall, and my impending danger; of his hastening to join me, but arriving just in time to snatch me from a watery grave; of the great difficulty in restoring me to animation; and of my being subsequently conveyed, in a state of insensibility, to this mansion.

"But where am I?" was the reiterated demand.

"In the house of Mr. Somerville."

"Somerville—Somerville!" I recollected to have heard that a gentleman of that name had recently taken up his residence at some distance from my father's abode, on the opposite side of the Hudson. He was commonly known by the name of "French Somerville," from having passed part of his early life in France, and from his exhibiting traces of French taste in his mode of living, and the arrangements of his house. In fact, it was in his pleasure-boat, which had got adrift, that I had made my fanciful and disastrous cruise. All this was simple, straightforward matter of fact, and threatened to demolish all the cobweb romance I had been spinning, when fortunately I again heard the tinkling of a harp. I raised myself in bed, and listened.

"Scipio," said I, with some little hesitation, "I heard some one singing just now. Who was it?"

"Oh, that was Miss Julia."

"Julia! Julia! Delightful! what a name! And, Scipio—is she—is she pretty?"

Scipio grinned from ear to ear. "Except Miss Sophy, she was the most beautiful young lady he had ever seen."

I should observe, that my sister Sophia was considered by all the servants a paragon of perfection.

Scipio now offered to remove the basket of flowers; he was afraid their odor might be too powerful; but Miss Julia had given them that morning to be placed in my room.

These flowers, then, had been gathered by the fairy fingers of my unseen beauty: that sweet breath, which had filled my ear with melody, had passed over them. I made Scipio hand them to me, culled several of the most delicate, and laid them on my bosom.

Mr. Somerville paid me a visit not long afterward. He was an interesting study for me, for he was the father of my unseen beauty, and probably resembled her. I scanned him closely. He was a tall and elegant man, with an open, affable manner, and an erect and graceful carriage. His eyes were bluish-gray, and, though not dark, yet at times were sparkling and expressive. His hair was dressed and powdered, and being lightly combed up from his forehead, added to the loftiness of his aspect. He was fluent in discourse, but his conversation had the quiet tone of polished society, without any of those bold flights of thought, and picturings of fancy, which I so much admired.

My imagination was a little puzzled, at first, to make out of this assemblage of personal and mental qualities, a picture that should harmonize with my previous idea of the fair unseen. By dint, however, of selecting what it liked, and rejecting what it did not like, and giving a touch here and a touch there, it soon finished out a satisfactory portrait.

"Julia must be tall," thought I, "and of exquisite grace and dignity. She is not quite so courtly as her father, for she has been brought up in the retirement of the country. Neither is she of such vivacious deportment; for the tones of her voice are soft and plaintive, and she loves pathetic music. She is rather pensive—yet not too pensive; just what is called interesting. Her eyes are like her father's, except that they are of a purer blue, and more tender and languishing. She has light hair—not exactly flaxen, for I do not like flaxen hair, but between that and auburn. In a word, she is a tall, elegant, imposing, languishing, blue-eyed, romantic-looking beauty." And having thus finished her picture, I felt ten times more in love with her than ever.

I felt so much recovered, that I would at once have left my room, but Mr. Somerville objected to it. He had sent early word to my family of my safety; and my father arrived in the course of the morning. He was shocked at learning the risk I had run, but rejoiced to find me so much restored, and was warm in his thanks to Mr. Somerville for his kindness. The other only required, in return, that I might remain two or three days as his guest, to give time for my recovery, and for our forming a closer acquaintance, a request which my father readily granted. Scipio accordingly accompanied my father home, and returned with a supply of clothes, and with affectionate letters from my mother and sisters.

The next morning, aided by Scipio, I made my toilet with rather more care than usual, and descended the stairs with some trepidation, eager to see the original of the portrait which had been so completely pictured in my imagination.

On entering the parlor, I found it deserted. Like the rest of the house, it was furnished in a foreign style. The curtains were of French silk; there were Grecian couches, marble tables, pier-glasses, and chandeliers. What chiefly attracted my eye, were documents of female taste that I saw around me, a piano—with an ample stock of Italian music; a book of poetry lying on the sofa; a vase of fresh flowers on a table, and a portfolio open with a skillful and half finished sketch of them. In the window was a Canary bird, in a gilt cage; and near by, the harp that had been in Julia's arms. Happy harp! But where was the being that reigned in this little empire of delicacies?— that breathed poetry and song, and dwelt among birds and flowers, and rose-colored curtains?

Suddenly I heard the hall-door fly open, the quick pattering of light steps, a wild, capricious strain of music, and the shrill barking of a dog. A light frolic nymph of fifteen came tripping into the room, playing on a flageolet, with a little spaniel romping after her. Her gypsy hat had fallen back upon her shoulders; a profusion of glossy brown hair was blown in rich ringlets about her face, which beamed through them with the brightness of smiles and dimples.

At sight of me she stopped short, in the most beautiful confusion, stammered out a word or two about looking for her father, glided out of the door, and I heard her bounding up the staircase, like a frightened fawn, with the little dog barking after her.

When Miss Somerville returned to the parlor, she was quite a different being. She entered, stealing along by her mother's side, with noiseless step and sweet timidity; her hair was prettily adjusted, and a soft blush mantled on her damask cheek. Mr. Somerville accompanied the ladies, and introduced me regularly to them. There were many kind inquiries, and much sympathy expressed on the subject of my nautical accident, and some remarks upon the wild scenery of the neighborhood, with which the ladies seemed perfectly acquainted.

"You must know," said Mr. Somerville, "that we are great navigators, and delight in exploring every nook and corner of the river. My daughter, too, is a great hunter of the picturesque, and transfers every rock and glen to her portfolio. By the way, my dear, show Mr. Mountjoy that pretty scene you have lately sketched." Julia complied, blushing, and drew from her portfolio a colored sketch. I almost started at the sight. It was my favorite brook. A sudden thought darted across my mind. I glanced down my eye, and beheld the divinest little foot in the world. Oh, blissful conviction! The struggle of my affections was at an end. The voice and the footstep were no longer at variance. Julia Somerville was the nymph of the fountain!

What conversation passed during breakfast I do not recollect, and hardly was conscious of at the time, for my thoughts were in complete confusion. I wished to gaze on Miss Somerville, but did not dare. Once, indeed, I ventured a glance. She was at that moment darting a similar one from under a covert of ringlets. Our eyes seemed shocked by the rencontre, and fell; hers through the natural modesty of her sex, mine through a bashfulness produced by the previous workings of my imagination. That glance, however, went like a sunbeam to my heart.

A convenient mirror favored my diffidence, and gave me the reflection of Miss Somerville's form. It is true it only presented the back of her head, but she had the merit of an ancient statue; contemplate her from any point of view, she was beautiful. And yet she was totally different from everything I had before conceived of beauty. She was not the serene, meditative maid that I had pictured the nymph of the fountain; nor the tall, soft, languishing, blue-eyed, dignified being that I had fancied the minstrel of the harp. There was nothing of dignity about her; she was girlish in her appearance, and scarcely of the middle size; but then there was the tenderness of budding youth; the sweetness of the half-blown rose, when not a tint of perfume has been withered or exhaled; there were smiles and dimples, and all the soft witcheries of ever varying expression. I wondered that I could ever have admired any other style of beauty.

After breakfast, Mr. Somerville departed to attend to the concerns of his estate, and gave me in charge of the ladies. Mrs. Somerville also was called away by her household cares, and I was left alone with Julia! Here then was the situation which of all others I had most coveted. I was in the presence of the lovely being that had so long been the desire of my heart. We were alone; propitious opportunity for a lover! Did I seize upon it? Did I break out in one of my accustomed rhapsodies? No such thing! Never was being more awkwardly embarrassed.

"What can be the cause of this?" thought I. "Surely I cannot stand in awe of this young girl. I am of course her superior in intellect, and am never embarrassed in company with my tutor, notwithstanding all his wisdom."

It was passing strange. I felt that if she were an old woman, I should be quite at my ease; if she were even an ugly woman, I should make out very well; it was her beauty that overpowered me. How little do lovely women know what awful beings they are, in the eyes of inexperienced youth! Young men brought up in the fashionable circles of our cities will smile at all this. Accustomed to mingle incessantly in female society, and to have the romance of the heart deadened by a thousand frivolous flirtations, women are nothing but women in their eyes; but to a susceptible youth like myself, brought up in the country, they are perfect divinities.

Miss Somerville was at first a little embarrassed herself; but, somehow or other, women have a natural adroitness in recovering their self-possession; they are more alert in their minds and graceful in their manners. Besides, I was but an ordinary personage in Miss Somerville's eyes; she was not under the influence of such a singular course of imaginings as had surrounded her, in my eyes, with the illusions of romance. Perhaps, too, she saw the confusion in the opposite camp, and gained courage from the discovery. At any rate she was the first to take the field.

Her conversation, however, was only on commonplace topics, and in an easy, well-bred style. I endeavored to respond in the same manner; but I was strangely incompetent to the task. My ideas were frozen up; even words seemed to fail me. I was excessively vexed at myself, for I wished to be uncommonly elegant. I tried two or three times to turn a pretty thought, or to utter a fine sentiment; but it would come forth so trite, so forced, so mawkish, that I was ashamed of it. My very voice sounded discordantly, though I sought to modulate it into the softest tones. "The truth is," thought I to myself, "I cannot bring my mind down to the small talk necessary for young girls; it is too masculine and robust for the mincing measure of parlor gossip. I am a philosopher; and that accounts for it."

The entrance of Mrs. Somerville at length gave me relief. I at once breathed freely, and felt a vast deal of confidence come over me. "This is strange," thought I, "that the appearance of another woman should revive my courage; that I should be a better match for two women than one. However, since it is so, I will take advantage of the circumstance, and let this young lady see that I am not so great a simpleton as she probably thinks me."

I accordingly took up the book of poetry which lay upon the sofa. It was Milton's *Paradise Lost*. Nothing could have been more fortunate; it afforded a fine scope for my favorite vein of grandiloquence. I went largely into a discussion of its merits, or rather an enthusiastic eulogy of them. My observations were addressed to Mrs. Somerville, for I found I could talk to her with more ease than to her daughter.

She appeared perfectly alive to the beauties of the poet, and disposed to meet me in the discussion; but it was not my object to hear her talk; it was to talk myself. I anticipated all she had to say, overpowered her with the copiousness of my ideas, and supported and illustrated them by long citations from the author.

While thus holding forth, I cast a side-glance to see how Miss Somerville was affected. She had some embroidery stretched on a frame before her, but had paused in her labor, and was looking down, as if lost in mute attention. I felt a glow of self-satisfaction, but I rec-ollected, at the same time, with a kind of pique, the advantage she had enjoyed over me in our *tête-à-tête*. I determined to push my tri-umph, and accordingly kept on with redoubled ardor, until I had fairly exhausted my subject, or rather my thoughts.

I had scarce come to a full stop, when Miss Somerville raised her eyes from the work on which they had been fixed, and turning to her mother, observed: "I have been considering, mamma, whether to work these flowers plain, or in colors."

Had an ice-bolt shot to my heart, it could not have chilled me more effectually. "What a fool," thought I, "have I been making myself,—squandering away fine thoughts and fine language upon a light mind and an ignorant ear! This girl knows nothing of poetry. She has no soul, I fear, for its beauties. Can any one have real sensibil-ity of heart, and not be alive to poetry? However, she is young; this part of her education has been neglected; there is time enough to remedy it. I will be her preceptor. I will kindle in her mind the sacred flame, and lead her through the fairy land of song. But, after all, it is rather unfortunate that I should have fallen in love with a woman who knows nothing of poetry."

I passed a day not altogether satisfactory. I was a little disappointed that Miss Somerville did not show more poetical feeling. "I am afraid, after all," said I to myself, "she is light and girlish, and more fitted to pluck wild flowers, play on the flageolet, and romp with little dogs, than to converse with a man of my turn."

I believe, however, to tell the truth, I was more out of humor with myself. I thought I had made the worst first appearance that ever hero made, either in novel or fairy tale. I was out of all patience when I called to mind my awkward attempts at ease and elegance, in the *tête-à-tête*. And then my intolerable long lecture about poetry, to catch the applause of a heedless auditor! But there I was not to blame. I had certainly been eloquent; it was her fault that the eloquence was wasted. To meditate upon the embroidery of a flower, when I was expatiating on the beauties of Milton! She might at least have admired the poetry, if she did not relish the manner in which it was delivered;

though that was not despicable, for I had recited passages in my best style, which my mother and sisters had always considered equal to a play. "Oh, it is evident," thought I, "Miss Somerville has very little soul!"

Such were my fancies and cogitations during the day, the greater part of which was spent in my chamber; for I was still languid. My evening was passed in the drawing-room, where I overlooked Miss Somerville's portfolio of sketches. They were executed with great taste, and showed a nice observation of the peculiarities of Nature. They were all her own, and free from those cunning tints and touches of the drawing-master, by which young ladies' drawings, like their heads, are dressed up for company. There was no garish and vulgar trick of colors, either; all was executed with singular truth and simplicity.

"And yet," thought I, "this little being, who has so pure an eye to take in, as in a limpid brook, all the graceful forms and magic tints of Nature, has no soul for poetry!"

Mr. Somerville, toward the latter part of the evening, observing my eye to wander occasionally to the harp, interpreted and met my wishes with his accustomed civility.

"Julia, my dear," said he, "Mr. Mountjoy would like to hear a little music from your harp; let us hear, too, the sound of your voice."

Julia immediately complied, without any of that hesitation and difficulty by which young ladies are apt to make the company pay dear for bad music. She sang a sprightly strain, in a brilliant style, that came trilling playfully over the ear; and the bright eye and dimpling smile showed that her little heart danced with the song. Her pet Canary bird, who hung close by, was awakened by the music, and burst forth into an emulating strain. Julia smiled with a pretty air of defiance, and played louder.

After some time the music changed, and ran into a plaintive strain, in a minor key. Then it was that all the former witchery of her voice came over me; then it was that she seemed to sing from the heart and to the heart. Her fingers moved about the chords as if they scarcely touched them. Her whole manner and appearance changed; her eyes beamed with the softest expression; her countenance, her frame,—all seemed subdued into tenderness. She rose from the harp, leaving it still vibrating with sweet sounds, and moved toward her father to bid him good-night.

His eyes had been fixed on her intently during her performance. As she came before him, he parted her shining ringlets with both his hands, and looked down with the fondness of a father on her innocent face. The music seemed still lingering in its lineaments, and the action of her father brought a moist gleam in her eye. He kissed her fair forehead, after the French mode of parental caressing: "Good-night, and God bless you," said he, "my good little girl!"

Julia tripped away with a tear in her eye, a dimple in her cheek, and a light heart in her bosom. I thought it the prettiest picture of paternal and filial affection I had ever seen.

When I retired to bed a new train of thoughts crowded into my brain. "After all," said I to myself, "it is clear this girl has a soul, though she was not moved by my eloquence. She has all the outward signs and evidences of poetic feeling. She paints well, and has an eye for Nature. She is a fine musician, and enters into the very soul of song. What a pity that she knows nothing of poetry! But we will see what is to be done. I am irretrievably in love with her; what then am I to do? Come down to the level of her mind, or endeavor to raise her to some kind of intellectual equality with myself? That is the most generous course. She will look up to me as a benefactor. I shall become associated in her mind with the lofty thoughts and harmonious graces of poetry. She is apparently docile; besides the difference of our ages will give me an ascendency over her. She cannot be above six-teen years of age, and I am full turned to twenty." So, having built this most delectable of air-castles, I fell asleep.

The next morning I was quite a different being. I no longer felt fearful of stealing a glance at Julia; on the contrary, I contemplated her steadily, with the benignant eye of a benefactor. Shortly after breakfast I found myself alone with her, as I had on the preceding morning; but I felt nothing of the awkwardness of our previous *tête-à-tête*. I was elevated by the consciousness of my intellectual superiority, and should almost have felt a sentiment of pity for the ignorance of the lovely little being, if I had not felt also the assurance that I should be able to dispel it. "But it is time," thought I, "to open school."

Julia was occupied in arranging some music on her piano. I looked over two or three songs; they were *Moore's Irish Melodies*.

"These are pretty things," said I, flirting the leaves over lightly, and giving a slight shrug, by way of qualifying the opinion.

"Oh, I love them of all things!" said Julia, "they're so touching!"

"Then you like them for the poetry?" said I, with an encouraging smile.

"Oh, yes; she thought them charmingly written."

Now was my time. "Poetry," said I, assuming a didactic attitude and air,—"poetry is one of the most pleasing studies to occupy a youthful mind. It renders us susceptible of the gentle impulses of humanity, and cherishes a delicate perception of all that is virtuous and elevated in morals, and graceful and beautiful in physics. It—"

I was going on in a style that would have graced a professor of rhetoric, when I saw a light smile playing about Miss Somerville's mouth, and that she began to turn over the leaves of a music-book. I recollected her inattention to my discourse of the preceding morning. "There is no fixing her light mind," thought I, "by abstract theory; we will proceed practically." As it happened, the identical volume of Milton's *Paradise Lost* was lying at hand.

"Let me recommend to you, my young friend," said I, in one of those tones of persuasive admonition, which I had so often loved in Glencoe,—"let me recommend to you this admirable poem: you will find in it sources of intellectual enjoyment far superior to those songs which have delighted you." Julia looked at the book, and then at me, with a whimsically dubious air. "Milton's *Paradise Lost?*" said she; "oh, I know the greater part of that by heart."

I had not expected to find my pupil so far advanced; however, the *Paradise Lost* is a kind of school-book, and its finest passages are given to young ladies as tasks.

"I find," said I to myself, "I must not treat her as so complete a novice; her inattention, yesterday, could not have proceeded from absolute ignorance, but merely from a want of poetic feeling. I'll try her again."

I now determined to dazzle her with my own erudition, and launched into a harangue that would have done honor to an institute. Pope, Spenser, Chaucer, and the old dramatic writers were all dipped into, with the excursive flight of a swallow. I did not confine myself to English poets, but gave a glance at the French and Italian schools: I passed over Ariosto in full wing, but paused on Tasso's *Jerusalem Delivered*. I dwelt on the character of Clorinda: "There's a character," said I, "that you will find well worthy a woman's study. It shows to what exalted heights of heroism the sex can rise; how gloriously they may share even in the stern concerns of men."

"For my part," said Julia, gently taking advantage of a pause,—"for my part, I prefer the character of Sophronia."

I was thunderstruck. She then had read Tasso! This girl that I had been treating as an ignoramus in poetry! She proceeded, with a slight glow of the cheek, summoned up perhaps by a casual glow of feeling:—

"I do not admire those masculine heroines," said she, "who aim at the bold qualities of the opposite sex. Now Sophronia only exhibits the real qualities of a woman, wrought up to their highest excitement. She is modest, gentle, and retiring, as it becomes a woman to be; but she has all the strength of affection proper to a woman. She cannot fight for her people, as Clorinda does, but she can offer herself up, and die, to serve them. You may admire Clorinda, but you surely would be more apt to love Sophronia; at least," added she, suddenly appearing to recollect herself, and blushing at having launched into such a discussion,—"at least that is what papa observed when we read the poem together."

"Indeed," said I, dryly, for I felt disconcerted and nettled at being unexpectedly lectured by my pupil,—"indeed, I do not exactly recollect the passage."

"Oh," said Julia, "I can repeat it to you;" and she immediately gave it in Italian.

Heavens and earth!—here was a situation! I knew no more of Italian than I did of the language of Psalmanazar. What a dilemma for a would-be-wise man to be placed in! I saw Julia waited for my opinion.

"In fact," said I, hesitating, "I—I do not exactly understand Italian."

"Oh," said Julia, with the utmost *naïveté*, "I have no doubt it is very beautiful in the translation."

I was glad to break up school and get back to my chamber, full of the mortification which a wise man in love experiences on finding his mistress wiser than himself. "Translation! translation!" muttered I to myself, as I jerked the door shut behind me. "I am surprised my father has never had me instructed in the modern languages. They are all important. What is the use of Latin and Greek? No one speaks them; but here, the moment I make my appearance in the world, a little girl slaps Italian in my face. However, thank Heaven, a language is easily learned. The moment I return home, I'll set about studying Italian; and to prevent future surprise, I will study Spanish and German at the same time; and if any young lady attempts to quote Italian upon me again, I'll bury her under a heap of High Dutch poetry!"

I felt now like some mighty chieftain, who has carried the war into a weak country, with full confidence of success, and been repulsed and obliged to draw off his forces from before some inconsiderable fortress.

"However," thought I, "I have as yet brought only my light artillery into action; we shall see what is to be done with my heavy ordnance. Julia is evidently well versed in poetry; but it is natural she should be so; it is allied to painting and music, and is congenial to the light graces of the female character. We will try her on graver themes."

I felt all my pride awakened; it even for a time swelled higher than my love. I was determined completely to establish my mental superiority, and subdue the intellect of this little being: it would then be time to sway the sceptre of gentle empire, and win the affections of her heart.

Accordingly, at dinner I again took the field *en potence*. I now addressed myself to Mr. Somerville, for I was about to enter upon topics in which a young girl like her could not be well versed. I led, or rather forced, the conversation into a vein of historical erudition, discussing several of the most prominent facts of ancient history and accompanying them with sound, indisputable apothegms.

Mr. Somerville listened to me with the air of a man receiving information. I was encouraged, and went on gloriously from theme to theme of school declamation. I sat with Marius on the ruins of Carthage; I defended the bridge with Horatius Cocles; thrust my hand into the flame with Martius Scævola, and plunged with Curtius into the yawning gulf; I fought side by side with Leonidas, at the straits of Thermopylæ; and was going full drive into the battle of Plataea, when my memory, which is the worst in the world, failed me, just as I wanted the name of the Lacedæmonian commander.

"Julia, my dear," said Mr. Somerville, "perhaps you may recollect the name of which Mr. Mountjoy is in quest?"

Julia colored slightly: "I believe," said she, in a low voice,—"I believe it was Pausanias."

This unexpected sally, instead of reinforcing me, threw my whole scheme of battle into confusion, and the Athenians remained unmolested in the field.

I am half inclined, since, to think Mr. Somerville meant this as a sly hit at my schoolboy pedantry; but he was too well-bred not to seek to relieve me from my mortification. "Oh!" said he, "Julia is our family book of reference for names, dates, and distances, and has an excellent memory for history and geography."

I now became desperate; as a last resource, I turned to metaphysics. "If she is a philosopher in petticoats," thought I, "it is all over with me."

Here, however, I had the field to myself. I gave chapter and verse of my tutor's lectures, heightened by all his poetical illustrations; I even went farther than he had ever ventured, and plunged into such depths of metaphysics, that I was in danger of sticking in the mire at the bottom. Fortunately, I had auditors who apparently could not detect my flounderings. Neither Mr. Somerville nor his daughter offered the least interruption.

When the ladies had retired, Mr. Somerville sat some time with me; and as I was no longer anxious to astonish, I permitted myself to listen, and found that he was really agreeable. He was quite communicative, and from his conversation I was enabled to form a juster idea of his daughter's character, and the mode in which she had been brought up. Mr. Somerville had mingled much with the world, and with what is termed fashionable society. He had experienced its cold elegancies, and gay insincerities; its dissipation of the spirits, and squanderings of the heart. Like many men of the world, though he had wandered too far from Nature ever to return to it, yet he had the good taste and good feeling to look back fondly to its simple delights, and to determine that his child, if possible, should never leave them. He had superintended her education with scrupulous care, storing her mind with the graces of polite literature, and with such knowledge as would enable it to furnish its own amusement and occupation, and giving her all the accomplishments that sweeten and enliven the circle of domestic life. He had been particularly sedulous to exclude fashionable affectations; all false sentiment, false sensibility, and false romance. "Whatever advantages she may possess," said he, "she is quite unconscious of them. She is a capricious little being, in everything but her affections; she is, however, free from art; simple, ingenuous, amiable, and, I thank God! happy."

Such was the eulogy of a fond father, delivered with a tenderness that touched me. I could not help making a casual inquiry whether, among the graces of polite literature, he had included a slight tincture of metaphysics. He smiled, and told me he had not.

On the whole, when, as usual, that night I summed up the day's observations on my pillow, I was not altogether dissatisfied. "Miss Somerville," said I, "loves poetry, and I like her the better for it. She has the advantage of me in Italian: agreed; what is it to know a variety of languages, but merely to have a variety of sounds to express the same idea? Original thought is the ore of the mind; language is but the accidental stamp and coinage, by which it is put into circulation. If I can furnish an original idea, what care I how many languages she can translate it into? She may be able, also, to quote names, and dates, and latitudes, better than I; but that is a mere effort of the memory. I admit she is more accurate in history and geography than I; but then she knows nothing of metaphysics."

I had now sufficiently recovered to return home; yet I could not think of leaving Mr. Somerville's without having a little farther conversation with him on the subject of his daughter's education.

"This Mr. Somerville," thought I, "is a very accomplished, elegant man; he has seen a good deal of the world, and, upon the whole, has profited by what he has seen. He is not without information, and, as far as he thinks, appears to think correctly; but after all, he is rather superficial, and does not think profoundly. He seems to take no delight in those metaphysical abstractions that are the proper aliment of masculine minds." I called to mind various occasions in which I had indulged largely in metaphysical discussions, but could recollect no instance where I had been able to draw him out. He had listened, it is true, with attention, and smiled as if in acquiescence, but had always appeared to avoid reply. Besides, I had made several sad blunders in the glow of eloquent declamation; but he had never interrupted me, to notice and correct them, as he would have done had he been versed in the theme.

"Now, it is really a great pity," resumed I, "that he should have the entire management of Miss Somerville's education. What a vast advantage it would be if she could be put for a little time under the superintendence of Glencoe. He would throw some deeper shades of thought into her mind, which at present is all sunshine; not but that Mr. Somerville has done very well, as far as he has gone; but then he has merely prepared the soil for the strong plants of useful knowledge. She is well versed in the leading facts of history, and the general course of belles-lettres," said I; "a little more philosophy would do wonders."

I accordingly took occasion to ask Mr. Somerville for a few moments' conversation in his study, the morning I was to depart. When we were alone, I opened the matter fully to him. I commenced with the warmest eulogium of Glencoe's powers of mind, and vast acquirements, and ascribed to him all my proficiency in the higher branches of knowledge. I begged, therefore, to recommend him as a friend calculated to direct the studies of Miss Somerville; to lead her mind, by degrees, to the contemplation of abstract principles, and to produce habits of philosophical analysis; "which," added I, gently smiling, "are not often cultivated by young ladies." I ventured to hint, in addition, that he would find Mr. Glencoe a most valuable and interesting acquaintance for himself; one who would stimulate and evolve the powers of his mind; and who might open to him tracts of inquiry and speculation to which perhaps he had hitherto been a stranger.

Mr. Somerville listened with grave attention. When I had finished, he thanked me in the politest manner for the interest I took in the welfare of his daughter and himself. He observed that, as regarded himself, he was afraid he was too old to benefit by the instructions of Mr. Glencoe, and that as to his daughter, he was afraid her mind was but little fitted for the study of metaphysics. "I do not wish," continued he, "to strain her intellects with subjects they cannot grasp, but to make her familiarly acquainted with those that are within the limits of her capacity. I do not pretend to prescribe the boundaries of female genius, and am far from indulging the vulgar opinion that women are unfitted by Nature for the highest intellectual pursuits. I speak only with reference to my daughter's taste and talents. She will never make a learned woman; nor in truth do I desire it; for such is the jealousy of our sex, as to mental as well as physical ascendency, that a learned woman is not always the happiest. I do not wish my daughter to excite envy, or to battle with the prejudices of the world; but to glide peaceably through life, on the good-will and kind opinion of her friends. She has ample employment for her little head in the course I have marked out for her; and is busy at present with some branches of natural history, calculated to awaken her perceptions to the beauties and wonders of Nature, and to the inexhaustible volume of wisdom constantly spread open before her eyes. I consider that woman most likely to make an agreeable companion, who can draw topics of pleasing remark from every natural object; and most likely to be cheerful and contented, who is continually sensible of the order, the harmony, and the invariable beneficence that reign throughout the beautiful world we inhabit.

"But," added he, smiling, "I am betraying myself into a lecture, instead of merely giving a reply to your kind offer. Permit me to take the liberty, in return, of inquiring a little about your own pursuits. You speak of having finished your education; but of course you have a line of private study and mental occupation marked out; for you must know the importance, both in point of interest and happiness, of keeping the mind employed. May I ask what system you observe in your intellectual exercises?"

"Oh, as to system," I observed, "I could never bring myself into anything of the kind. I thought it best to let my genius take it own course, as it always acted the most vigorously when stimulated by inclination."

Mr. Somerville shook his head. "This same genius," said he, "is a wild quality, that runs away with our most promising young men. It has become so much the fashion, too, to give it the reins, that it is now thought an animal of too noble and generous a nature to be brought to the harness. But it is all a mistake. Nature never designed these high endowments to run riot through society, and throw the whole system into confusion. No, my dear sir; genius, unless it acts upon system, is very apt to be a useless quality to society; sometimes an injurious, and certainly a very uncomfortable one, to its possessor. I have had many opportunities of seeing the progress through life of young men who were accounted geniuses, and have found it too often end in early exhaustion and bitter disappointment; and have as often noticed that these effects might be traced to a total want of

system. There were no habits of business, of steady purpose, and
regular application superinduced upon the mind; everything was left
to chance and impulse, and native luxuriance, and everything of
course ran to waste and wild entanglement. Excuse me if I am tedious
on this point, for I feel solicitous to impress it upon you, being an
error extremely prevalent in our country, and one into which too
many of our youth have fallen. I am happy, however, to observe the
zeal which still appears to actuate you for the acquisition of knowledge, and augur every good from the elevated bent of your ambition.
May I ask what has been your course of study for the last six
months?"

Never was question more unluckily timed. For the last six months
I had been absolutely buried in novels and romances.

Mr. Somerville perceived that the question was embarrassing, and
with his invariable good breeding, immediately resumed the conversation, without waiting for a reply. He took care, however, to turn it
in such a way as to draw from me an account of the whole manner
in which I had been educated, and the various currents of reading
into which my mind had run. He then went on to discuss briefly, but
impressively, the different branches of knowledge most important to
a young man in my situation; and to my surprise I found him a complete master of those studies on which I had supposed him ignorant,
and on which I had been descanting so confidently.

He complimented me, however, very graciously, upon the progress I had made, but advised me for the present to turn my attention
to the physical rather than the moral sciences. "These studies," said
he, "store a man's mind with valuable facts, and at the same time
repress self-confidence, by letting him know how boundless are the
realms of knowledge, and how little we can possibly know. Whereas
metaphysical studies, though of an ingenious order of intellectual
employment, are apt to bewilder some minds with vague speculations. They never know how far they have advanced, or what may
be the correctness of their favorite theory. They render many of our
young men verbose and declamatory, and prone to mistake the aber-
rations of their fancy for the inspirations of divine philosophy."

I could not but interrupt him, to assent to the truth of these remarks, and to say that it had been my lot, in the course of my limited
experience, to encounter young men of the kind, who had overwhelmed me by their verbosity.

Mr. Somerville smiled. "I trust," said he kindly, "that you will
guard against these errors. Avoid the eagerness with which a young
man is apt to hurry into conversation, and to utter the crude and ill-
digested notions which he has picked up in his recent studies. Be

assured that extensive and accurate knowledge is the slow acquisition of a studious lifetime; that a young man, however pregnant his wit and prompt his talent, can have mastered but the rudiments of learning, and, in a manner attained the implements of study. Whatever may have been your past assiduity, you must be sensible that as yet you have but reached the threshold of true knowledge; but at the same time, you have the advantage that you are still very young, and have ample time to learn."

Here our conference ended. I walked out of the study, a very different being from what I was on entering it. I had gone in with the air of a professor about to deliver a lecture; I came out like a student, who had failed in his examination, and been degraded in his class.

"Very young," and "on the threshold of knowledge!" This was extremely flattering to one who had considererd himself an accomplished scholar and a profound philosopher!

"It is singular," thought I; "there seems to have been a spell upon my faculties ever since I have been in this house. I certainly have not been able to do myself justice. Whenever I have undertaken to advise, I have had the tables turned upon me. It must be that I am strange and diffident among people I am not accustomed to. I wish they could hear me talk at home!"

"After all," added I, on farther reflection,—"after all, there is a great deal of force in what Mr. Somerville has said. Somehow or other, these men of the world do now and then hit upon remarks that would do credit to a philosopher. Some of his general observations came so home, that I almost thought they were meant for myself. His advice about adopting a system of study, is very judicious. I will immediately put it in practice. My mind shall operate henceforward with the regularity of clock-work."

How far I succeeded in adopting this plan, how I fared in the farther pursuit of knowledge, and how I succeeded in my suit to Julia Somerville, may afford matter for a farther communication to the public, if this simple record of my early life is fortunate enough to excite any curiosity.

ADVENTURE OF THE GERMAN STUDENT

ON A STORMY NIGHT, in the tempestuous times of the French revolution, a young German was returning to his lodgings, at a late hour, across the old part of Paris. The lightning gleamed, and the loud claps of thunder rattled through the lofty narrow streets—but I should first tell you something about this young German.

Gottfried Wolfgang was a young man of good family. He had studied for some time at Göttingen, but being of a visionary and enthusiastic character, he had wandered into those wild and speculative doctrines which have so often bewildered German students. His secluded life, his intense application, and the singular nature of his studies, had an effect on both mind and body. His health was impaired; his imagination diseased. He had been indulging in fanciful speculations on spiritual essences, until, like Swedenborg, he had an ideal world of his own around him. He took up a notion, I do not know from what cause, that there was an evil influence hanging over him; an evil genius or spirit seeking to ensnare him and ensure his perdition. Such an idea working on his melancholy temperament, produced the most gloomy effects. He became haggard and desponding. His friends discovered the mental malady preying upon him, and determined that the best cure was a change of scene; he was sent, therefore, to finish his studies amidst the splendors and gayeties of Paris.

Wolfgang arrived at Paris at the breaking out of the revolution. The popular delirium at first caught his enthusiastic mind, and he was captivated by the political and philosophical theories of the day: but the scenes of blood which followed shocked his sensitive nature, disgusted him with society and the world, and made him more than ever a recluse. He shut himself up in a solitary apartment in the *Pays Latin,* the quarter of students. There, in a gloomy street not far from the monastic walls of the Sorbonne, he pursued his favorite speculations. Sometimes he spent hours together in the great libraries of Paris, those catacombs of departed authors, rummaging among their hoards

113

of dusty and obsolete works in quest of food for his unhealthy appetite. He was, in a manner, a literary ghoul, feeding in the charnel-house of decayed literature.

Wolfgang, though solitary and recluse, was of an ardent temperament, but for a time it operated merely upon his imagination. He was too shy and ignorant of the world to make any advances to the fair, but he was a passionate admirer of female beauty, and in his lonely chamber would often lose himself in reveries on forms and faces which he had seen, and his fancy would deck out images of loveliness far surpassing the reality.

While his mind was in this excited and sublimated state, a dream produced an extraordinary effect upon him. It was of a female face of transcendent beauty. So strong was the impression made, that he dreamt of it again and again. It haunted his thoughts by day, his slumbers by night; in fine, he became passionately enamoured of this shadow of a dream. This lasted so long that it became one of those fixed ideas which haunt the minds of melancholy men, and are at times mistaken for madness.

Such was Gottfried Wolfgang, and such his situation at the time I mentioned. He was returning home late one stormy night, through some of the old and gloomy streets of the *Marais,* the ancient part of Paris. The loud claps of thunder rattled among the high houses of the narrow streets. He came to the Place de Grève, the square where public executions are performed. The lightning quivered about the pinnacles of the ancient Hôtel de Ville, and shed flickering gleams over the open space in front. As Wolfgang was crossing the square, he shrank back with horror at finding himself close by the guillotine. It was the height of the reign of terror, when this dreadful instrument of death stood ever ready, and its scaffold was continually running with the blood of the virtuous and the brave. It had that very day been actively employed in the work of carnage, and there it stood in grim array, amidst a silent and sleeping city, waiting for fresh victims.

Wolfgang's heart sickened within him, and he was turning shuddering from the horrible engine, when he beheld a shadowy form, cowering as it were at the foot of the steps which led up to the scaffold. A succession of vivid flashes of lightning revealed it more distinctly. It was a female figure, dressed in black. She was seated on one of the lower steps of the scaffold, leaning forward, her face hid in her lap; and her long dishevelled tresses hanging to the ground, streaming with the rain which fell in torrents. Wolfgang paused. There was something awful in this solitary monument of woe. The female had the appearance of being above the common order. He knew the times to be full of vicissitude, and that many a fair head, which had once been pillowed on down, now wandered houseless. Perhaps this was some poor mourner whom the dreadful axe had rendered desolate, and who sat here heart-broken on the strand of existence, from which all that was dear to her had been launched into eternity.

He approached, and addressed her in the accents of sympathy. She raised her head and gazed wildly at him. What was his astonishment at beholding, by the bright glare of the lightning, the very face which had haunted him in his dreams. It was pale and disconsolate, but ravishingly beautiful.

Trembling with violent and conflicting emotions, Wolfgang again accosted her. He spoke something of her being exposed at such an hour of the night, and to the fury of such a storm, and offered to conduct her to her friends. She pointed to the guillotine with a gesture of dreadful signification.

"I have no friend on earth!" said she.

"But you have a home," said Wolfgang.

"Yes—in the grave!"

The heart of the student melted at the words.

"If a stranger dare make an offer," said he, "without danger of being misunderstood, I would offer my humble dwelling as a shelter; myself as a devoted friend. I am friendless myself in Paris, and a stranger in the land; but if my life could be of service, it is at your disposal, and should be sacrificed before harm or indignity should come to you."

There was an honest earnestness in the young man's manner that had its effect. His foreign accent, too, was in his favor; it showed him not to be a hackneyed inhabitant of Paris. Indeed, there is an eloquence in true enthusiasm that is not to be doubted. The homeless stranger confided herself implicitly to the protection of the student.

He supported her faltering steps across the Pont Neuf, and by the place where the statue of Henry the Fourth had been overthrown by the populace. The storm had abated, and the thunder rumbled at a distance. All Paris was quiet; that great volcano of human passion slumbered for a while, to gather fresh strength for the next day's eruption. The student conducted his charge through the ancient streets of the *Pays Latin,* and by the dusky walls of the Sorbonne, to the great dingy hotel which he inhabited. The old portress who admitted them stared with surprise at the unusual sight of the melancholy Wolfgang with a female companion.

On entering his apartment, the student, for the first time, blushed at the scantiness and indifference of his dwelling. He had but one chamber—an old-fashioned saloon—heavily carved, and fantastically furnished with the remains of former magnificence, for it was one of those hotels in the quarter of the Luxembourg palace, which had once belonged to nobility. It was lumbered with books and papers, and all the usual apparatus of a student, and his bed stood in a recess at one end.

When lights were brought, and Wolfgang had a better opportunity of contemplating the stranger, he was more than ever intoxicated by her beauty. Her face was pale, but of a dazzling fairness, set off by a profusion of raven hair that hung clustering about it. Her eyes were large and brilliant, with a singular expression approaching almost to wildness. As far as her black dress permitted her shape to be seen, it was of perfect symmetry. Her whole appearance was highly striking, though she was dressed in the simplest style. The only thing approaching to an ornament which she wore, was a broad black band round her neck, clasped by diamonds.

The perplexity now commenced with the student how to dispose of the helpless being thus thrown upon his protection. He thought of abandoning his chamber to her, and seeking shelter for himself elsewhere. Still, he was so fascinated by her charms, there seemed to be such a spell upon his thoughts and senses, that he could not tear himself from her presence. Her manner, too, was singular and unaccountable. She spoke no more of the guillotine. Her grief had abated. The attentions of the student had first won her confidence, and then, apparently, her heart. She was evidently an enthusiast like himself, and enthusiasts soon understand each other.

In the infatuation of the moment, Wolfgang avowed his passion for her. He told her the story of his mysterious dream, and how she had possessed his heart before he had even seen her. She was strangely affected by his recital, and acknowledged to have felt an impulse towards him equally unaccountable. It was the time for wild theory and wild actions. Old prejudices and superstitions were done away; everything was under the sway of the "Goddess of Reason." Among other rubbish of the old times, the forms and ceremonies of marriage began to be considered superfluous bonds for honorable minds. Social compacts were the vogue. Wolfgang was too much of a theorist not to be tainted by the liberal doctrines of the day.

"Why should we separate?" said he: "our hearts are united; in the eye of reason and honor we are as one. What need is there of sordid forms to bind high souls together?"

The stranger listened with emotion: she had evidently received illumination at the same school.

"You have no home or family," continued he: "let me be everything to you, or rather let us be everything to one another. If form is

necessary, form shall be observed—there is my hand. I pledge myself
to you forever."

"Forever?" said the stranger, solemnly.

"Forever!" repeated Wolfgang.

The stranger clasped the hand extended to her: "Then I am yours,"
murmured she, and sank upon his bosom.

The next morning the student left his bride sleeping, and sallied
forth at an early hour to seek more spacious apartments suitable to the
change in his situation. When he returned, he found the stranger
lying with her head hanging over the bed, and one arm thrown over
it. He spoke to her, but received no reply. He advanced to awaken
her from her uneasy posture. On taking her hand, it was cold—there
was no pulsation—her face was pallid and ghastly. In a word, she was
a corpse.

Horrified and frantic, he alarmed the house. A scene of confusion
ensued. The police were summoned. As the officer of police entered
the room, he started back on beholding the corpse.

"Great heaven!" cried he, "how did this woman come here?"

"Do you know anything about her?" said Wolfgang eagerly.

"Do I?" exclaimed the officer: "she was guillotined yesterday."

He stepped forward; undid the black collar round the neck of the
corpse, and the head rolled on the floor!

The student burst into a frenzy. "The fiend! the fiend has gained
possession of me!" shrieked he: "I am lost forever."

They tried to soothe him, but in vain. He was possessed with the
frightful belief that an evil spirit had reanimated the dead body to
ensnare him. He went distracted, and died in a mad-house.

Here the old gentleman with the haunted head finished his
narrative.

"And is this really a fact?" said the inquisitive gentleman.

"A fact not to be doubted," replied the other. "I had it from the
best authority. The student told it to me himself. I saw him in a mad-
house in Paris."

ADVENTURE OF THE
MYSTERIOUS STRANGER

MANY YEARS SINCE, when I was a young man, and had just left Oxford, I was sent on the grand tour to finish my education. I believe my parents had tried in vain to inoculate me with wisdom; so they sent me to mingle with society, in hopes that I might take it the natural way. Such, at least, appears the reason for which nine-tenths of our youngsters are sent abroad. In the course of my tour I remained some time at Venice. The romantic character of the place delighted me; I was very much amused by the air of adventure and intrigue that prevalent in this region of masks and gondolas; and I was exceedingly smitten by a pair of languishing black eyes, that played upon my heart from under an Italian mantle; so I persuaded myself that I was lingering at Venice to study men and manners; at least I persuaded my friends so, and that answered all my purposes.

I was a little prone to be struck by peculiarities in character and conduct, and my imagination was so full of romantic associations with Italy that I was always on the look-out for adventure. Everything chimed in with such a humor in this old mermaid of a city. My suite of apartments were in a proud, melancholy palace on the grand canal, formerly the residence of a Magnifico, and sumptuous with the traces of decayed grandeur. My gondolier was one of the shrewdest of his class, active, merry, intelligent, and, like his brethren, secret as the grave; that is to say, secret to all the world except his master. I had not had him a week before he put me behind all the curtains in Venice. I liked the silence and mystery of the place, and when I sometimes saw from my window a black gondola gliding mysteriously along in the dusk of the evening, with nothing visible but its little glimmering lantern, I would jump into my own zendeletta, and give a signal for pursuit.—"But I am running away from my subject with the recollection of youthful follies," said the Baronet, checking himself. "Let us come to the point."

Among my familiar resorts was a casino under the arcades on one

side of the grand square of St. Mark. Here I used frequently to lounge
and take my ice, on those warm summer-nights, when in Italy everybody lives abroad until morning. I was seated here one evening, when
a group of Italians took their seat at a table on the opposite side of the
saloon. Their conversation was gay and animated, and carried on with
Italian vivacity and gesticulation. I remarked among them one young
man, however, who appeared to take no share, and find no enjoyment in the conversation, though he seemed to force himself to attend to it. He was tall and slender, and of extremely prepossessing
appearance. His features were fine, though emaciated. He had a profusion of black glossy hair, that curled lightly about his head, and
contrasted with the extreme paleness of his countenance. His brow
was haggard; deep furrows seemed to have been ploughed into his
visage by care, not by age, for he was evidently in the prime of youth.
His eye was full of expression and fire, but wild and unsteady. He
seemed to be tormented by some strange fancy or apprehension. In
spite of every effort to fix his attention on the conversation of his
companions, I noticed that every now and then he would turn his
head slowly round, give a glance over his shoulder, and then with-
draw it with a sudden jerk, as if something painful met his eye. This
was repeated at intervals of about a minute, and he appeared hardly to
have recovered from one shock, before I saw him slowly preparing to
encounter another.

After sitting some time in the casino, the party paid for the refreshment they had taken, and departed. The young man was the last to
leave the saloon, and I remarked him glancing behind him in the
same way, just as he passed out at the door. I could not resist the
impulse to rise and follow him; for I was at an age when a romantic
feeling of curiosity is easily awakened. The party walked slowly down
the arcades, talking and laughing as they went. They crossed the
Piazetta, but paused in the middle of it to enjoy the scene. It was one
of those moonlight nights, so brilliant and clear in the pure atmosphere of Italy. The moonbeams streamed on the tall tower of St.
Mark, and lighted up the magnificent front and swelling domes of the
cathedral. The party expressed their delight in animated terms. I kept
my eye upon the young man. He alone seemed abstracted and self-
occupied. I noticed the same singular and, as it were, furtive glance
over the shoulder, which had attracted my attention in the casino.
The party moved on, and I followed; they passed along the walk
called the Broglio; turned the corner of the Ducal palace, and getting
into a gondola, glided swiftly away.

The countenance and conduct of this young man dwelt upon my
mind, and interested me exceedingly. I met him a day or two after-

wards in a gallery of paintings. He was evidently a connoisseur, for he always singled out the most masterly productions, and a few remarks drawn from him by his companions showed an intimate acquaintance with the art. His own taste, however, ran on singular extremes. On Salvator Rosa, in his most savage and solitary scenes; on Raphael, Titian, and Correggio, in their softest delineations of female beauty; on these he would occasionally gaze with transient enthusiasm. But this seemed only a momentary forgetfulness. Still would recur that cautious glance behind, and always quickly withdrawn, as though something terrible had met his view.

I encountered him frequently afterwards at the theatre, at balls, at concerts; at promenades in the gardens of San Georgio; at the grotesque exhibitions in the square of St. Mark; among the throng of merchants on the exchange by the Rialto. He seemed, in fact, to seek crowds; to hunt after bustle and amusement; yet never to take any interest in either the business or the gayety of the scene. Ever an air of painful thought, of wretched abstraction; and ever that strange and recurring movement of glancing fearfully over the shoulder. I did not know at first but this might be caused by apprehension of arrest; or, perhaps, from dread of assassination. But if so, why should he go thus continually abroad? why expose himself at all times and in all places?

I became anxious to know this stranger. I was drawn to him by that romantic sympathy that sometimes draws young men towards each other. His melancholy threw a charm about him, no doubt heightened by the touching expression of his countenance, and the manly graces of his person; for manly beauty has its effect even upon men. I had an Englishman's habitual diffidence and awkwardness to contend with; but from frequently meeting him in the casinos, I gradually edged myself into his acquaintance. I had no reserve on his part to contend with. He seemed, on the contrary, to court society; and in fact, to seek any thing rather than be alone.

When he found that I really took an interest in him, he threw himself entirely upon my friendship. He clung to me like a drowning man. He would walk with me for hours up and down the place of St. Mark—or he would sit, until night was far advanced, in my apartments. He took rooms under the same roof with me; and his constant request was that I would permit him, when it did not incommode me, to sit by me in my saloon. It was not that he seemed to take a particular delight in my conversation, but rather that he craved the vicinity of a human being; and, above all, of a being that sympathized with him. "I have often heard," said he, "of the sincerity of Englishmen—thank God I have one at length for a friend!"

Yet he never seemed disposed to avail himself of my sympathy other than by mere companionship. He never sought to unbosom himself to me: there appeared to be a settled corroding anguish in his bosom that neither could be soothed "by silence nor by speaking."

A devouring melancholy preyed upon his heart, and seemed to be drying up the very blood in his veins. It was not a soft melancholy, the disease of the affections, but a parching, withering agony. I could see at times that his mouth was dry and feverish; he panted rather than breathed; his eyes were bloodshot; his cheeks pale and livid; with now and then faint streaks of red athwart them, baleful gleams of the fire that was consuming his heart. As my arm was within his, I felt him press it at times with a convulsive motion to his side; his hands would clinch themselves involuntarily, and a kind of shudder would run through his frame.

I reasoned with him about his melancholy, and sought to draw from him the cause; he shrunk from all confiding: "Do not seek to know it," said he, "you could not relieve it if you knew it; you would not even seek to relieve it. On the contrary, I should lose your sympathy, and that," said he, pressing my hand convulsively, "that I feel has become too dear to me to risk."

I endeavored to awaken hope within him. He was young; life had a thousand pleasures in store for him; there is a healthy reaction in the youthful heart; it medicines all its own wounds; "Come, come" said I, "there is no grief so great that youth cannot outgrow it."—"No! no!" said he, clinching his teeth, and striking repeatedly, with the energy of despair, upon his bosom,—"it is here! here! deep-rooted; draining my heart's blood. It grows and grows, while my heart withers and withers. I have a dreadful monitor that gives me no repose—that follows me step by step—and will follow me step by step, until it pushes me into my grave!"

As he said this he gave involuntarily one of those fearful glances over his shoulder, and shrunk back with more than usual horror. I could not resist the temptation, to allude to this movement, which I supposed to be some mere malady of the nerves. The moment I mentioned it, his face became crimsoned and convulsed; he grasped me by both hands—

"For God's sake," exclaimed he, with a piercing agony of voice, "never allude to that again.—Let us avoid this subject, my friend; you cannot relieve me, indeed you cannot relieve me; but you may add to the torments I suffer.—At some future day you shall know all."

I never resumed the subject; for however much my curiosity might be roused, I felt too true a compassion for his sufferings to increase them by my intrusion. I sought various ways to divert his mind, and to arouse him from the constant meditations in which he was plunged. He saw my efforts, and seconded them as far as in his power, for there was nothing moody or wayward in his nature. On the contrary, there was something frank, generous, unassuming, in his whole deportment. All the sentiments that he uttered were noble and lofty. He claimed no indulgence, asked no toleration, but he seemed content to carry his load of misery in silence, and only sought to carry it by my side. There was a mute beseeching manner about him, as if he craved companionship as a charitable boon; and a tacit thankfulness in his looks, as if he felt grateful to me for not repulsing him.

I felt this melancholy to be infectious. It stole over my spirits; interfered with all my gay pursuits, and gradually saddened my life; yet I could not prevail upon myself to shake off a being who seemed to hang upon me for support. In truth, the generous traits of character which beamed through all this gloom had penetrated to my heart. His bounty was lavish and open-handed; his charity melting and spontaneous; not confined to mere donations, which humiliate as much as they relieve. The tone of his voice, the beam of his eye, enhanced every gift, and surprised the poor suppliant with that rarest and sweetest of charities, the charity not merely of the hand, but of the heart. Indeed, his liberality seemed to have something in it of self-abasement and expiation. He, in a manner, humbled himself before the mendicant. "What right have I to ease and affluence"—would he murmur to himself—"when innocence wanders in misery and rags?"

The carnival-time arrived. I hoped the gay scenes then presented might have some cheering effect. I mingled with him in the motley throng that crowded the place of St. Mark. We frequented operas, masquerades, balls—all in vain. The evil kept growing on him. He became more and more haggard and agitated. Often, after we had returned from one of these scenes of revelry, I have entered his room and found him lying on his face on the sofa; his hands clinched in his fine hair, and his whole countenance bearing traces, of the convulsions of his mind.

The carnival passed away; the time of Lent succeeded; passion-week arrived; we attended one evening a solemn service in one of the churches, in the course of which a grand piece of vocal and instrumental music was performed relating to the death of our Savior.

I had remarked that he was always powerfully affected by music; on this occasion he was so in an extraordinary degree. As the pealing notes swelled through the lofty aisles, he seemed to kindle up with fervor; his eyes rolled upwards, until nothing but the whites were visible; his hands were clasped together, until the fingers were deeply imprinted in the flesh. When the music expressed the dying agony, his face gradually sank upon his knees; and at the touching words resounding through the church "*Gesu mori,*" sobs burst from him uncontrolled—I had never seen him weep before. His had always been agony rather than sorrow. I augured well from the circumstance, I let him weep on uninterrupted. When the service was ended, we left the church. He hung on my arm as we walked homewards with something of a softer and more subdued manner, instead of that nervous agitation I had been accustomed to witness. He alluded to the service we had heard. "Music," said he, "is indeed the voice of heaven; never before have I felt more impressed by the story of the atonement of our Savior. Yes, my friend," said he, clasping his hands with a kind of transport, "I know that my Redeemer liveth!"

We parted for the night. His room was not far from mine, and I heard him for some time busied in it. I fell asleep, but was awakened before daylight. The young man stood by my bedside, dressed for travelling. He held a sealed packet and a large parcel in his hand, which he laid on the table.

"Farewell, my friend," said he, "I am about to set forth on a long journey; but, before I go, I leave with you these remembrances. In this packet you will find the particulars of my story. When you read them I shall be far away; do not remember me with aversion. You have been indeed a friend to me. You have poured oil into a broken heart, but you could not heal it. Farewell! let me kiss your hand—I am unworthy to embrace you." He sank on his knees, seized my hand in despite of my efforts to the contrary, and covered it with kisses. I was so surprised by all the scene, that I had not been able to say a word. "But we shall meet again," said I, hastily, as I saw him hurrying towards the door. "Never, never, in this world!" said he, solemnly.—He sprang once more to my bedside—seized my hand, pressed it to his heart and to his lips, and rushed out of the room.

Here the Baronet paused. He seemed lost in thought, and sat looking upon the floor, and drumming with his fingers on the arm of his chair.

"And did this mysterious personage return?" said the inquisitive gentleman.

"Never!" replied the Baronet, with a pensive shake of the head,— "I never saw him again."

"And pray what has all this to do with the picture?" inquired the old gentleman with the nose.

"True," said the questioner; "is it the portrait of this crack-brained Italian?"

"No!" said the Baronet, dryly, not half liking the appellation given to his hero; "but this picture was enclosed in the parcel he left with me. The sealed packet contained its explanation. There was a request on the outside that I would not open it until six months had elapsed. I kept my promise in spite of my curiosity. I have a translation of it by me, and had meant to read it, by way of accounting for the mystery of the chamber; but I fear I have already detained the company too long."

Here there was a general wish expressed to have the manuscript read, particularly on the part of the inquisitive gentleman; so the worthy Baronet drew out a fairly-written manuscript, and, wiping his spectacles, read aloud the following story.—

THE ADVENTURE OF MY UNCLE

MANY YEARS SINCE, some time before the French Revolution, my uncle had passed several months at Paris. The English and French were on better terms in those days than at present, and mingled cordially in society. The English went abroad to spend money then, and the French were always ready to help them: they go abroad to save money at present, and that they can do without French assistance. Perhaps the travelling English were fewer and choicer than at present, when the whole nation has broke loose and inundated the continent. At any rate, they circulated more readily and currently in foreign society, and my uncle, during his residence in Paris, made many very intimate acquaintances among the French noblesse.

Some time afterwards, he was making a journey in the winter-time in that part of Normandy called the Pays de Caux, when, as evening was closing in, he perceived the turrets of an ancient chateau rising out of the trees of its walled park; each turret with its high conical roof of gray slate, like a candle with an extinguisher on it.

"To whom does that chateau belong, friend?" cried my uncle to a meagre but fiery postilion, who, with tremendous jack-boots and cocked hat, was floundering on before him.

"To Monseigneur the Marquis de——," said the postilion, touching his hat, partly out of respect to my uncle, and partly out of reverence to the noble name pronounced.

My uncle recollected the Marquis for a particular friend in Paris, who had often expressed a wish to see him at his paternal chateau. My uncle was an old traveller, one who knew how to turn things to account. He revolved for a few moments in his mind, how agreeable it would be to his friend the Marquis to be surprised in this sociable way by a pop visit; and how much more agreeable to himself to get into snug quarters in a chateau, and have a relish of the Marquis's well-known kitchen, and a smack of his superior Champagne and Burgundy, rather than take up with the miserable lodgement, and miserable fare of a provincial inn. In a few minutes, therefore, the meagre postilion was cracking his whip like a very devil, or like a true Frenchman, up the long straight avenue that led to the chateau.

You have no doubt all seen French chateaus, as everybody travels in France nowadays. This was one of the oldest; standing naked and alone in the midst of a desert of gravel walks and cold stone terraces; with a cold-looking, formal garden, cut into angles and rhomboids; and a cold, leafless park, divided geometrically by straight alleys; and two or three cold-looking noseless statues; and fountains spouting cold water enough to make one's teeth chatter. At least such was the feeling they imparted on the wintry day of my uncle's visit; though, in hot summer weather, I'll warrant there was glare enough to scorch one's eyes out.

The smacking of the postilion's whip, which grew more and more intense the nearer they approached, frightened a flight of pigeons out of a dove-cot, and rooks out of the roofs, and finally a crew of servants out of the chateau, with the Marquis at their head. He was enchanted to see my uncle, for his chateau, like the house of our worthy host, had not many more guests at the time than it could accommodate. So he kissed my uncle on each cheek, after the French fashion, and ushered him into the castle.

The Marquis did the honors of the house with the urbanity of his country. In fact, he was proud of his old family chateau, for part of it was extremely old. There was a tower and chapel that had been built almost before the memory of man; but the rest was more modern, the castle having been nearly demolished during the wars of the league. The Marquis dwelt upon this event with great satisfaction, and seemed really to entertain a grateful feeling towards Henry the Fourth, for having thought his paternal mansion worth battering down. He had many stories to tell of the prowess of his ancestors; and several skull-caps, helmets, and cross-bows, and divers huge boots and buff jerkins, to show which had been worn by the leaguers. Above all, there was a two-handled sword, which he could hardly wield, but which he displayed as a proof that there had been giants in his family.

In truth, he was but a small descendant from such great warriors. When you looked at their bluff visages and brawny limbs, as depicted in their portraits, and then at the little Marquis, with his spindle shanks, his sallow lanthern visage, flanked with a pair of powdered earlocks, or *aîles de pigeon,* that seemed ready to fly away with it, you could hardly believe him to be of the same race. But when you looked at the eyes that sparkled out like a beetle's from each side of his hooked nose, you saw at once that he inherited all the fiery spirit of his fore-fathers. In fact, a Frenchman's spirit never exhales, however his body may dwindle. It rather rarifies, and grows more inflammable, as the earthly particles diminish; and I have seen valour enough in a little fiery hearted French dwarf to have furnished out a tolerable giant.

When once the Marquis, as he was wont, put on one of the old helmets that were stuck up in his hall; though his head no more filled it than a dry pea its peascod, yet his eyes flashed from the bottom of the iron cavern with the brilliancy of carbuncles; and when he poised the ponderous two-handed sword of his ancestors, you would have thought you saw the doughty little David wielding the sword of Goliath, which was unto him like a weaver's beam.

However, gentlemen, I am dwelling too long on this description of the Marquis and his chateau, but you must excuse me; he was an old friend of my uncle; and whenever my uncle told the story, he was always fond of talking a great deal about his host.—Poor little Marquis! He was one of that handful of gallant courtiers who made such a devoted but hopeless stand in the cause of their sovereign, in the chateau of the Tuileries, against the irruption of the mob on the sad tenth of August. He displayed the valour of a *preux* French chevalier to the last; flourishing feebly his little court-sword with a *sa-sa!* in face of a whole legion of *sans-culottes;* but was pinned to the wall like a butterfly, by the pike of a *poissarde,* and his heroic soul was borne up to heaven on his *aîles de pigeon.*

But all this has nothing to do with my story. To the point then. When the hour arrived for retiring for the night, my uncle was shown to his room in a venerable old tower. It was the oldest part of the chateau, and had in ancient times been the donjon or stronghold; of course the chamber was none of the best. The Marquis had put him there, however, because he knew him to be a traveller of taste, and fond of antiquities; and also because the better apartments were already occupied. Indeed, he perfectly reconciled my uncle to his quarters by mentioning the great personages who had once inhabited them, all of whom were, in some way or other, connected with the family. If you would take his word for it, John Baliol, or as he called him Jean de Bailleul, had died of chagrin in this very chamber, on hearing of the success of his rival, Robert de Bruce, at the battle of Bannockburn. And when he added that the Duke de Guise had slept in it, my uncle was fain to felicitate himself on being honoured with such distinguished quarters.

The night was shrewd and windy, and the chamber none of the warmest. An old long-faced, long-bodied servant, in quaint livery, who attended upon my uncle, threw down an armful of wood beside the fireplace, gave a queer look about the room, and then wished him *bon repos,* with a grimace and a shrug that would have been suspicious from any other than an old French servant.

The chamber had indeed a wild, crazy look, enough to strike any one who had read romances with apprehension and foreboding. The windows were high and narrow, and had once been loop-holes, but had been rudely enlarged, as well as the extreme thickness of the walls would permit; and the ill-fitted casements rattled to every breeze. You would have thought, on a windy night, some of the old leaguers were tramping and clanking about the apartment in their huge boots and rattling spurs. A door which stood ajar, and, like a true French door, would stand ajar in spite of every reason and effort to the contrary, opened upon a long dark corridor, that led the Lord knows whither, and seemed just made for ghosts to air themselves in, when they turned out of their graves at midnight. The wind would spring up into a hoarse murmur through this passage, and creak the door to and fro, as if some dubious ghost were balancing in its mind whether to come in or not. In a word, it was precisely the kind of comfortless apartment that a ghost, if ghost there were in the chateau, would single out for its favorite lounge.

My uncle, however, though a man accustomed to meet with strange adventures, apprehended none at the time. He made several attempts to shut the door, but in vain. Not that he apprehended anything, for he was too old a traveller to be daunted by a wild-looking apartment; but the night, as I have said, was cold and gusty, and the wind howled about the old turret pretty much as it does round this old mansion at this moment, and the breeze from the long dark corridor came in as damp and as chilly as if from a dungeon. My uncle, therefore, since he could not close the door, threw a quantity of wood on the fire, which soon sent up a flame in the great wide-mouthed chimney that illumined the whole chamber; and made the shadow of the tongs on the opposite wall look like a long-legged giant. My uncle now clambered on the top of the half-score of mattresses which form a French bed, and which stood in a deep recess; then tucking himself snugly in, and burying himself up to the chin in the bed-clothes, he lay looking at the fire, and listening to the wind, and thinking how knowingly he had come over his friend the Marquis for a night's lodging—and so he fell asleep.

He had not taken above half of his first nap when he was awakened by the clock of the chateau, in the turret over his chamber, which struck midnight. It was just such an old clock as ghosts are fond of. It had a deep, dismal tone, and struck so slowly and tediously that my uncle thought it would never have done. He counted and counted till he was confident he counted thirteen, and then it stopped.

The fire had burnt low, and the blaze of the last fagot was almost expiring, burning in small blue flames, which now and then lengthened up into little white gleams. My uncle lay with his eyes half closed, and his nightcap drawn almost down to his nose. His fancy was already wandering, and began to mingle up the present scene with the crater of Vesuvius, the French Opera, the Coliseum at Rome, Dolly's chop-house in London, and all the farrago of noted places with which the brain of a traveller is crammed,—in a word, he was just falling asleep.

Suddenly he was roused by the sound of footsteps, slowly pacing along the corridor. My uncle, as I have often heard him say himself, was a man not easily frightened. So he lay quiet, supposing this some other guest, or some servant on his way to bed. The footsteps, however, approached the door; the door gently opened; whether of its own accord, or whether pushed open, my uncle could not distinguish: a figure all in white glided in. It was a female, tall and stately, and of a commanding air. Her dress was of an ancient fashion, ample in volume and sweeping the floor. She walked up to the fireplace, without regarding my uncle; who raised his nightcap with one hand, and stared earnestly at her. She remained for some time standing by the fire, which, flashing up at intervals, cast blue and white gleams of light, that enabled my uncle to remark her appearance minutely.

Her face was ghastly pale, and perhaps rendered still more so by the bluish light of the fire. It possessed beauty, but its beauty was saddened by care and anxiety. There was the look of one accustomed to trouble, but of one whom trouble could not cast down nor subdue; for there was still the predominating air of proud, unconquerable resolution. Such at least was the opinion formed by my uncle, and he considered himself a great physiognomist.

The figure remained, as I said, for some time by the fire, putting out first one hand, then the other, then each foot alternately, as if warming itself; for your ghosts, if ghost it really was, are apt to be cold. My uncle furthermore remarked that it wore high-heeled shoes, after an ancient fashion, with paste or diamond buckles, that sparkled as though they were alive. At length the figure turned gently round, casting a glassy look about the apartment, which, as it passed over my uncle, made his blood run cold, and chilled the very marrow in his bones. It then stretched its arms towards heaven, clasped its hands, and wringing them in a supplicating manner, glided slowly out of the room.

My uncle lay for some time meditating on this visitation, for (as he remarked when he told me the story) though a man of firmness, he was also a man of reflection, and did not reject a thing because it was out of the regular course of events. However, being as I have before said, a great traveller, and accustomed to strange adventures, he drew his nightcap resolutely over his eyes, turned his back to the door, hoisted the bedclothes high over his shoulders, and gradually fell asleep.

How long he slept he could not say, when he was awakened by the voice of some one at his bedside. He turned round, and beheld the old French servant, with his ear-locks in tight buckles on each side of a long lantern face, on which habit had deeply wrinkled an everlasting smile. He made a thousand grimaces, and asked a thousand pardons for disturbing Monsieur, but the morning was considerably advanced. While my uncle was dressing, he called vaguely to mind the visitor of the preceding night. He asked the ancient domestic what lady was in the habit of rambling about this part of the chateau at night. The old valet shrugged his shoulders as high as his head, laid one hand on his bosom, threw open the other with every finger extended, made a most whimsical grimace which he meant to be complimentary, and replied, that it was not for him to know anything of *les bonnes fortunes* of Monsieur.

My uncle saw there was nothing satisfactory to be learned in this quarter. After breakfast, he was walking with the Marquis through the modern apartments of the chateau, sliding over the well-waxed floors of silken saloons, amidst furniture rich in gilding and brocade, until they came to a long picture-gallery, containing many portraits, some in oil and some in chalks.

Here was an ample field for the eloquence of his host, who had all the pride of a nobleman of the *ancien régime*. There was not a grand name in Normandy, and hardly one in France, that was not, in some way or other, connected with his house. My uncle stood listening with inward impatience, resting sometimes on one leg, sometimes on the other, as the little Marquis descanted, with his usual fire and vivacity, on the achievements of his ancestors, whose portraits hung along the wall; from the martial deeds of the stern warriors in steel, to the gallantries and intrigues of the blue-eyed gentlemen, with fair smiling faces, powdered ear-locks, laced ruffles, and pink and blue silk coats and breeches;—not forgetting the conquests of the lovely shepherdesses, with hoop petticoats, and waists no thicker than an hourglass, who appeared ruling over their sheep and their swains, with dainty crooks decorated with fluttering ribbons.

In the midst of his friend's discourse, my uncle was started on beholding a full-length portrait, the very counterpart of his visitor of the preceding night.

"Methinks," said he, pointing to it, "I have seen the original of this portrait."

"*Pardonnez moi,*" replied the Marquis politely, "that can hardly be, as the lady has been dead more than a hundred years. That was the beautiful Duchess de Longueville, who figured during the minority of Louis the Fourteenth."

"And was there anything remarkable in her history?"

Never was question more unlucky. The little Marquis immediately threw himself into the attitude of a man about to tell a long story. In fact, my uncle had pulled upon himself the whole history of the civil war of the Fronde, in which the beautiful Duchess had played so distinguished a part. Turenne, Coligni, Mazarin, were called up from their graves to grace his narration; nor were the affairs of the Barricadoes, nor the chivalry of the Port Cochères forgotten. My uncle began to wish himself a thousand leagues off from the Marquis and his merciless memory, when suddenly the little man's recollections took a more interesting turn. He was relating the imprisonment of the Duke de Longueville with the Princes Condé and Conti in the chateau of Vincennes, and the ineffectual efforts of the Duchess to rouse the sturdy Normans to their rescue. He had come to that part where she was invested by the royal forces in the Castle of Dieppe.

"The spirit of the Duchess," proceeded the Marquis, "rose from her trials. It was astonishing to see so delicate and beautiful a being buffet so resolutely with hardships. She determined on a desperate means of escape. You may have seen the château in which she logs mewed up,—an old ragged wart of an edifice, standing on the knuckle of a hill, just above the rusty little town of Dieppe. One dark unruly night she issued secretly out of a small postern gate of the castle, which the enemy had neglected to guard. The postern gate is there to this very day; opening upon a narrow bridge over a deep fosse between the castle and the brow of the hill. She was followed by her female attendants, a few domestics, and some gallant cavaliers, who still remained faithful to her fortunes. Her object was to gain a small port about two leagues distant, where she had privately provided a vessel for her escape in case of emergency.

"The little band of fugitives were obliged to perform the distance on foot. When they arrived at the port the wind was high and stormy, the tide contrary, the vessel anchored far off in the road, and no means of getting on board, but by a fishing-shallop which lay tossing like a cockle-shell on the edge of the surf. The Duchess determined to risk the attempt. The seamen endeavoured to dissuade her, but the imminence of her danger on shore, and the magnanimity of her spirit urged her on. She had to be borne to the shallop in the arms of a mariner. Such was the violence of the wind and waves that he faltered, lost his foothold, and let his precious burden fall into the sea.

"The Duchess was nearly drowned, but partly through her own struggles, partly by the exertions of the seamen, she got to land. As soon as she had a little recovered strength, she insisted on renewing the attempt. The storm, however, had by this time become so violent as to set all efforts at defiance. To delay, was to be discovered and taken prisoner. As the only resource left, she procured horses, mounted with her female attendants, *en croupe,* behind the gallant gentlemen who accompanied her, and scoured the country to seek some temporary asylum.

"While the Duchess," continued the Marquis, laying his forefinger on my uncle's breast to arouse his flagging attention,—"while the Duchess, poor lady, was wandering amid the tempest in this disconsolate manner, she arrived at this chateau. Her approach caused some uneasiness; for the clattering of a troop of horse at dead of night up the avenue of a lonely chateau, in those unsettled times, and in a troubled part of the country, was enough to occasion alarm.

"A tall, broad-shouldered chasseur, armed to the teeth, galloped ahead, and announced the name of the visitor. All uneasiness was dispelled. The household turned out with flambeaux to receive her, and never did torches gleam on a more weather-beaten, travel-stained band than came tramping into the court. Such pale, careworn faces, such bedraggled dresses, as the poor Duchess and her females presented, each seated behind her cavalier: while half-drenched, half-drowsy pages and attendants seemed ready to fall from their horses with sleep and fatigue.

"The Duchess was received with a hearty welcome by my ancestor. She was ushered into the hall of the chateau, and the fires soon crackled and blazed, to cheer herself and her train; and every spit and stew-pan was put in requisition to prepare ample refreshments for the wayfarers.

"She had a right to our hospitalities," continued the Marquis, drawing himself up with a slight degree of stateliness, "for she was related to our family. I'll tell you how it was. Her father, Henry de Bourbon, Prince of Condé—"

"But did the Duchess pass the night in the chateau?" said my uncle rather abruptly, terrified at the idea of getting involved in one of the Marquis's genealogical discussions.

"Oh, as to the Duchess, she was put into the apartment you occupied last night, which at that time was a kind of state-apartment. Her followers were quartered in the chambers opening upon the neighboring corridor, and her favorite page slept in an adjoining closet. Up and down the corridor walked the great chasseur, who had announced her arrival, and who acted as a kind of sentinel or guard.

He was a dark, stern, powerful-looking fellow; and as the light of a lamp in the corridor fell upon his deeply marked face and sinewy form, he seemed capable of defending the castle with his single arm.

"It was a rough, rude night; about this time of the year—apropos!—now I think of it, last night was the anniversary of her visit. I may well remember the precise date, for it was a night not to be forgotten by our house. There is a singular tradition concerning it in our family." Here the Marquis hesitated, and a cloud seemed to gather about his bushy eyebrows. "There is a tradition—that a strange occurrence took place that night.—A strange, mysterious, inexplicable occurrence——" Here he checked himself, and paused.

"Did it relate to that lady?" inquired my uncle, eagerly.

"It was past the hour of midnight," resumed the Marquis,—"when the whole chateau——" Here he paused again. My uncle made a movement of anxious curiosity.

"Excuse me," said the Marquis, a slight blush streaking his sallow visage. "There are some circumstances connected with our family history which I do not like to relate. That was a rude period. A time of great crimes among great men: for you know high blood, when it runs wrong, will not run tamely, like blood of the *canaille*—poor lady!—But I have a little family pride, that—excuse me—we will change the subject if you please—"

My uncle's curiosity was piqued. The pompous and magnificent introduction had led him to expect something wonderful in the story to which it served as a kind of avenue. He had no idea of being cheated out of it by a sudden fit of unreasonable squeamishness. Besides, being a traveller in quest of information, he considered it his duty to inquire into everything.

The Marquis, however, evaded every question.

"Well," said my uncle, a little petulantly, "whatever you may think of it, I saw that lady last night."

The Marquis stepped back and gazed at him with surprise.

"She paid me a visit in my bedchamber."

The Marquis pulled out his snuff-box with a shrug and a smile; taking it no doubt for an awkward piece of English pleasantry, which politeness required him to be charmed with.

My uncle went on gravely, however, and related the whole circumstance. The Marquis heard him through with profound attention, holding his snuff-box unopened in his hand. When the story was finished he tapped on the lid of his box deliberately took a long sonorous pinch of snuff—

"Bah!" said the Marquis, and walked towards the other end of the gallery.—

Here the narrator paused. The company waited for some time for him to resume his narration; but he continued silent.

"Well," said the inquisitive gentleman,—"and what did your uncle say then?"

"Nothing," replied the other.

"And what did the Marquis say farther?"

"Nothing."

"And is that all?"

"That is all," said the narrator, filling a glass of wine.

"I surmise," said the shrewd old gentleman with the waggish nose,—"I surmise the ghost must have been the old housekeeper, walking her rounds to see that all was right."

"Bah!" said the narrator. "My uncle was too much accustomed to strange sights not to know a ghost from a housekeeper."

There was a murmur round the table, half of merriment, half of disappointment. I was inclined to think the old gentleman had really an after-part of his story in reserve; but he sipped his wine and said nothing more; and there was an odd expression about his dilapidated countenance which left me in doubt whether he were in drollery or earnest.

"Egad," said the knowing gentleman, with the flexible nose, "this story of your uncle puts me in mind of one that used to be told of an aunt of mine, by the mother's side; though I don't know that it will bear a comparison; as the good lady was not so prone to meet with strange adventures. But at any rate you shall have it."

THE ADVENTURE OF MY AUNT

MY AUNT WAS a lady of large frame, strong mind, and great resolution: she was what might be termed a very manly woman. My uncle was a thin, puny little man, very meek and acquiescent, and no match for my aunt. It was observed that he dwindled and dwindled gradually away, from the day of his marriage. His wife's powerful mind was too much for him; it wore him out. My aunt, however, took all possible care of him: had half the doctors in town to prescribe for him; made him take all their prescriptions, and dosed him with physic enough to cure a whole hospital. All was in vain. My uncle grew worse and worse the more dosing and nursing he underwent, until in the end he added another to the long list of matrimonial victims who have been killed with kindness.

"And was it his ghost that appeared to her?" asked the inquisitive gentleman, who had questioned the former story-teller.

"You shall hear," replied the narrator.—My aunt took on mightily for the death of her poor dear husband. Perhaps she felt some compunction at having given him so much physic, and nursed him into the grave. At any rate, she did all that a widow could do to honor his memory. She spared no expense in either the quantity or quality of her mourning weeds; wore a miniature of him about her neck as large as a little sun dial; and she had a full-length portrait of him always hanging in her bed-chamber. All the world extolled her conduct to the skies; and it was determined, that a woman who behaved so well to the memory of one husband deserved soon to get another.

It was not long after this that she went to take up her residence in an old country-seat in Derbyshire, which had long been in the care of merely a steward and housekeeper. She took most of her servants with her, intending to make it her principal abode. The house stood in a lonely wild part of the country, among the gray Derbyshire hills, with a murderer hanging in chains on a bleak height in full view.

The servants from town were half frightened out of their wits at the idea of living in such a dismal, pagan-looking place; especially when they got together in the servants' hall in the evening, and compared notes on all the hobgoblin stories picked up in the course of the day. They were afraid to venture alone about the gloomy black-looking chambers. My lady's maid, who was troubled with nerves, declared she could never sleep alone in such a "gashly rummaging old building"; and the footman, who was a kind-hearted young fellow, did all in his power to cheer her up.

My aunt was struck with the lonely appearance of the house. Before going to bed, therefore, she examined well the fastenesses of the doors and windows; locked up the plate with her own hands, and carried the keys, together with a little box of money and jewels, to her own room; for she was a notable woman, and always saw to all things herself. Having put the keys under her pillow, and dismissed her maid, she sat by her toilet arranging her hair; for, being, in spite of her grief for my uncle, rather a buxom widow, she was somewhat particular about her person. She sat for a little while looking at her face in the glass, first on one side, then on the other, as ladies are apt to do when they would ascertain whether they have been in good looks; for a roystering country squire of the neighborhood, with whom she had flirted when a girl, had called that day to welcome her to the country.

All of a sudden she thought she heard something move behind her. She looked hastily round, but there was nothing to be seen. Nothing but the grimly painted portrait of her poor dear man, hanging against the wall.

She gave a heavy sigh to his memory, as she was accustomed to do, whenever she spoke of him in company, and went on adjusting her night-dress, and thinking of the squire. Her sigh was re-echoed, or answered by a long-drawn breath. She looked round again, but no one was to be seen. She ascribed these sounds to the wind oozing through the ratholes of the old mansion, and proceeded leisurely to put her hair in papers, when, all at once, she thought she perceived one of the eyes of the portrait move.

"The back of her head being towards it!" said the story-teller with the ruined head,—"good!"

"Yes sir!" replied dryly the narrator, "her back being towards the portrait, but her eyes fixed on its reflection in the glass."—Well, as I was saying, she perceived one of the eyes of the portrait move. So strange a circumstance, as you may well suppose, gave her a sudden shock. To assure herself of the fact, she put one hand to her forehead as if rubbing it; peeped through her fingers, and moved the candle with the other hand. The light of the taper gleamed on the eye, and was reflected from it. She was sure it moved. Nay, more, it seemed to give her a wink, as she had sometimes known her husband to do when living! It struck a momentary chill to her heart; for she was a lone woman, and felt herself fearfully situated.

The chill was but transient. My aunt, who was almost as resolute a personage as your uncle, sir, (turning to the old story-teller,) became instantly calm and collected. She went on adjusting her dress. She even hummed an air, and did not make a single false note. She casually overturned a dressing-box; took a candle and picked up the articles one by one from the floor; pursued a rolling pin-cushion that was making the best of its way under the bed; then opened the door; looked for an instant into the corridor, as if in doubt whether to go; and then walked quietly out.

She hastened down-stairs, ordered the servants to arm themselves with the weapons first at hand, placed herself at their head, and returned almost immediately.

Her hastily levied army presented a formidable force. The steward had a rusty blunder-buss, the coachman a loaded whip; the footman a pair of horse pistols; the cook a huge chopping-knife, and the butler a bottle in each hand. My aunt led the van with a red-hot poker, and in my opinion she was the most formidable of the party. The waiting maid who dreaded to stay alone in the servant's hall brought up the rear, smelling to a broken bottle of volatile salts, and expressing her terror of the ghostesses. "Ghosts!" said my aunt resolutely, "I'll singe their whiskers for them!"

They entered the chamber. All was still and undisturbed as when she left it. They approached the portrait of my uncle.

"Pull down that picture!" cried my aunt. A heavy groan, and a sound like the chattering of teeth, issued from the portrait. The servants shrunk back; the maid uttered a faint shriek, and clung to the footman for support.

"Instantly!" added my aunt, with a stamp of the foot.

The picture was pulled down, and from a recess behind it, in which had formerly stood a clock, they hauled forth a round-shouldered, black-bearded varlet, with a knife as long as my arm, but trembling all over like an aspen-leaf.

"Well, and who was he? No ghost, I suppose!" said the inquisitive gentleman.

"A Knight of the Post," replied the narrator, "who had been smitten with the worth of the wealthy widow; or rather a marauding Tarquin, who had stolen into her chamber to violate her purse, and rifle her strong box, when all the house should be asleep. In plain terms," continued he, "the vagabond was a loose idle fellow of the neighborhood, who had once been a servant in the house, and had been employed to assist in arranging it for the reception of its mistress. He confessed that he had contrived this hiding-place for his nefarious purpose, and had borrowed an eye from the portrait by way of a reconnoitering-hole."

"And what did they do with him?—did they hang him?" resumed the questioner.

"Hang him!—how could they?" exclaimed a beetle-browed barrister, with a hawk's nose. "The offense was not capital. No robbery, no assault had been committed. No forcible entry or breaking into the premises—"

"My aunt," said the narrator, "was a woman of spirit, and apt to take the law in her own hands. She had her own notions of cleanliness also. She ordered the fellow to be drawn through the horsepond, to cleanse away all offenses, and then to be well rubbed down with an oaken towel."

"And what became of him afterwards?" said the inquisitive gentleman.

"I do not exactly know. I believe he was sent on a voyage of improvement to Botany Bay."

"And your aunt," said the inquisitive gentleman; "I'll warrant she took care to make her maid sleep in the room with her after that."

"No, sir, she did better; she gave her hand shortly after to the roistering squire; for she used to observe, that it was a dismal thing for a woman to sleep alone in the country."

"She was right," observed the inquisitive gentleman, nodding sagaciously; "but I am sorry they did not hang that fellow."

It was agreed on all hands that the last narrator had brought his tale to the most satisfactory conclusion, though a country clergyman present regretted that the uncle and aunt, who figured in the different stories, had not been married together; they certainly would have been well matched.

"But I don't see, after all," said the inquisitive gentleman, "that there was any ghost in this last story."

"Oh! If it's ghosts you want, honey," cried the Irish captain of Dragoons, "if it's ghosts you want, you shall have a whole regiment of them. And since these gentlemen have been giving the adventures of their uncles and aunts, faith, and I'll even give you a chapter out of my own family-history."

THE STORY OF THE YOUNG ITALIAN

I WAS BORN at Naples. My parents, though of noble rank, were limited in fortune, or rather, my father was ostentatious beyond his means, and expended so much on his palace, his equipage, and his retinue, that he was continually straitened in his pecuniary circumstances. I was a younger son, and looked upon with indifference by my father, who, from a principle of family-pride, wished to leave all his property to my elder brother. I showed, when quite a child, an extreme sensibility. Everything affected me violently. While yet an infant in my mother's arms, and before I had learned to talk, I could be wrought upon to a wonderful degree of anguish or delight by the power of music. As I grew older, my feelings remained equally acute, and I was easily transported into paroxysms of pleasure or rage. It was the amusement of my relations and of the domestics to play upon this irritable temperament. I was moved to tears, tickled to laughter, provoked to fury, for the entertainment of company, who were amused by such a tempest of mighty passion in a pigmy frame;—they little thought, or perhaps little heeded the dangerous sensibilities they were fostering. I thus became a little creature of passion before reason was developed. In a short time I grew too old to be a plaything, and then I became a torment. The tricks and passions I had been teased into became irksome, and I was disliked by my teachers for the very lessons they had taught me. My mother died; and my power as a spoiled child was at an end. There was no longer any necessity to humor or tolerate me, for there was nothing to be gained by it, as I was no favorite of my father. I therefore experienced the fate of a spoiled child in such situation, and was neglected, or noticed only to be crossed and contradicted. Such was the early treatment of a heart which, if I can judge of it at all, was naturally disposed to the extremes of tenderness and affection.

My father, as I have already said, never liked me—in fact, he never understood me; he looked upon me as wilful and wayward, as deficient in natural affection. It was the stateliness of his own manner, the loftiness and grandeur of his own look, which had repelled me from his arms. I always pictured him to myself as I had seen him, clad in his senatorial robes, rustling with pomp and pride. The magnificence of his person had daunted my young imagination. I could never approach him with the confiding affection of a child.

My father's feelings were wrapped up in my elder brother. He was to be the inheritor of the family-title and the family-dignity, and every thing was sacrificed to him—I, as well as everything else. It was determined to devote me to the Church, that so my humors and myself might be removed out of the way, either of tasking my father's time and trouble, or interfering with the interests of my brother. At an early age, therefore, before my mind had dawned upon the world and its delights, or known anything of it beyond the precincts of my father's palace, I was sent to a convent, the superior of which was my uncle, and was confided entirely to his care.

My uncle was a man totally estranged from the world: he had never relished, for he had never tasted its pleasures; and he regarded rigid self-denial as the great basis of Christian virtue. He considered every one's temperament like his own; or at least he made them conform to it. His character and habits had an influence over the fraternity of which he was superior: a more gloomy, saturnine set of beings were never assembled together. The convent, too, was calculated to awaken sad and solitary thoughts. It was situated in a gloomy gorge of those mountains away south of Vesuvius. All distant views were shut out by sterile volcanic heights. A mountain-stream raved beneath its walls, and eagles screamed about its turrets.

I had been sent to this place at so tender an age as soon to lose all distinct recollection of the scenes I had left behind. As my mind expanded, therefore, it formed its idea of the world from the convent and its vicinity, and a dreary world it appeared to me. An early tinge of melancholy was thus infused into my character; and the dismal stories of the monks, about devils and evil spirits, with which they affrighted my young imagination, gave me a tendency to superstition, which I could never effectually shake off. They took the same delight to work upon my ardent feelings, that had been so mischievously executed by my father's household. I can recollect the horrors with which they fed my heated fancy during an eruption of Vesuvius. We were distant from that volcano, with mountains between us; but its convulsive throes shook the solid foundations of nature. Earthquakes threatened to topple down our convent-towers. A lurid, baleful light hung in the heavens at night, and showers of ashes, borne by the wind, fell in our narrow valley. The monks talked of the earth being honeycombed beneath us; of streams of molten lava raging through its veins; of caverns of sulphurous flames roaring in the centre, the abodes of demons and the damned; of fiery gulfs ready to yawn beneath our feet. All these tales were told to the doleful accompaniment of the mountain's thunders, whose low bellowing made the walls of our convent vibrate.

One of the monks had been a painter, but had retired from the world, and embraced this dismal life in expiation of some crime. He was a melancholy man, who pursued his art in the solitude of his cell, but made it a source of penance to him. His employment was to portray, either on canvass or in waxen models, the human face and human form, in the agonies of death, and in all the stages of dissolution and decay. The fearful mysteries of the charnel house were unfolded in his labors; the loathsome banquet of the beetle and the worm. I turn with shuddering even from the recollection of his works; yet, at the time, my strong but ill-directed imagination seized with ardor upon his instructions in his art. Anything was a variety from the dry studies and monotonous duties of the cloister. In a little while I became expert with my pencil, and my gloomy productions were thought worthy of decorating some of the altars of the chapel.

In this dismal way was a creature of feeling and fancy brought up. Everything genial and amiable in my nature was repressed, and nothing brought out but what was unprofitable and ungracious. I was ardent in my temperament; quick, mercurial, impetuous, formed to be a creature all love and adoration; but a leaden hand was laid on all my finer qualities. I was taught nothing but fear and hatred. I hated my uncle. I hated the monks. I hated the convent in which I was immured. I hated the world; and I almost hated myself for being, as I supposed, so hating and hateful an animal.

When I had nearly attained the age of sixteen, I was suffered, on one occasion, to accompany one of the brethren on a mission to a distant part of the country. We soon left behind us the gloomy valley in which I had been pent up for so many years, and after a short journey among the mountains, emerged upon the voluptuous landscape that spreads itself about the Bay of Naples. Heavens! how transported was I, when I stretched my gaze over a vast reach of delicious sunny country, gay with groves and vineyards; with Vesuvius rearing its forked summit to my right; the blue Mediterranean to my left, with its enchanting coast, studded with shining towns and sumptuous villas; and Naples, my native Naples, gleaming far, far in the distance.

Good God! was this the lovely world from which I had been excluded! I had reached that age when the sensibilities are in all their bloom and freshness. Mine had been checked and chilled. They now burst forth with the suddenness of a retarded spring-time. My heart, hitherto unnaturally shrunk up, expanded into a riot of vague but delicious emotions. The beauty of nature intoxicated—bewildered me. The song of the peasants; their cheerful looks; their happy avocations; the picturesque gayety of their dresses; their rustic music; their dances; all broke upon me like witchcraft. My soul responded to the music, my heart danced in my bosom. All the men appeared amiable, all the women lovely.

I returned to the convent; that is to say, my body returned, but my heart and soul never entered there again. I could not forget this glimpse of a beautiful and a happy world—a world so suited to my natural character. I had felt so happy while in it; so different a being from what I felt myself when in the convent—that tomb of the living. I contrasted the countenances of the beings I had seen, full of fire and freshness and enjoyment, with the pallid, leaden, lack-lustre visages of the monks: the dance with the droning chant of the chapel. I had before found the exercises of the cloister wearisome, they now became intolerable. The dull round of duties wore away my spirit; my nerves became irritated by the fretful tinkling of the convent-bell, evermore dinging among the mountain-echoes; evermore calling me from my repose at night, my pencil by day, to attend to some tedious and mechanical ceremony of devotion.

I was not of a nature to meditate long without putting my thoughts into action. My spirit had been suddenly aroused, and was now all awake within me. I watched my opportunity, fled from the convent, and made my way on foot to Naples. As I entered its gay and crowded streets, and beheld the variety and stir of life around me, the luxury of palaces, the splendor of equipages, and the pantomimic animation of the motley populace, I seemed as if awakened to a world of enchantment, and solemnly vowed that nothing should force me back to the monotony of the cloister.

I had to inquire my way to my father's palace, for I had been so young on leaving it that I knew not its situation. I found some difficulty in getting admitted to my father's presence; for the domestics scarcely knew that there was such a being as myself in existence, and my monastic dress did not operate in my favor. Even my father entertained no recollection of my person. I told him my name, threw myself at his feet, implored his forgiveness, and entreated that I might not be sent back to the convent.

He received me with the condescension of a patron rather than the fondness of a parent; listened patiently, but coldly, to my tale of monastic grievances and disgusts, and promised to think what else could be done for me. This coldness blighted and drove back all the frank affection of my nature, that was ready to spring forth at the least warmth of parental kindness. All my early feelings towards my father revived. I again looked up to him as the stately magnificent being that had daunted my childish imagination, and felt as if I had no pretensions to his sympathies. My brother engrossed all his care and love; he inherited his nature, and carried himself towards me with a protecting rather than a fraternal air. It wounded my pride, which was great. I could brook condescension from my father, for I looked up to him with awe, as a superior being; but I could not brook patronage from a brother, who I felt was intellectually my inferior. The servants perceived that I was an unwelcome intruder in the paternal mansion, and, menial-like, they treated me with neglect. Thus baffled at every point, my affections outraged wherever they would attach themselves, I became sullen, silent, and desponding. My feelings, driven back upon myself, entered and preyed upon my own heart. I remained for some days an unwelcome guest rather than a restored son in my father's house. I was doomed never to be properly known there. I was made, by wrong treatment, strange even to myself, and they judged of me from my strangeness.

I was startled one day at the sight of one of the monks of my convent gliding out of my father's room. He saw me, but pretended not to notice me, and this very hypocrisy made me suspect something. I had become sore and susceptible in my feelings, everything inflicted a wound on them. In this state of mind, I was treated with marked disrespect by a pampered minion, the favorite servant of my father. All the pride and passion of my nature rose in an instant, and I struck him to the earth. My father was passing by; he stopped not to inquire the reason, nor indeed could he read the long course of mental sufferings which were the real cause. He rebuked me with anger and scorn; summoning all the haughtiness of his nature and grandeur of his look to give weight to the contumely with which he treated me. I felt I had not deserved it. I felt that I was not appreciated. I felt that I had that within me which merited better treatment; my heart swelled against a father's injustice. I broke through my habitual awe of him—I replied to him with impatience. My hot spirit flushed in my cheek and kindled in my eye; but my sensitive heart swelled as quickly, and before I had half vented my passion, I felt it suffocated and quenched in my tears. My father was astonished and incensed at this turning of the worm, and ordered me to my chamber. I retired in silence, choking with contending emotions.

I had not been long there when I overheard voices in an adjoining apartment. It was a consultation between my father and the monk, about the means of getting me back quietly to the convent. My resolution was taken. I had no longer a home nor a father. That very night I left the paternal roof. I got on board a vessel about making sail from the harbor, and abandoned myself to the wide world. No matter to what port she steered; any part of so beautiful a world was better than my convent. No matter where I was cast by fortune; any place would be more a home to me than the home I had left behind. The vessel was bound to Genoa. We arrived there after a voyage of a few days.

As I entered the harbor, between the moles which embrace it, and beheld the amphitheatre of palaces, and churches, and splendid gardens, rising one above another, I felt at once its title to the appellation of Genoa the Superb. I landed on the mole an utter stranger, without knowing what to do, or whither to direct my steps. No matter: I was released from the thraldom of the convent and the humiliations of home. When I traversed the Strada Balbi and the Strada Nuova, those streets of palaces, and gazed at the wonders of architecture around me; when I wandered at close of day amid a gay throng of the brilliant and the beautiful, through the green alleys of the Aquaverde, or among the colonnades and terraces of the magnificent Doria gardens; I thought it impossible to be ever otherwise than happy in Genoa. A few days sufficed to show me my mistake. My scanty purse was exhausted, and for the first time in my life I experienced the sordid distress of penury. I had never known the want of money, and had never adverted to the possibility of such an evil. I was ignorant of the world and all its ways; and when first the idea of destitution came over my mind, its effect was withering. I was wandering penniless through the streets which no longer delighted my eyes, when chance led my steps into the magnificent church of the Annunciata.

A celebrated painter of the day was at that moment superintending the placing of one of his pictures over an altar. The proficiency which I had acquired in his art during my residence in the convent, had made me an enthusiastic amateur. I was struck, at the first glance, with the painting. It was the face of a Madonna. So innocent, so lovely, such a divine expression of maternal tenderness! I lost, for the moment, all recollection of myself in the enthusiasm of my art. I clasped my hands together, and uttered an ejaculation of delight. The painter perceived my emotion. He was flattered and gratified by it. My air and manner pleased him, and he accosted me. I felt too much the want of friendship to repel the advances of a stranger; and there was something in this one so benevolent and winning, that in a moment he gained my confidence.

I told him my story and my situation, concealing only my name and rank. He appeared strongly interested by my recital, invited me to his house, and from that time I became his favorite pupil. He thought he perceived in me extraordinary talents for the art, and his encomiums awakened all my ardor. What a blissful period of my existence was it that I passed beneath his roof! Another being seemed created within me; or rather, all that was amiable and excellent was drawn out. I was as recluse as ever I had been at the convent, but how different was my seclusion. My time was spent in storing my mind with lofty and poetical ideas; in meditating on all that was striking and noble in history and fiction; in studying and tracing all that was sublime and beautiful in nature. I was always a visionary, imaginative being, but now my reveries and imaginings all elevated me to rapture. I looked up to my master as to a benevolent genius that had opened to me a region of enchantment. He was not a native of Genoa, but had been drawn thither by the solicitations of several of the nobility, and had resided there but a few years, for the completion of certain works. His health was delicate, and he had to confide much of the filling up of his designs to the pencils of his scholars. He considered me as particularly happy in delineating the human countenance; in seizing upon characteristic though fleeting expressions, and fixing them powerfully upon my canvas. I was employed continually, therefore, in sketching faces, and often, when some particular grace of beauty or expression was wanted in a countenance, it was entrusted to my pencil. My benefactor was fond of bringing me forward; and partly, perhaps, through my actual skill, and partly through his partial praises, I began to be noted for the expression of my countenances.

Among the various works which he had undertaken, was an historical piece for one of the palaces of Genoa, in which were to be introduced the likenesses of several of the family. Among these was one intrusted to my pencil. It was that of a young girl, as yet in a convent for her education. She came out for the purpose of sitting for the picture. I first saw her in an apartment of one of the sumptuous palaces of Genoa. She stood before a casement that looked out upon the bay; a stream of vernal sunshine fell upon her, and shed a kind of glory round her, as it lit up the rich crimson chamber. She was but sixteen years of age—and oh, how lovely! The scene broke upon me like a mere vision of spring and youth and beauty. I could have fallen down and worshipped her. She was like one of those fictions of poets and painters, when they would express the *beau ideal* that haunts their minds with shapes of indescribable perfection. I was permitted to watch her countenance in various positions, and I fondly protracted the study that was undoing me. The more I gazed on her, the more I became enamored; there was something almost painful in my intense admiration. I was but nineteen years of age, shy, diffident, and inexperienced. I was treated with attention by her mother; for my youth and my enthusiasm in my art had won favor for me; and I am inclined to think something in my air and manner inspired interest and respect. Still the kindness with which I was treated could not dispel the embarrassment into which my own imagination threw me when in presence of this lovely being. It elevated her into something almost more than mortal. She seemed too exquisite for earthly use; too delicate and exalted for human attainment. As I sat tracing her charms on my canvas, with my eyes occasionally riveted on her features, I drank in delicious poison that made me giddy. My heart alternately gushed with tenderness, and ached with despair. Now I became more than ever sensible of the violent fires that had lain dormant at the bottom of my soul. You who were born in a more temperate climate and under a cooler sky, have little idea of the violence of passion in our southern bosoms.

A few days finished my task. Bianca returned to her convent, but her image remained indelibly impressed upon my heart. It dwelt on my imagination; it became my pervading idea of beauty. It had an effect even upon my pencil. I became noted for my felicity in depicting female loveliness: it was but because I multiplied the image of Bianca. I soothed, and yet fed my fancy by introducing her in all the productions of my master. I have stood, with delight, in one of the chapels of the Annunciata, and heard the crowd extol the seraphic beauty of a saint which I had painted; I have seen them bow down in adoration before the painting; they were bowing before the loveliness of Bianca.

I existed in this kind of dream, I might almost say delirium, for upwards of a year. Such is the tenacity of my imagination, that the image formed in it continued in all its power and freshness. Indeed, I was a solitary, meditative being, much given to reverie, and apt to foster ideas which had once taken strong possession of me. I was roused from this fond, melancholy, delicious dream by the death of my worthy benefactor. I cannot describe the pangs his death occasioned me. It left me alone, and almost broken-hearted. He bequeathed to me his little property, which, from the liberality of his disposition, and his expensive style of living, was indeed but small; and he most particularly recommended me, in dying, to the protection of a nobleman who had been his patron.

The latter was a man who passed for munificent. He was a lover and an encourager of the arts, and evidently wished to be thought so. He fancied he saw in me indications of future excellence; my pencil had already attracted attention; he took me at once under his protection. Seeing that I was overwhelmed with grief, and incapable of exerting myself in the mansion of my late benefactor, he invited me to sojourn for a time at a villa which he possessed on the border of the sea, in the picturesque neighborhood of Sestri de Ponente.

I found at the villa the count's only son Filippo. He was nearly of my age; prepossessing in his appearance, and fascinating in his manners, he attached himself to me, and seemed to court my good opinion. I thought there was something of profession in his kindness, and of caprice in his disposition; but I had nothing else near me to attach myself to, and my heart felt the need of something to repose upon. His education had been neglected; he looked upon me as his superior in mental powers and acquirements, and tacitly acknowledged my superiority. I felt that I was his equal in birth, and that gave independence to my manners, which had its effect. The caprice and tyranny I saw sometimes exercised on others, over whom he had power, were never manifested towards me. We became intimate friends and frequent companions. Still I loved to be alone, and to indulge in the reveries of my own imagination among the scenery by which I was surrounded. The villa commanded a wide view of the Mediterranean, and of the picturesque Ligurian coast. It stood alone in the midst of ornamental grounds, finely decorated with statues and fountains, and laid out in groves and alleys and shady lawns. Everything was assembled here that could gratify the taste, or agreeably occupy the mind. Soothed by the tranquillity of this elegant retreat, the turbulence of my feelings gradually subsided, and blending with the romantic spell which still reigned over my imagination, produced a soft, voluptuous melancholy.

I had not been long under the roof of the count, when our solitude was enlivened by another inhabitant. It was a daughter of a relative of the count, who had lately died in reduced circumstances, bequeathing this only child to his protection. I had heard much of her beauty from Filippo, but my fancy had become so engrossed by one idea of beauty, as not to admit of any other. We were in the central saloon of the villa when she arrived. She was still in mourning, and approached, leaning on the count's arm. As they ascended the marble portico, I was struck by the elegance of her figure and movement, by the grace with which the *mezzaro,* the bewitching veil of Genoa, was folded about her slender form. They entered. Heavens! what was my surprise when I beheld Bianca before me! It was herself; pale with grief; but still more matured in loveliness than when I had last beheld her. The time that had elapsed had developed the graces of her person, and the sorrow she had undergone had diffused over her countenance an irresistible tenderness.

She blushed and trembled at seeing me, and tears rushed into her eyes, for she remembered in whose company she had been accustomed to behold me. For my part, I cannot express what were my emotions. By degrees I overcame the extreme shyness that had formerly paralyzed me in her presence. We were drawn together by sympathy of situation. We had each lost our best friend in the world; we were each, in some measure, thrown upon the kindness of others. When I came to know her intellectually, all my ideal picturings of her were confirmed. Her newness to the world, her delightful susceptibility to everything beautiful and agreeable in nature, reminded me of my own emotions when first I escaped from the convent. Her rectitude of thinking delighted my judgment; the sweetness of her nature wrapped itself round my heart; and then her young, and tender, and budding loveliness, sent a delicious madness to my brain.

I gazed upon her with a kind of idolatry, as something more than mortal; and I felt humiliated at the idea of my comparative unworthiness. Yet she was mortal; and one of mortality's most susceptible and loving compounds;—for she loved me!

How first I discovered the transporting truth I cannot recollect. I believe it stole upon me by degrees as a wonder past hope or belief. We were both at such a tender and loving age; in constant intercourse with each other; mingling in the same elegant pursuits,—for music, poetry, and painting were our mutual delights; and we were almost separated from society among lovely and romantic scenery. Is it strange that two young hearts, thus brought together, should readily twine round each other?

Oh, gods! what a dream—a transient dream of unalloyed delight then passed over my soul! Then it was that the world around me was indeed a paradise; for I had woman—lovely, delicious woman, to share it with me! How often have I rambled over the picturesque shores of Sestri, or climbed its wild mountains, with the coast gemmed with villas, and the blue sea far below me, and the slender Faro of Genoa on its romantic promontory in the distance; and as I sustained the faltering steps of Bianca, have thought there could no unhappiness enter into so beautiful a world! How often have we listened together to the nightingale, as it poured forth its rich notes among the moonlight bowers of the garden, and have wondered that poets could ever have fancied anything melancholy in its song! Why, oh why is this budding season of life and tenderness so transient!— why is this rosy cloud of love, that sheds such a glow over the morning of our days, so prone to brew up into the whirlwind and the storm!

I was the first to awaken from this blissful delirium of the affections. I had gained Bianca's heart, what was I to do with it? I had no wealth nor prospects to entitle me to her hand; was I to take advantage of her ignorance of the world, of her confiding affection, and draw her down to my own poverty? Was this requiting the hospitality of the count? was this requiting the love of Bianca?

Now first I began to feel that even successful love may have its bitterness. A corroding care gathered about my heart. I moved about the palace like a guilty being. I felt as if I had abused its hospitality, as if I were a thief within its walls. I could no longer look with unembarrassed mien in the countenance of the count. I accused myself of perfidy to him, and I thought he read it in my looks, and began to distrust and despise me. His manner had always been ostentatious and condescending; it now appeared cold and haughty. Filippo, too, became reserved and distant; or at least I suspected him to be so. Heavens! was this mere coinage of my brain? Was I to become suspicious of all the world? a poor, surmising wretch; watching looks and gestures; and torturing myself with misconstructions. Or, if true, was I to remain beneath a roof where I was merely tolerated, and linger there on sufferance? "This is not to be endured!" exclaimed I: "I will tear myself from this state of self-abasement; I will break through this fascination and fly—Fly?—Whither? from the world? for where is the world when I leave Bianca behind me?"

My spirit was naturally proud, and swelled within me at the idea of being looked upon with contumely. Many times I was on the point of declaring my family and rank, and asserting my equality in the presence of Bianca, when I thought her relatives assumed an air of superiority. But the feeling was transient. I considered myself discarded and condemned by my family; and had solemnly vowed never to own relationship to them until they themselves should claim it.

The struggle of my mind preyed upon my happiness and my health. It seemed as if the uncertainty of being loved would be less intolerable than thus to be assured of it, and yet not dare to enjoy the conviction. I was no longer the enraptured admirer of Bianca; I no longer hung in ecstacy on the tones of her voice, nor drank in with insatiate gaze the beauty of her countenance. Her very smiles ceased to delight me, for I felt culpable in having won them.

She could not but be sensible of the change in me, and inquired the cause with her usual frankness and simplicity. I could not evade the inquiry, for my heart was full to aching. I told her all the conflict of my soul; my devouring passion, my bitter self-upbraiding. "Yes!" said I, "I am unworthy of you. I am an offcast from my family—a wanderer—a nameless, homeless wanderer—with nothing but poverty for my portion; and yet I have dared to love you—have dared to aspire to your love."

My agitation moved her to tears, but she saw nothing in my situation so hopeless as I had depicted it. Brought up in a convent, she knew nothing of the world—its wants—its cares: and indeed what woman is a worldly casuist in the matters of the heart? Nay, more, she kindled into a sweet enthusiasm when she spoke of my fortunes and myself. We had dwelt together on the works of the famous masters. I had related to her their histories; the high reputation, the influence, the magnificence to which they had attained. The companions of princes, the favorites of kings, the pride and boast of nations. All this she applied to me. Her love saw nothing in their great productions that I was not able to achieve; and when I beheld the lovely creature glow with fervor, and her whole countenance radiant with the visions of my glory, I was snatched up for the moment into the heaven of her own imagination.

I am dwelling too long upon this part of my story; yet I cannot help lingering over a period of my life on which, with all its cares and conflicts, I look back with fondness, for as yet my soul was unstained by a crime. I do not know what might have been the result of this struggle between pride, delicacy, and passion, had I not read in a Neapolitan gazette an account of the sudden death of my brother. It was accompanied by an earnest inquiry for intelligence concerning me, and a prayer, should this meet my eye, that I would hasten to Naples to comfort an infirm and afflicted father.

I was naturally of an affectionate disposition; but my brother had never been as a brother to me. I had long considered myself as disconnected from him, and his death caused me but little emotion. The thoughts of my father, infirm and suffering, touched me, however, to the quick; and when I thought of him, that lofty, magnificent being, now bowed down and desolate, and suing to me for comfort, all my resentment for past neglect was subdued, and a glow of filial affection was awakened within me.

The predominant feeling, however, that overpowered all others, was transport at the sudden change in my whole fortunes. A home, a name, rank, wealth, awaited me; and love painted a still more rapturous prospect in the distance. I hastened to Bianca, and threw myself at her feet. "Oh, Bianca!" exclaimed I, "at length I can claim you for my own. I am no longer a nameless adventurer, a neglected, rejected outcast. Look—read—behold the tidings that restore me to my name and to myself!"

I will not dwell on the scene that ensued. Bianca rejoiced in the reverse of my situation, because she saw it lightened my heart of a load of care; for her own part, she had loved me for myself, and had never doubted that my own merits would command both fame and fortune.

I now felt all my native pride buoyant within me. I no longer walked with my eyes bent to the dust; hope elevated them to the skies—my soul was lit up with fresh fires, and beamed from my countenance.

I wished to impart the change in my circumstances to the count; to let him know who and what I was—and to make formal proposals for the hand of Bianca; but he was absent on a distant estate. I opened my whole soul to Filippo. Now first I told him of my passion, of the doubts and fears that had distracted me, and of the tidings that had suddenly dispelled them. He overwhelmed me with congratulations and with the warmest expressions of sympathy; I embraced him in the fullness of my heart;—I felt compunctious for having suspected him of coldness, and asked him forgiveness for ever having doubted his friendship.

Nothing is so warm and enthusiastic as a sudden expansion of the heart between young men. Filippo entered into our concerns with the most eager interest. He was our confidant and counsellor. It was determined that I should hasten at once to Naples, to reëstablish myself in my father's affections, and my paternal home; and the moment the reconciliation was effected, and my father's consent insured, I should return and demand Bianca of the count. Filippo engaged to secure his father's acquiescence; indeed, he undertook to watch over our interest, and was the channel through which we were to correspond.

My parting with Bianca was tender—delicious—agonizing. It was in a little pavilion of the garden which had been one of our favorite resorts. How often and often did I return to have one more adieu, to have her look once more on me in speechless emotion; to enjoy once more the rapturous sight of those tears streaming down her lovely cheeks; to seize once more on that delicate hand, the frankly accorded pledge of love, and cover it with tears and kisses? Heavens! There is a delight even in the parting agony of two lovers, worth a thousand tame pleasures of the world. I have her at this moment before my eyes—at the window of the pavilion, putting aside the vines which clustered about the casement, her form beaming forth in virgin light, her countenance all tears and smiles, sending a thousand and a thousand adieus after me, as hesitating, in a delirium of fondness and agitation, I faltered my way down the avenue.

As the bark bore me out of the harbor of Genoa, how eagerly my eye stretched along the coast of Sestri, till it discovered the villa gleaming from among the trees at the foot of the mountain. As long as day lasted I gazed and gazed upon it, till it lessened and lessened to a mere white speck in the distance; and still my intense and fixed gaze discerned it, when all other objects of the coast had blended into indistinct confusion, or were lost in the evening gloom.

On arriving at Naples, I hastened to my paternal home. My heart yearned for the long-withheld blessing of a father's love. As I entered the proud portal of the ancestral palace, my emotions were so great that I could not speak. No one knew me, the servants gazed at me with curiosity and surprise. A few years of intellectual elevation and development had made a prodigious change in the poor fugitive stripling from the convent. Still, that no one should know me in my rightful home was overpowering. I felt like the prodigal son returned. I was a stranger in the house of my father. I burst into tears and wept aloud. When I made myself known, however, all was changed. I, who had once been almost repulsed from its walls, and forced to fly as an exile, was welcomed back with acclamation, with servility. One of the servants hastened to prepare my father for my reception; my eagerness to receive the paternal embrace was so great that I could not await his return; but hurried after him. What a spectacle met my eyes as I entered the chamber! My father, whom I had left in the pride of vigorous age, whose noble and majestic bearing had so awed my young imagination, was bowed down and withered into decrepitude. A paralysis had ravaged his stately form, and left it a shaking ruin. He sat propped up in his chair, with pale, relaxed visage, and glassy, wandering eye. His intellect had evidently shared in the ravages of his frame. The servant was endeavoring to make him comprehend that a visitor was at hand. I tottered up to him, and sunk at his feet. All his past coldness and neglect were forgotten in his present sufferings. I remembered only that he was my parent, and that I had deserted him. I clasped his knee: my voice was almost stifled with convulsive sobs. "Pardon—pardon! oh! my father!" was all that I could utter. His apprehension seemed slowly to return to him. He gazed at me for some moments with a vague, inquiring look; a convulsive tremor quivered about his lips; he feebly extended a shaking hand; laid it upon my head, and burst into an infantine flow of tears.

From that moment he would scarcely spare me from his sight. I appeared the only object that his heart responded to in the world; all else was as a blank to him. He had almost lost the power of speech, and the reasoning faculty seemed at an end. He was mute and passive, excepting that fits of childlike weeping would sometimes come over him without any immediate cause. If I left the room at any time, his eye was incessantly fixed on the door till my return, and on my entrance there was another gush of tears.

To talk with him of my concerns, in this ruined state of mind, would have been worse than useless; to have left him for ever so short a time would have been cruel, unnatural. Here then was a new trial for my affections. I wrote to Bianca an account of my return, and of my actual situation, painting in colors vivid, for they were true, the torments I suffered at our being thus separated; for to the youthful lover every day of absence is an age of love lost. I enclosed the letter in one to Filippo, who was the channel of our correspondence. I received a reply from him full of friendship and sympathy; from Bianca, full of assurances of affection and constancy. Week after week, month after month elapsed, without making any change in my circumstances. The vital flame which had seemed nearly extinct when first I met my father, kept fluttering on without any apparent diminution. I watched him constantly, faithfully, I had almost said patiently. I knew that his death alone would set me free—yet I never at any moment wished it. I felt too glad to be able to make any atonement for past disobedience; and denied, as I had been, all endearments of relationship in my early days, my heart yearned towards a father, who in his age and helplessness, had thrown himself entirely on me for comfort.

My passion for Bianca gained daily more force from absence: by constant meditation it wore itself a deeper and deeper channel. I made no new friends nor acquaintances; sought none of the pleasures of Naples, which my rank and fortune threw open to me. Mine was a heart that confined itself to few objects, but dwelt upon them with the intenser passion. To sit by my father, and administer to his wants, and to meditate on Bianca in the silence of his chamber, was my constant habit. Sometimes I amused myself with my pencil, in portraying the image ever present to my imagination. I transferred to canvas every look and smile of hers that dwelt in my heart. I showed them to my father, in hopes of awakening an interest in his bosom for the mere shadow of my love; but he was too far sunk in intellect to take any notice of them. When I received a letter from Bianca, it was a new source of solitary luxury. Her letters, it is true, were less and less frequent, but they were always full of assurances of unabated affection. They breathed not the frank and innocent warmth with which she expressed herself in conversation, but I accounted for it from the embarrassment which inexperienced minds have often to express themselves upon paper. Filippo assured me of her unaltered constancy. They both lamented, in the strongest terms, our continued separation, though they did justice to the filial piety that kept me by my father's side.

Nearly two years elapsed in this protracted exile. To me they were so many ages. Ardent and impetuous by nature, I scarcely know how I should have supported so long an absence, had I not felt assured that the faith of Bianca was equal to my own. At length my father died. Life went from him almost imperceptibly. I hung over him in mute affliction, and watched the expiring spasms of nature. His last faltering accents whispered repeatedly a blessing on me. Alas! how has it been fulfilled!

When I had paid due honors to his remains, and laid them in the tomb of our ancestors, I arranged briefly my affairs, put them in a posture to be easily at my command from a distance, and embarked once more with a bounding heart for Genoa.

Our voyage was propitious, and oh! what was my rapture, when first, in the dawn of morning, I saw the shadowy summits of the Apennines rising almost like clouds above the horizon! The sweet breath of summer just moved us over the long wavering billows that were rolling us on towards Genoa. By degrees the coast of Sestri rose like a creation of enchantment from the silver bosom of the deep. I beheld the line of villages and palaces studding its borders. My eye reverted to a well-known point, and at length, from the confusion of distant objects, it singled out the villa which contained Bianca. It was a mere speck in the landscape, but glimmering from afar, the polar star of my heart.

Again I gazed at it for a livelong summer's day, but oh! how different the emotions between departure and return. It now kept growing and growing, instead of lessening and lessening on my sight. My heart seemed to dilate with it. I looked at it through a telescope. I gradually defined one feature after another. The balconies of the central saloon where first I met Bianca beneath its roof; the terrace where we so often had passed the delightful summer evenings; the awning which shaded her chamber window; I almost fancied I saw her form beneath it. Could she but know her lover was in the bark whose white sail now gleamed on the sunny bosom of the sea! My fond impatience increased as we neared the coast; the ship seemed to lag lazily over the billows; I could almost have sprang into the sea and swam to the desired shore.

The shadows of evening gradually shrouded the scene; but the moon arose in all her fullness and beauty, and shed the tender light so dear to lovers, over the romantic coast of Sestri. My soul was bathed in unutterable tenderness. I anticipated the heavenly evenings I should pass in once more wandering with Bianca by the light of that blessed moon.

It was late at night before we entered the harbor. As early next morning as I could get released from the formalities of landing, I threw myself on horseback, and hastened to the villa. As I galloped round the rocky promontory on which stands the Faro, and saw the coast of Sestri opening upon me, a thousand anxieties and doubts suddenly sprang up in my bosom. There is something fearful in returning to those we love, while yet uncertain what ills or changes absence may have effected. The turbulence of my agitation shook my very frame. I spurred my horse to redoubled speed; he was covered with foam when we both arrived panting at the gateway that opened to the grounds around the villa. I left my horse at a cottage and walked through the grounds, that I might regain tranquillity for the approaching interview. I chid myself for having suffered mere doubts and surmises thus suddenly to overcome me; but I was always prone to be carried away by these gusts of the feelings.

On entering the garden, everything bore the same look as when I had left it; and this unchanged aspect of things reassured me. There were the alleys in which I had so often walked with Bianca, as we listened to the song of the nightingale; the same shades under which we had so often sat during the noontide heat. There were the same flowers of which she was fond; and which appeared still to be under the ministry of her hand. Everything around looked and breathed of Bianca; hope and joy flushed in my bosom at every step. I passed a little arbor in which we had often sat and read together;—a book and a glove lay on the bench;— it was Bianca's glove; it was a volume of the "Metestasio" I had given her. The glove lay in my favorite passage. I clasped them to my heart with rapture. "All is safe!" exclaimed I; "she loves me! she is still my own!"

I bounded lightly along the avenue, down which I had faltered slowly at my departure. I beheld her favorite pavilion, which had witnessed our parting-scene. The window was open, with the same vine clambering about it, precisely as when she waved and wept me an adieu. O how transporting was the contrast in my situation! As I passed near the pavilion, I heard the tones of a female voice: they thrilled through me with an appeal to my heart not to be mistaken. Before I could think, I *felt* they were Bianca's. For an instant I paused, overpowered with agitation. I feared to break in suddenly upon her. I softly ascended the steps of the pavilion. The door was open. I saw Bianca seated at a table; her back was towards me, she was warbling a soft melancholy air, and was occupied in drawing. A glance sufficed to show me that she was copying one of my own paintings. I gazed on her for a moment in a delicious tumult of emotions. She paused in her singing: a heavy sigh, almost a sob, followed. I could no longer contain myself. "Bianca!" exclaimed I, in a half-smothered voice. She started at the sound, brushed back the ringlets that hung clustering about her face, darted a glance at me, uttered a piercing shriek, and would have fallen to the earth, had I not caught her in my arms.

"Bianca! my own Bianca!" exclaimed I, folding her to my bosom, my voice stifled in sobs of convulsive joy. She lay in my arms without sense or motion. Alarmed at the effects of my own precipitation, I scarce knew what to do. I tried by a thousand endearing words to call her back to consciousness. She slowly recovered, and half opened her eyes.—"Where am I?" murmured she faintly. "Here," exclaimed I, pressing her to my bosom, "here—close to the heart that adores you—in the arms of your faithful Ottavio!" "Oh no! no! no!" shrieked she, starting into sudden life and terror,—"away! away! leave me! leave me!"

She tore herself from my arms; rushed to a corner of the saloon, and covered her face with her hands, as if the very sight of me were baleful. I was thunderstruck. I could not believe my senses. I followed her, trembling—confounded. I endeavored to take her hand; but she shrunk from my very touch with horror.

"Good heavens, Bianca!" exclaimed I, "what is the meaning of this? Is this my reception after so long an absence? Is this the love you professed for me?"

At the mention of love, a shuddering ran through her. She turned to me a face wild with anguish: "No more of that! no more of that!" gasped she—"talk not to me of love—I—I—am married!"

I reeled as if I had received a mortal blow—a sickness struck to my very heart. I caught at a window-frame for support. For a moment or two everything was chaos around me. When I recovered, I beheld Bianca lying on a sofa, her face buried in the pillow, and sobbing convulsively. Indignation at her fickleness for a moment overpowered every other feeling.

"Faithless! perjured!" cried I, striding across the room. But another glance at that beautiful being in distress checked all my wrath. Anger could not dwell together with her idea in my soul.

"Oh! Bianca," exclaimed I, in anguish, could I have dreamt of this? Could I have suspected you would have been false to me?"

She raised her face all streaming with tears, all disordered with emotion, and gave me one appealing look. "False to you!—They told me you were dead!"

"What," said I, "in spite of our constant correspondence?"

She gazed wildly at me: "Correspondence!—what correspondence!"

"Have you not repeatedly received and replied to my letters?"

She clasped her hands with solemnity and fervor. "As I hope for mercy—never!"

A horrible surmise shot through my brain. "Who told you I was dead?"

"It was reported that the ship in which you embarked for Naples perished at sea."

"But who told you the report?"

She paused for an instant, and trembled;—"Filippo!"

"May the God of heaven curse him!" cried I, extending my clinched fists aloft.

"Oh do not curse him, do not curse him!" exclaimed she, "he is—he is—my husband!"

This was all that was wanting to unfold the perfidy that had been practised upon me. My blood boiled like liquid fire in my veins. I gasped with rage too great for utterance—I remained for a time bewildered by the whirl of horrible thoughts that rushed through my mind. The poor victim of deception before me thought it was with her I was incensed. She faintly murmured forth her exculpation. I will not dwell upon it. I saw in it more than she meant to reveal. I saw with a glance how both of us had been betrayed.

"'Tis well," muttered I to myself in smothered accents of concentrated fury. "He shall render an account of all this."

Bianca overheard me. New terror flashed in her countenance. "For mercy's sake, do not meet him!—say nothing of what has passed—for my sake say nothing to him—I only shall be the sufferer!"

A new suspicion darted across my mind.—"What!" exclaimed I, "do you then *fear* him? is he *unkind* to you? Tell me," reiterated I, grasping her hand, and looking her eagerly in the face, "tell me—*dares* he to use you harshly?"

"No! no! no!" cried she, faltering and embarrassed; but the glance at her face had told volumes. I saw in her pallid and wasted features, in the prompt terror and subdued agony of her eye, a whole history of a mind broken down by tyranny. Great God! and was this beauteous flower snatched from me to be thus trampled upon? The idea roused me to madness. I clinched my teeth and hands; I foamed at the mouth; every passion seemed to have resolved itself into the fury that like a lava boiled within my heart. Bianca shrunk from me in speechless affright. As I strode by the window, my eye darted down the alley. Fatal moment! I beheld Filippo at a distance! my brain was in delirium—I sprang from the pavilion, and was before him with the quickness of lightning. He saw me as I came rushing upon him—he turned pale, looked wildly to right and left, as if he would have fled, and trembling, drew his sword.

"Wretch!" cried I, "well may you draw your weapon!"

I spoke not another word—I snatched forth a stiletto, put by the sword which trembled in his hand, and buried my poniard in his bosom. He fell with the blow, but my rage was unsated. I sprang upon him with the bloodthirsty feeling of a tiger; redoubled my blows; mangled him in my frenzy, grasped him by the throat, until, with reiterated wounds and strangling convulsions, he expired in my grasp. I remained glaring on the countenance, horrible in death, that seemed to stare back with its protruded eyes upon me. Piercing shrieks roused me from my delirium. I looked round and beheld Bianca flying distractedly towards us. My brain whirled—I waited not to meet her; but fled from the scene of horror. I fled forth from the garden like another Cain,—a hell within my bosom, and a curse upon my head. I fled without knowing whither, almost without knowing why. My only idea was to get farther and farther from the horrors I had left behind; as if I could throw space between myself and my conscience. I fled to the Apennines, and wandered for days and days among their savage heights. How I existed, I cannot tell; what rocks and precipices I braved, and how I braved them, I know not. I kept on and on, trying to out-travel the curse that clung to me. Alas! the shrieks of Bianca rung forever in my ears. The horrible countenance of my victim was for ever before my eyes. The blood of Filippo cried to me from the ground. Rocks, trees, and torrents, all resounded with my crime. Then it was I felt how much more insupportable is the anguish of remorse than every other mental pang. Oh! could I but have cast off this crime that festered in my heart—could I but have regained the innocence that reigned in my breast as I entered the garden at Sestri—could I but have restored my victim to life, I felt as if I could look on with transport, even though Bianca were in his arms.

By degrees this frenzied fever of remorse settled into a permanent malady of the mind—into one of the most horrible that ever poor wretch was cursed with. Wherever I went, the countenance of him I had slain appeared to follow me. Wherever I turned my head, I beheld it behind me, hideous with the contortions of the dying moment. I have tried in every way to escape from this horrible phantom, but in vain. I know not whether it be an illusion of the mind, the consequence of my dismal education at the convent, or whether a phantom really sent by Heaven to punish me, but there it ever is—at all times—in all places. Nor has time nor habit had any effect in familiarizing me with its terrors. I have travelled from place to place—plunged into amusements—tried dissipation and distraction of every kind—all—all in vain. I once had recourse to my pencil, as a desperate experiment. I painted an exact resemblance of this phantom-face. I placed it before me, in hopes that by constantly contemplating the copy, I might diminish the effect of the original. But I only doubled instead of diminishing the misery. Such is the curse that has clung to my footsteps—that has made my life a burden—but the thought of death terrible. God knows what I have suffered—what days and days, and nights and nights of sleepless torment—what a never-dying worm has preyed upon my heart—what an unquenchable fire has burned within my brain! He knows the wrongs that wrought upon my poor weak nature; that converted the tenderest of affections into the deadliest of fury. He knows best whether a frail erring creature has expiated by long-enduring torture and measureless remorse, the crime of a moment of madness. Often, often have I prostrated myself in the dust, and implored that he would give me a sign of his forgiveness, and let me die——

Thus far had I written some time since. I had meant to leave this record of misery and crime with you, to be read when I should be no more.

My prayer to Heaven has at length been heard. You were witness to my emotions last evening at the church, when the vaulted temple resounded with the words of atonement and redemption. I heard a voice speaking to me from the midst of the music; I heard it rising above the pealing of the organ and the voices of the choir—it spoke to me in tones of celestial melody—it promised mercy and forgiveness, but demanded from me full expiation. I go to make it. To-morrow I shall be on my way to Genoa, to surrender myself to justice. You who have pitied my sufferings, who have poured the balm of sympathy into my wounds, do not shrink from my memory with abhorrence now that you know my story. Recollect, when you read of my crime I shall have atoned for it with my blood!

When the Baronet had finished, there was an universal desire expressed to see the painting of this frightful visage. After much entreaty the Baronet consented, on condition that they should only visit it one by one. He called his housekeeper, and gave her charge to conduct the gentlemen, singly, to the chamber. They all returned varying in their stories: some affected in one way, some in another; some more, some less; but all agreeing that there was a certain something about the painting that had a very odd effect upon the feelings.

I stood in a deep bow-window with the Baronet, and could not help expressing my wonder. "After all," said I, "there are certain mysteries in our nature, certain inscrutable impulses and influences, that warrant one in being superstitious. Who can account for so many persons of different characters being thus strangely affected by a mere painting?"

"And especially when not one of them has seen it!" said the Baronet, with a smile.

"How!" exclaimed I, "not seen it?"

"Not one of them!" replied he, laying his finger on his lips, in sign of secrecy. "I saw that some of them were in a bantering vein, and did not choose that the momento of the poor Italian should be made a jest of. So I gave the housekeeper a hint to show them all to a different chamber!"

Thus end the stories of the Nervous Gentleman.

THE DEVIL AND TOM WALKER

A FEW MILES from Boston in Massachusetts, there is a deep inlet, winding several miles into the interior of the country from Charles Bay, and terminating in a thickly-wooded swamp or morass. On one side of this inlet is a beautiful dark grove; on the opposite side the land rises abruptly from the water's edge into a high ridge, on which grow a few scattered oaks of great age and immense size. Under one of these gigantic trees, according to old stories, there was a great amount of treasure buried by Kidd the pirate. The inlet allowed a facility to bring the money in a boat secretly and at night to the very foot of the hill; the elevation of the place permitted a good lookout to be kept that no one was at hand; while the remarkable trees formed good landmarks by which the place might easily be found again. The old stories add, moreover, that the devil presided at the hiding of the money, and took it under his guardianship; but this, it is well known, he always does with buried treasure, particularly when it has been ill-gotten. Be that as it may, Kidd never returned to recover his wealth; being shortly after seized at Boston, sent out to England, and there hanged for a pirate.

About the year 1727, just at the time that earthquakes were prevalent in New England, and shook many tall sinners down upon their knees, there lived near this place a meagre, miserly fellow of the name of Tom Walker. He had a wife as miserly as himself: they were so miserly that they even conspired to cheat each other. Whatever the woman could lay hands on, she hid away; a hen could not cackle but she was on the alert to secure the new-laid egg. Her husband was continually prying about to detect her secret hoards, and many and fierce were the conflicts that took place about what ought to have been common property. They lived in a forlorn-looking house, that stood alone, and had an air of starvation. A few straggling savin-trees, emblems of sterility, grew near it; no smoke ever curled from its chimney; no traveller stopped at its door. A miserable horse, whose ribs were as articulate as the bars of a gridiron, stalked about a field where a thin carpet of moss, scarcely covering the ragged beds of pudding-stone, tantalized and balked his hunger; and sometimes he would lean his head over the fence, look piteously at the passer-by, and seem to petition deliverance from this land of famine.

The house and its inmates had altogether a bad name. Tom's wife was a tall termagant, fierce of temper, loud of tongue, and strong of arm. Her voice was often heard in wordy warfare with her husband; and his face sometimes showed signs that their conflicts were not confined to words. No one ventured, however, to interfere between them. The lonely wayfarer shrunk within himself at the horrid clamor and clapper-clawing; eyed the den of discord askance; and hurried on his way, rejoicing, if a bachelor, in his celibacy.

One day that Tom Walker had been to a distant part of the neighborhood, he took what he considered a short cut homeward, through the swamp. Like most short cuts, it was an ill-chosen route. The swamp was thickly grown with great gloomy pines and hemlocks, some of them ninety feet high, which made it dark at noonday, and a retreat for all the owls of the neighborhood. It was full of pits and quagmires, partly covered with weeds and mosses, where the green surface often betrayed the traveller into a gulf of black smothering mud: there were also dark and stagnant pools, the abodes of the tadpole, the bull-frog, and the water-snake, where the trunks of pines and hemlocks lay half-drowned, half-rotting, looking like alligators sleeping in the mire.

Tom had long been picking his way cautiously through this treacherous forest; stepping from tuft to tuft of rushes and roots, which afforded precarious foothold among deep sloughs; or pacing carefully, like a cat, along the prostrate trunks of trees; startled now and then by the sudden screaming of the bittern, or the quacking of a wild duck rising on the wing from some solitary pool. At length he arrived at a firm piece of ground, which ran out like a peninsula into the deep bosom of the swamp. It had been one of the strongholds of the Indians during their wars with the first colonists. Here they had thrown up a kind of fort, which they had looked upon as almost impregnable, and had used as a place of refuge for their squaws and children. Nothing remained of the old Indian fort but a few embankments, gradually sinking to the level of the surrounding earth, and already overgrown in part by oaks and other forest trees, the foliage of which formed a contrast to the dark pines and hemlocks of the swamp.

It was late in the dusk of evening that Tom Walker reached the old fort, and he paused there for awhile to rest himself. Any one but he would have felt unwilling to linger in this lonely, melancholy place, for the common people had a bad opinion of it, from the stories handed down from the time of the Indian wars; when it was asserted that the savages held incantations here, and made sacrifices to the evil spirit.

Tom Walker, however, was not a man to be troubled with any fears of the kind. He reposed himself for some time on the trunk of a fallen hemlock, listening to the boding cry of the tree-toad, and delving with his walking-staff into a mound of black mould at his feet. As he turned up the soil unconsciously, his staff struck against something hard. He raked it out of the vegetable mould, and lo! a cloven skull, with an Indian tomahawk buried deep in it, lay before him. The rust on the weapon showed the time that had elapsed since this death blow had been given. It was a dreary memento of the fierce struggle that had taken place in this last foothold of the Indian warriors.

"Humph!" said Tom Walker, as he gave it a kick to shake the dirt from it.

"Let that skull alone!" said a gruff voice. Tom lifted up his eyes, and beheld a great black man seated directly opposite him, on the stump of a tree. He was exceedingly surprised, having neither heard nor seen any one approach; and he was still more perplexed on observing, as well as the gathering gloom would permit, that the stranger was neither negro nor Indian. It is true he was dressed in a rude half Indian garb, and had a red belt or sash swathed round his body, but his face was neither black nor copper-color, but swarthy and dingy and begrimed with soot, as if he had been accustomed to toil among fires and forges. He had a shock of coarse black hair, that stood out from his head in all directions, and bore an axe on his shoulder.

He scowled for a moment at Tom with a pair of great red eyes.

"What are you doing in my grounds?" said the black man, with a hoarse growling voice.

"Your grounds!" said Tom, with a sneer, "no more your grounds than mine: they belong to Deacon Peabody."

"Deacon Peabody be d——d," said the stranger, "as I flatter myself he will be, if he does not look more to his own sins and less to those of his neighbors. Look yonder, and see how Deacon Peabody is faring."

Tom looked in the direction that the stranger pointed and beheld one of the great trees, fair and flourishing without, but rotten at the core, and saw that it had been nearly hewn through, so that the first high wind was likely to below it down. On the bark of the tree was scored the name of Deacon Peabody, an eminent man, who had waxed wealthy by driving shrewd bargains with the Indians. He now looked around, and found most of the tall trees marked with the name of some great man of the colony, and all more or less scored by the axe. The one on which he had been seated, and which had evidently just been hewn down, bore the name of Crowninshield; and he recollected a mighty rich man of that name, who made a vulgar display of wealth, which it was whispered he had acquired by buccaneering.

"He's just ready for burning!" said the black man with a growl of triumph. "You see I am likely to have a good stock of firewood for winter."

"But what right have you," said Tom, "to cut down Deacon Peabody's timber?"

"The right of a prior claim," said the other. "This woodland belonged to me long before one of your white-faced race put foot upon the soil."

"And pray, who are you, if I may be so bold?" said Tom.

"Oh, I go by various names. I am the wild huntsman in some countries; the black miner in others. In this neighborhood I am known by the name of the black woodsman. I am he to whom the red men devoted this spot, and in honor of whom they now and then roasted a white man, by way of sweet-smelling sacrifice. Since the red men have been exterminated by you white savages, I amuse myself by presiding at the persecutions of Quakers and Anabaptists; I am the great patron and prompter of slave-dealers, and the grand-master of the Salem witches."

"The upshot of all which is, that, if I mistake not," said Tom, sturdily, "you are he commonly called Old Scratch."

"The same at your service!" replied the black man, with a half civil nod.

Such was the opening of this interview, according to the old story; though it has almost too familiar an air to be credited. One would think that to meet with such a singular personage, in this wild lonely place, would have shaken any man's nerves; but Tom was a hard-minded fellow, not easily daunted, and he had lived so long with a termagant wife, that he did not even fear the devil.

It is said that after this commencement they had a long and earnest conversation together, as Tom returned homeward. The black man told him of great sums of money buried by Kidd the pirate, under the oak-trees on the high ridge, not far from the morass. All these were under his command and protected by his power, so that none could find them but such as propitiated his favour. These he offered to place within Tom Walker's reach, having conceived an especial kindness for him: but they were to be had only on certain conditions. What these conditions were may be easily surmised, though Tom never disclosed them publicly. They must have been very hard, for he required time to think of them, and he was not a man to stick at trifles where money was in view. When they had reached the edge of the swamp, the stranger paused. "What proof have I that all you have been telling me is true?" said Tom. "There's my signature," said the black man, pressing his finger on Tom's forehead. So saying, he turned off among the thickets of the swamp, and seemed, as Tom said, to go down, down, down, into the earth, until nothing but his head and shoulders could be seen, and so on until he totally disappeared.

When Tom reached home, he found the black print of a finger burnt, as it were, into his forehead, which nothing could obliterate.

The first news his wife had to tell him was the sudden death of Absalom Crowninshield, the rich buccaneer. It was announced in the papers with the usual flourish, that "A great man had fallen in Israel."

Tom recollected the tree which his black friend had just hewn down, and which was ready for burning. "Let the freebooter roast," said Tom, "who cares!" He now felt convinced that all he had heard and seen was no illusion.

He was not prone to let his wife into his confidence; but as this was an uneasy secret, he willingly shared it with her. All her avarice was awakened at the mention of hidden gold, and she urged her husband to comply with the black man's terms, and secure what would make them wealthy for life. However Tom might have felt disposed to sell himself to the Devil, he was determined not to do so to oblige his wife; so he flatly refused, out of the mere spirit of contradiction. Many and bitter were the quarrels they had on the subject, but the more she talked, the more resolute was Tom not to be damned to please her.

At length she determined to drive the bargain on her own account, and if she succeeded, to keep all the gain to herself. Being of the same fearless temper as her husband, she set off for the old Indian fort towards the close of a summer's day. She was many hours absent. When she came back, she was reserved and sullen in her replies. She spoke something of a black man, whom she had met about twilight hewing at the root of a tall tree. He was sulky, however, and would not come to terms: she was to go again with a propitiatory offering, but what it was she forebore to say.

The next evening she set off again for the swamp, with her apron heavily laden. Tom waited and waited for her, but in vain; midnight came, but she did not make her appearance: morning, noon, night returned, but still she did not come. Tom now grew uneasy for her safety, especially as he found she had carried off in her apron the silver tea-pot and spoons and every portable article of value. Another night elapsed, another morning came; but no wife. In a word, she was never heard of more.

What was her real fate nobody knows, in consequence of so many pretending to know. It is one of those facts which have become confounded by a variety of historians. Some asserted that she lost her way among the tangled mazes of the swamp, and sunk into some pit or slough; others, more uncharitable, hinted that she had eloped with the household booty, and made off to some other province; while others surmised that the tempter had decoyed her into a dismal quagmire, on top of which her hat was found lying. In confirmation of this, it was said a great black man, with an axe on his shoulder, was seen late that very evening coming out of the swamp, carrying a bundle tied in a check apron, with an air of surly triumph.

The most current and probable story, however, observes that Tom Walker grew so anxious about the fate of his wife and his property, that he sat out at length to seek them both at the Indian fort. During a long summer's afternoon he searched about the gloomy place, but no wife was to be seen. He called her name repeatedly, but she was nowhere to be heard. The bittern alone responded to his voice, as he flew screaming by; or the bull-frog croaked dolefully from a neighboring pool. At length, it is said, just in the brown hour of twilight, when the owls began to hoot, and the bats to flit about, his attention was attracted by the clamor of carrion crows hovering about a cypress-tree. He looked up, and beheld a bundle tied in a check apron, and hanging in the branches of the tree, with a great vulture perched hard by, as if keeping watch upon it. He leaped with joy; for he recognized his wife's apron, and supposed it to contain the household valuables.

"Let us get hold of the property," said he, consolingly to himself, "and we will endeavor to do without the woman."

As he scrambled up the tree, the vulture spread its wide wings, and sailed off, screaming, into the deep shadows of the forest. Tom seized the check apron, but, woful sight! found nothing but a heart and liver tied up in it!

Such, according to the most authentic old story, was all that was to be found of Tom's wife. She had probably attempted to deal with the black man as she had been accustomed to deal with her husband; but though a female scold is generally considered a match for the devil, yet in this instance she appears to have had the worst of it. She must have died game, however; for it is said Tom noticed many prints of cloven feet deeply stamped about the tree, and found handfuls of hair, that looked as if they had been plucked from the coarse black shock of the woodman. Tom knew his wife's prowess by experience. He shrugged his shoulders, as he looked at the signs of a fierce clapper-clawing. "Egad," said he to himself, "Old Scratch must have had a tough time of it!"

Tom consoled himself for the loss of his property, with the loss of his wife, for he was a man of fortitude. He even felt something like gratitude towards the black woodman, who, he considered, had done him a kindness. He sought, therefore, to cultivate a further acquaintance with him, but for some time without success; the old black-legs played shy, for whatever people may think, he is not always to be had for calling for: he knows how to play his cards when pretty sure of his game.

At length, it is said, when delay had whetted Tom's eagerness to the quick, and prepared him to agree to anything rather than not gain the promised treasure, he met the black man one evening in his usual woodman's dress, with his axe on his shoulder, sauntering along the swamp, and humming a tune. He affected to receive Tom's advance with great indifference, made brief replies, and went on humming his tune.

By degrees, however, Tom brought him to business, and they began to haggle about the terms on which the former was to have the pirate's treasure. There was one condition which need not be mentioned, being generally understood in all cases where the devil grants favors; but there were others about which, though of less importance, he was inflexibly obstinate. He insisted that the money found through his means should be employed in his service. He proposed, therefore, that Tom should employ it in the black traffic; that is to say, that he should fit out a slave-ship. This, however, Tom resolutely refused; he was bad enough in all conscience; but the devil himself could not tempt him to turn slave-trader.

Finding Tom so squeamish on this point, he did not insist upon it, but proposed, instead, that he should turn usurer; the devil being extremely anxious for the increase of usurers, looking upon them as his peculiar people.

To this no objections were made, for it was just to Tom's taste.

"You shall open a broker's shop in Boston next month," said the black man.

"I'll do it to-morrow, if you wish," said Tom Walker.

"You shall lend money at two per cent. a month."

"Egad, I'll charge four!" replied Tom Walker.

"You shall extort bonds, foreclose mortgages, drive the merchant to bankruptcy—"

"I'll drive him to the d——l," cried Tom Walker.

"You are the usurer for my money!" said the black-legs, with delight. "When will you want the rhino?"

"This very night."

"Done!" said the devil.

"Done!" said Tom Walker.—So they shook hands and struck a bargain.

A few days' time saw Tom Walker seated behind his desk in a counting-house in Boston.

His reputation for a ready-moneyed man, who would lend money out for a good consideration, soon spread abroad. Everybody remembers the time of Governor Belcher, when money was particularly scarce. It was a time of paper credit. The country had been deluged with government bills, the famous Land Bank had been established; there had been a rage for speculating; the people had run mad with schemes for new settlements; for building cities in the wilderness; land-jobbers went about with maps of grants, and townships, and Eldorados, lying nobody knew where, but which everybody was ready to purchase. In a word, the great speculating fever which breaks out every now and then in the country, had raged to an alarming degree, and everybody was dreaming of making sudden fortunes from nothing. As usual the fever had subsided; the dream had gone off, and the imaginary fortunes with it; the patients were left in doleful plight, and the whole country resounded with the consequent cry of "hard times."

At this propitious time of public distress did Tom Walker set up as a usurer in Boston. His door was soon thronged by customers. The needy and adventurous; the gambling speculator; the dreaming land-jobber; the thriftless tradesman; the merchant with cracked credit; in short, every one driven to raise money by desperate means and desperate sacrifices, hurried to Tom Walker.

Thus Tom was the universal friend of the needy, and acted like a "friend in need"; that is to say, he always exacted good pay and good security. In proportion to the distress of the applicant was the hardness of his terms. He accumulated bonds and mortgages; gradually squeezed his customers closer and closer: and sent them at length, dry as a sponge from his door.

In this way he made money hand over hand; became a rich and mighty man, and exalted his cocked hat upon Change. He built himself, as usual, a vast house, out of ostentation; but left the greater part of it unfinished and unfurnished, out of parsimony. He even set up a carriage in the fullness of his vainglory, though he nearly starved the horses which drew it; and as the ungreased wheels groaned and screeched on the axletrees, you would have thought you heard the souls of the poor debtors he was squeezing.

As Tom waxed old, however, he grew thoughtful. Having secured the good things of this world, he began to feel anxious about those of the next. He thought with regret on the bargain he had made with his black friend, and set his wits to work to cheat him out of the conditions. He became, therefore, all of a sudden, a violent church-goer. He prayed loudly and strenuously as if heaven were to be taken by force of lungs. Indeed, one might always tell when he had sinned most during the week, by the clamor of his Sunday devotion. The quiet Christians who had been modestly and steadfastly travelling Zionward, were struck with self-reproach at seeing themselves so suddenly outstripped in their career by this new-made convert. Tom was as rigid in religious as in money matters; he was a stern supervisor and censurer of his neighbors, and seemed to think every sin entered up to their account became a credit on his own side of the page. He even talked of the expediency of reviving the persecution of Quakers and Anabaptists. In a word, Tom's zeal became as notorious as his riches.

Still, in spite of all this strenuous attention to forms, Tom had a lurking dread that the devil, after all, would have his due. That he might not be taken unawares, therefore, it is said he always carried a small Bible in his coat-pocket. He had also a great folio Bible on his counting-house desk, and would frequently be found reading it when people called on business; on such occasions he would lay his green spectacles on the book, to mark the place, while he turned round to drive some usurious bargain.

Some say that Tom grew a little crack-brained in his old days, and that, fancying his end approaching, he had his horse new shod, saddled and bridled, and buried with his feet uppermost; because he supposed that at the last day the world would be turned upside down; in which case he should find his horse standing ready for mounting, and he was determined at the worst to give his old friend a run for it. This, however, is probably a mere old wives' fable. If he really did take such a precaution it was totally superfluous; at least so says the authentic old legend which closes his story in the following manner.

One hot summer afternoon in the dog-days, just as a terrible black thundergust was coming up, Tom sat in his counting-house in his white linen cap and India silk morning-gown. He was on the point of foreclosing a mortgage, by which he would complete the ruin of an unlucky land-speculator for whom he had professed the greatest friendship. The poor land-jobber begged him to grant a few months' indulgence. Tom had grown testy and irritated, and refused another day.

"My family will be ruined, and brought upon the parish," said the land-jobber. "Charity begins at home," replied Tom; "I must take care of myself in these hard times."

"You have made so much money out of me," said the speculator.

Tom lost his patience and his piety. "The devil take me," said he, "if I have made a farthing!"

Just then there were three loud knocks at the street-door. He stepped out to see who was there. A black man was holding a black horse, which neighed and stamped with impatience.

"Tom, you're come for," said the black fellow, gruffly. Tom shrunk back, but too late. He had left his little Bible at the bottom of his coat-pocket, and his big Bible on the desk buried under the mortgage he was about to foreclose: never was sinner taken more unawares. The black man whisked him like a child into the saddle, gave the horse the lash, and away he galloped, with Tom on his back, in the midst of a thunder-storm. The clerks stuck their pens behind their ears, and stared after him from the windows. Away went Tom Walker, dashing down the streets; his white cap bobbing up and down; his morning-gown fluttering in the wind, and his steed striking fire out of the pavement at every bound. When the clerks turned to look for the black man, he had disappeared.

Tom Walker never returned to foreclose the mortgage. A countryman who lived on the border of the swamp, reported that in the height of the thunder-gust he had heard a great clattering of hoofs and a howling along the road, and running to the window just caught sight of a figure, such as I have described, on a horse that galloped like mad across the fields, over the hills, and down into the black hemlock swamp towards the old Indian fort; and that shortly after a thunder-bolt fell in that direction which seemed to set the whole forest in a blaze.

The good people of Boston shook their heads and shrugged their shoulders, but had been so much accustomed to witches and goblins, and tricks of the devil, in all kinds of shapes, from the first settlement of the colony, that they were not so much horror struck as might have been expected. Trustees were appointed to take charge of Tom's effects. There was nothing, however, to administer upon. On searching his coffers, all his bonds and mortgages were found reduced to cinders. In place of gold and silver his iron chest was filled with chips and shavings; two skeletons lay in his stable instead of his half-starved horses, and the very next day his great house took fire and was burnt to the ground.

Such was the end of Tom Walker and his ill-gotten wealth. Let all griping money-brokers lay this story to heart. The truth of it is not to be doubted. The very hole under the oak-trees, from whence he dug Kidd's money, is to be seen to this day; and the neighboring swamp and old Indian fort are often haunted in stormy nights by a figure on horseback, in a morning-gown and white cap, which is doubtless the troubled spirit of the usurer. In fact, the story has resolved itself into a proverb, and is the origin of that popular saying, prevalent throughout New England, of "The Devil and Tom Walker."